"I think I'll follow Dr. Willson's advice," Casey Ballard said, "and just rest the remainder of the day."

"That's wise," Sheriff Foster replied. "Say, is your car still at K.C.'s place?"

"Oh, damn—"

"Don't worry about it. I'll have someone bring it over."

"The keys are right here—" He thrust a hand into his pocket.

Foster laughed. "No need, Lieutenant. Someone will still bring it over."

"That'll be helpful," Casey said coldly. He started to get out of the squad car.

"Before you leave," the sheriff said emphatically, placing a restraining hand on Ballard's arm, "how do you propose to settle this matter about your grandfather's property?"

"I suppose I should sell."

"Yes, you should," Foster said quietly.

REDEMPTION
CHET HAGAN

TOR®

A TOM DOHERTY ASSOCIATES BOOK
NEW YORK

REDEMPTION

Reprinted by arrangement with Richardson & Steirman

A TOR Book
Published by Tom Doherty Associates, Inc.
49 West 24 Street
New York, NY 10010

ISBN: 0-812-58358-2   Can. ISBN: 0-812-58359-0

Library of Congress Catalog Card Number: 87-062-149

First Tor edition: November 1989

Printed in the United States of America

0 9 8 7 6 5 4 3 2 1

"See then that you walk circumspectly, not as fools but as wise, redeeming the time, because the days are evil . . ."

—Ephesians v:15, 16

1

i   Perhaps Casey Ballard was a paradox, dealing daily with the human sewage infesting the streets of Chicago and still believing he was doing some good—a cop who wasn't a cynic. A very strange animal indeed.

Which is not to say Lieutenant Casey Ballard, second in command of the Chicago Police Department's vice squad, was a hopeless Pollyanna. He didn't find good in everything and he wasn't irrepressibly optimistic; there were days—and this was one of them—when he raged at the idiocies of the system in which he worked.

He drove slowly now through the streets he knew so intimately, alone in his unmarked departmental coupe, trying to bring his anger under control. For three months his squad had been building a case against a pig named Charlie Montgomery, a slimy cretin whose profession it was to lure starry-eyed kids into his "talent agency" and cast them in the kind of sick pornographic movies no family newspaper dared to adequately describe. On this morning, a judge had thrown the case out of court, agreeing with the contention of Charlie's defense counsel that the undercover policewoman the vice squad had placed inside Montgomery's operation had acted improperly. The police, the judge decreed, had engaged in entrapment. Charles Montgomery went free.

In one sense it was even worse than that. The young policewoman, on the force only nine months, had been the kind of idealistic, committed, well-educated cop the police department bent over backwards to recruit. Casey Ballard had seen her anguished face when the judge ruled and had heard her bitter question: "What about the kids that bastard ruined?" Lieutenant Ballard had no answer for her. Too often, there were no answers. One thing he knew, however: no matter what would happen to the young woman in the future, she would never again be as good a cop as she had been that morning when she got out of bed and dressed to go to court.

Burdened with his baggage of despair, Casey tried to lose himself for a time, letting the hours burn away his ire. He had attempted, in twenty-nine years on the force, never to bring his problems, his angers, his frustrations, home to Rosalie; not to rely on his wife's strength to supplant his own. Maybe that was why, after a quarter of a century, they were still lovers. Rosie O'Hara Ballard was his island of sanity and he meant to keep it that way. Ballard knew all the sad statistics about the high divorce rate among police officers—twice the national average—and he was determined that he and Rosie would not be among those numbers.

She knew about his cases, of course, but he told her only enough to be honest with her. The sordid details he kept from her; his wife, in turn, didn't ask a lot of questions. The depth of her worries about his safety was never enunciated. Rosalie was, in sum, a good cop's wife and Casey appreciated that.

He had turned off the constant chatter of the police radio, listening instead to a disc jockey who played the "golden oldies" of their courting days. Those familiar songs were a catharsis. He hummed along with a recording of "Volare," trying to remember where they had been together when they first heard it.

That, friends, the D.J. was saying, *was a hot tune of of '58, and believe you me, we can use some heat right about now. Just in case you haven't stuck your nose outside today, let me tell you, we're fast approaching a record low for a January fifteenth. Those winds blowing off old Lake Michigan have tumbled the mercury way bee-low zero!* He chuckled. *And with what the weather mavens call the wind-chill factor, it feels like minus fifty! So draw yourself close and wrap yourself around a warm message from Eastern Airlines, offering bargain rates right now for flights to the sunny climes of Florida and the fantasies of Mickey Mouseland—*

Ballard's aimless driving had put him on Madison Street, going west out of the Loop and away from the lake. He crossed the bridge over the murky waters of the south branch of the Chicago River, coming to Canal Street, noting the people streaming into the Northwestern Station, filling the block between Canal and Clinton, intent on catching their commuter trains to the suburbs. Maybe it was time for him to go home, too.

Then he saw him—*Jack Carmen.*

Walking east on Madison toward the station entrance was a citizen Casey knew well: pimp, drug dealer, and most important to that moment, a wanted suspect in the shooting of a police officer in a South Side altercation two weeks earlier. Although he was bundled up against the bitter cold, a huge, mottled fur hat partially obscuring his features, there was no mistaking Jack Carmen. It was as if they were old friends, so familiar was Carmen to the vice cop.

Casey eased his coupe to the curb, sliding across the seat to get out on the sidewalk. Carmen was only ten yards from him, making his way through the crowd of people. Casey pushed closer to him, drawing his gun from the shoulder holster.

"Freeze right there, Jack!" he ordered. "You're under arrest!"

Carmen's head snapped up, his eyes wide in surprise. A woman screamed at the sight of the gun, suddenly pushing between them in her panic.

Given that slight opportunity, Carmen bolted away, darting through the crowd, pushing people out of his way, sending several of the commuters sprawling to the pavement. Casey whirled, his gun leveled in both hands, but there was no clear target. Too many bodies were in the way.

Sprinting to his coupe, Casey tore a sawed-off shotgun from the clips holding it to the inside of the roof, keeping the fleeing Carmen in sight. The pimp's distinctive fur hat made that possible.

Casey raced after him, seeing the fugitive enter the Northwestern Station. "Police officer!" Ballard yelled. "Out of the way! Out of the way!" Somehow, a narrow path was made for him and the pursuer gained ground, keeping the fur hat in sight.

In the middle of the crowded station, Carmen halted momentarily, a gun in his hand now, pointed in the general direction of the oncoming Ballard. He waved the weapon about menacingly but was unable to get off a shot because of the press of people. Turning again, he sped toward the restroom, bursting through the double doors of the men's lavatory.

"That's a mistake, my friend," Casey muttered under his breath.

In just seconds he was at the men's room doors, where he stopped. Putting his handgun in its holster, he double-checked the loads in the shotgun. Satisfied, he cautiously pushed open a door. To the distressed black attendant just inside, "I'm a police officer," he whispered, not bothering to show his shield. "A man just ran in here. Tall fellow, dark complexion, funny-colored fur hat. Maybe with a gun in his hand—"

The black man nodded.

"Where'd he go?"

His hand trembling, the attendant pointed down the aisle of toilet stalls. "At the end."

"Right or left?"

"Left."

"Okay, get everybody out of here," Casey ordered. "Quietly."

He watched as the attendant went to the half dozen men at the urinals to give them the urgent message. They hurriedly zipped up their flies and departed. The macabre humor of it wasn't lost on the lieutenant; he smiled.

The black man came back to him. "What about the guys in the toilets?"

"No." Ballard shook his head. "It'd be too dangerous to try to get them out. Just stand outside those doors and don't let anybody else in here."

"You can bet on that." The attendant fled.

Casey walked softly, slowly, along the double row of stalls, checking under each door for occupants. In several of the stalls he saw feet, trousers down around the ankles.

Let's hope they stay right there.

Halfway down the aisle, a toilet flushed. Casey froze in his tracks, waiting. When the stall door opened, and the occupant emerged, Ballard gestured with the shotgun, inclining his head toward the exit. He mouthed the words: *Get out.* A startled Oriental man scurried past him, his eyes showing his fright.

Slower now, Casey approached the end of the aisle, his own fears building. He checked under the doors of the last two stalls on the right; they were empty. So, too, was the second to last stall on the left.

The cop felt nauseous, his mind racing. *He's got to know I'm out here. Why in the hell doesn't he make a move?*

His shotgun ready, he glanced under the door of the last stall on the left. There were no feet!

Christ! The bastard's standing on the seat!

Casey took a quick half-step backwards, his eyes darting to the top of the stall, fully expecting to see Jack Carmen looking down at him, a pistol pointed in his direction. He saw nothing.

Maybe he's not in there. Doubt, the lack of knowing, wrenched at his gut. *Maybe the attendant was wrong. But if he's not in there, then he's in one of the other stalls.*

Swallowing hard against his ever-increasing nausea, Casey glanced back down the aisle, once more expecting to see Carmen with the drop on him. Again, nothing. Another toilet flushed.

Dear God, I can't wait!

He stepped directly in front of the last stall on the left, raised his foot and kicked in the door, simultaneously squeezing both triggers of the shotgun. It was one swift, deadly move. Booming sounds reverberated in the enclosed space as Jack Carmen's body slammed back against the tiled wall, his blood splattering it in a surrealistic pattern. Limply, the dead pimp fell down across the toilet, the gun he had held in his hand clattering to the hard-surfaced floor.

"You blew your chance, Jack," Casey breathed.

Then, suddenly, it wasn't Carmen's body there before him, but his father's—Patrolman Abel Ballard's body—lying lifeless and bleeding on the floor of a Loop currency exchange, shot dead by a drug-crazed robber. And he was hearing again the voice of the woman clerk of the exchange, an eyewitness to the shooting. *I don't know why he didn't shoot,* she sobbed, *but he just kept pleading with the kid to drop his gun and give up. He asked him that a couple of times, you know, begging him.* She swallowed hard. *He said, "Come on, kid, don't do anything stupid." And then that kid just stood up from behind a desk and started shooting—a lot of times. And the cop was hit bad. I guess he was dead right away, because he didn't make no sound. My God, I'll always remember how he kept pleading with that kid.*

"You okay, officer?" a voice said.

"What?" Casey was startled from his bitter reverie.

"I said, are you okay?" It was the black men's room attendant speaking.

"Oh . . . yeah . . . sure." Ballard looked around him. The men's room was filling with curious citizens, male and female. "Everybody get the hell out of here!" he screamed at them. "Now!" He made a threatening move with the empty shotgun. "This isn't a goddamned sideshow!"

The crowd retreated.

"Go find a cop," he said to the attendant. "Tell him Lieutenant Ballard needs assistance."

"Right away." He ran out.

Wearily, Casey moved to the row of washbowls, leaning on one of them, staring at the reflection of his chalk-white face in the big mirror. And then he vomited.

ii   It was nearly eight o'clock when Ballard let himself into his comfortable Old Town apartment, shedding his heavy overcoat. "Rosalie!" he called out.

She came to him, a freshly poured martini in her hand.

Her husband groaned. "You heard."

"Be hard not to. You're all over TV, darling," she answered soberly. "The number-one story on the evening news."

"That's because of my impeccable sense of timing," he said, trying to make light of it. "Be sure of the news deadlines before you act. They teach that now at police academies across the country."

They went into the living room, Casey gingerly lowering himself into a contour chair and pushing a lever to attain a reclining position. He winced in pain.

"The back again?"

"Yeah."

"You really ought to see a doctor, Casey."

"And he's going to tell me what—that I ought to stay away from tense situations?" He chuckled. "You've got to face it, lady, you're married to an old, creaking cop."

She leaned over him, kissing him. "Was it terrible, darling?"

"Bad enough."

Rosie sat down opposite him. "One of the TV reports said you've been suspended."

"Oh . . . that." He shrugged. "You know what that's all about—routine stuff in any shooting. Automatic suspension pending a departmental investigation. Carmen had a gun in his hand and—" He saw no need to explain further. Draining the martini glass, he held it out to her. "Can a guy get a refill in this joint?"

"If you're nice to the barmaid," she giggled, "you may get more than one."

"How nice?"

"We'll negotiate that later."

He watched her appreciatively as she went to the small bar to pour him another drink. She still had her figure and she still moved as provocatively as she did when he first met her. She was just out of a Catholic high school where the nuns had filled her head with warnings about the evils of sex—warnings, as it turned out, serving only to heighten her curiosity, her determination to know for sure. He thought now that she hadn't aged at all. The auburn hair, the creamy skin, the intense green eyes—all the same. There was a young girl's sensuousness in her still, but now matched by a mature woman's sensitivity. *You're a lucky bastard, Ballard.*

Casey himself was an attractive man. Most women might not have thought him handsome in any passionate way. Still, he was slim, well-made, his face pleasant, without critical flaws. His gray eyes were clear, suggesting an inner kindness. A lot of him was "inner," including the passion Rosie knew. No, he wasn't really outwardly handsome. Maybe he was just average in appearance. That suited him; he didn't stand out in a crowd. In his job it was an advantage not to be conspicuous.

Rosie brought the martini refill to him. "I also heard on the tube the judge threw out the Montgomery case."

"Uh huh." He sighed. "It's been a *wonderful* day."

"Does that finish you with Montgomery?"

"No, but it's back to square one."

She knew they had exhausted the conversation about what had transpired on that day. "Oh, I almost forgot—a letter came for you. From a law firm in Knoxville, Tennessee, it looks like." She retrieved it from an end table, handing it to him.

Casey tore it open, scanning it. "Well, I'll be damned!"

"What?"

"Listen to this: *I have the sad duty to inform you of the death of your grandfather, K.C. Ballard, at his home in Mountain County, Tennessee, on the fifth of January last. . . .* He looked up from the letter. "That's ten days ago." . . . *at the advanced age of ninety-three. His last will and testament, to be presented for probate by this office, names you as the principal heir. I respectfully request that you contact the writer as soon as it is convenient so that we may bring this matter to a satisfactory conclusion. You have my deepest sympathy in your loss.* And it's signed, *Winston Marshall, Attorney-at-Law.* What do you think of that?"

"I don't know what to think. I knew your dad came from somewhere in Tennessee—you told me that—but I had no idea there was still a grandfather around."

"That makes two of us."

"But . . . does that mean you're the only survivor?"

"It says I'm the 'principal heir,' so there must be others."

"Sons or daughters or other grandchildren—what?"

"Hell, Rosie, I just don't know! My old man never talked about his home. Or his family. Whenever he did mention Mountain County it was about the beauty of the place and the crisp, fresh air, and things like that. Christ, I was always under the impression I was named for my grandfather. But, now, this . . . " He tapped the letter. "And I learn his name wasn't Casey at all—not the way I write it—but just the initials K.C."

"Maybe the middle initial stands for 'Casey.' "

"Yeah, maybe."

Rosalie prodded him. "Don't you remember anything about other members of the family?"

Ballard thought for a moment. "Well, I remember when Dad was killed, Mother said something about having our lawyer notify Dad's father. But I don't think there was ever any response. Not that I heard of anyway. Let's see . . . at that time Mother spoke of some aunts and uncles—in other words, brothers and sisters of Dad. Biblical names, I think . . . Esther . . . Sarah . . . uh, Moses, I believe." He sighed. "Lord, Rosie, I was twenty when Dad was killed, so that was nearly *thirty* years ago. I'm amazed I remember even that much."

"But weren't you ever curious about the Ballards?"

"Not much. Dad was always so . . . uh . . . circumspect about his family, and they all seemed so far away. Perhaps if there'd been more talk about them I would have been curious, but—"

"And now you've inherited a fortune," Rosie said gaily.

"I doubt that. We're talking about hillbillies."

"Hillbillies can be rich."

Her husband laughed. "You've been influenced by that TV show."

"Well, I like to think we *will* be wealthy, with big cars, furs, jewelry, a retirement home in Arizona—" She giggled like a little girl.

"You're a greedy wench."

"Guilty."

"With my luck, I'll find the old man had nothing left but debts."

"You've got to think positively, darling."

"Hmmm, maybe so." He grinned at her. "The only positive thought I have right now is that I want another martini."

"Don't you think you ought to eat something, too?"

"Nope. I think maybe I'll just get sloshed and make improper advances to an Irish broad I know."

"What about the aching back?"

"Aching back?" Casey tried to affect a lecherous expression. "I didn't know you had an aching back."

2

i   It was eleven o'clock the next morning before Ballard awoke. Since eight o'clock Rosalie had been fending off the outside world. She had unplugged the telephone in the bedroom and had sat over the instrument on the desk in the living room, picking it up each time on the first ring. There had been many calls, all of a type—from newspapers, wire services, radio and television newsrooms—and she had told them all, "Lieutenant Ballard will not be available for comment today."

There was a somewhat bigger lie told to Captain Martin Sullivan, Casey's superior on the vice squad.

"There's a three P.M. meeting of the inquiry board on the Carmen shooting," Sullivan told her, "and I'd like to see Casey at two to go over—"

"That's not going to be possible," Rosie interrupted firmly. "He's ill.

"Oh?" There was a silence on the other end of the line. "Is he really ill, Rosie?"

"I'm telling you he is!" the wife answered angrily. "He's ill and he's not going to be there!"

"Some people might think—"

"I don't give a damn what *some people* might think. Postpone the hearing for a day or two, Marty. What possible difference will it make?"

"The media are raising hell."

"So that's the reason for all this haste," she said sarcastically. "You care more about the media than you do about the well-being of the best man you have."

"Don't put it that way, Rosie," Captain Sullivan pleaded.

"But I am, Marty."

"Okay . . . okay . . . I'll get a postponement."

"Good!"

"But not for long, Rosie, huh? My neck is going to be out far enough when I cancel today's meeting."

"I'll have Casey call you . . . " She hesitated. "When he's able."

Rosalie was preparing lunch when Casey shuffled into the kitchen, wearing only his shorts, rubbing his face. "Mornin', O'Hara," he mumbled.

"Jesus, you look like—" She stopped.

"Death warmed over?"

"I was trying to think of a less terminal description, but that one will do." She kissed him. "How do you feel?"

"Not too bad," he said easily. "Except for the remains of a martini head, not too bad at all. I slept well, I think."

Rosie handed him a steaming cup of coffee. "You did, and I'm glad." She didn't want to tell him he had thrashed around wildly for more than an hour, loudly muttering epithets, in the throes of an obvious nightmare.

"Any calls?" he asked without interest.

"Oh, the usual from the news people, but I told them Lieutenant Ballard wasn't available for comment."

"Thanks." He took a sip of the coffee. "Say, will you tell me something?"

"What?"

"When we went to bed last night did I . . . uh . . . did we—?"

12

"We did *not*, sir," she said, feigning disgust. "My date passed out on me."

Casey grinned sheepishly. "Well, another time then."

"I figured you were going to make a rash offer like that . . . " She put her arms around him, running her fingers down his bare back. "And I also figured, you being on suspension and all, that we might just consider a matinee."

"Gosh, I don't know," he teased. "Maybe I ought to go in and see Sullivan about—"

"Casey!"

He hugged her tightly, laughing with her. He loved the comfortable way they had with each other.

But he sobered quickly. "Didn't Marty call?"

"They wouldn't schedule the review board so quickly, would they?" She had adroitly sidestepped lying to him directly.

"No, I guess not."

"Anyway, there's something more important right now. Please—will you call that Knoxville lawyer? I'm dying to know how wealthy we are."

"Okay, but don't expect too much." He went to the telephone in the living room, direct-dialing the number on the attorney's letterhead. Within a very few seconds Winston Marshall was on the line.

"Mr. Ballard, I appreciate your prompt response to my letter."

"I'll have to admit it all came as something of a surprise."

"Yes, I thought it might. I gather you didn't know your grandfather?"

"No. I'd . . . well, lost track of my dad's branch of the family."

"The late Mr. Ballard was a man much loved in Mountain County," the lawyer explained pompously. "One of its leading citizens. Respected, you know. He was a fine old gentleman."

"That's nice to hear." Casey wanted to get to the heart of the matter. "Uh . . . could you tell me what's involved in this inheritance?"

13

"Certainly. There's a property of twenty-three acres just off Interstate 40, some eight or nine miles from Hillside, the county seat. Mostly wooded. But there's a rather substantial three-story frame house on it, and a large, sturdy barn."

"And I share that with the other members of the family there?"

"No, no. There are no other family members."

"But you used the phrase 'principal heir,' and I assumed—"

"I'm sorry about that misunderstanding," the lawyer interrupted. "You see, there's a tenant family on the property by the name of Staley who cared for your grandfather in his declining years, and there was a small savings account which he left to Mrs. Staley. Something less than three thousand dollars. You are, for all intents and purposes, the *sole* heir."

"I see." Casey pondered about what he ought to say next.

"Mr. Ballard," the Knoxville attorney went on, "I've been authorized by the Staleys to make you an offer for the property. You would, I believe, net something in the neighborhood of forty thousand dollars, once the mortgage is retired."

"Uh huh. And the amount of the mortgage?"

"A token one—fifteen thousand." Marshall cleared his throat. "I realize this may be a difficult decision for you to make, you being up there in Chicago and all, but I respectfully recommend you accept the offer."

"Make it nice and neat for everyone, right?" Casey chuckled.

"You might characterize it in that manner," the lawyer answered with no hint of humor. "But I could handle the entire matter through the mails, if you wish."

"Uh huh." Casey paused. "Maybe I should see the property first."

"Have you ever been to Mountain County, Mr. Ballard?"

There was something about the way the man on the other end of the line had asked the question that made Casey uneasy. His policeman's antennae had picked up some strange signals. "No, I haven't," he replied. "Is there something you're not telling me?"

"No, no, not at all. It's just that . . . uh . . . the people of Mountain County are different, you know. Good Christian people, you understand, but . . . uh . . . how shall I put this? . . . jealous of their heritage."

Ballard had to laugh. "You mean they don't like outsiders, Mr. Marshall?"

"I wouldn't put it exactly like that. There's a great pride among the people of Mountain County in their own way of life."

"A clever explanation, sir. Let me think about it. I'll get back to you."

The attorney was clearly annoyed. "May I ask how soon?"

"In a reasonable time."

"Very well." Coldly.

"Mr. Marshall, one more question: how did you know where to send the letter?"

"Actually, we didn't know at first. In the will, drawn several years ago, old Mr. Ballard simply referred to you as 'Casey Ballard, a son of Abel Ballard, of Chicago.' Hoping you were still in Chicago, we asked a correspondent law firm there to find you. In light of their quick response to our query, I'm assuming they simply found you in the city directory."

"Hmmm. Well, thank you, Mr. Marshall. You'll be hearing from me."

"Keep in mind, please," the lawyer added forcefully, "that I'll be most happy to handle this matter without the necessity of your making a long, time-consuming trip. Perhaps you won't find it convenient to take time away from your business—"

It was evident the correspondent law firm hadn't told the Tennessean the new-found heir was on the Chicago police force. Casey decided to keep him ignorant on that point. "As I said, you'll be hearing from me, Mr. Marshall." He hung up the telephone, remaining at the desk, drumming his fingers. Deep in thought.

"So—?" Rosie asked impatiently.

Casey laughed. "You're *not* married to a millionaire, O'Hara." He joined her on the sofa. "He says I've inherited twenty-three acres in the woods, with a house and a barn, and that he believes it could net me forty thousand if I sold it."

"Well, it's not big cars and furs, but it's better than a sharp stick in the eye." His wife loved that cliché.

"I don't know," Ballard replied, shaking his head doubtfully. "That lawyer seems too damned eager to settle this thing quickly."

"Meaning what?"

"I'm not sure," he had to admit. "It's just something I feel in my gut."

Rosalie leaned over, kissing him on the cheek. "Casey, darling, stop being a cop, will you? Take this for what it is. A grandfather you never knew leaves you an estate of forty thousand dollars and right away you begin to see a foul plot. Why don't you just take the money and be grateful for it? We certainly can find a use for it."

"Yeah."

There was a silence.

"Say, listen, Rosie," he said finally, "I'm probably going to have some time while this suspension runs its course. Why don't we just get on a plane and go down there to look at my property? Maybe have some fun, huh?"

Rosie thought of Captain Sullivan's call. "Do you think this is a good time for you to be away?"

"No . . . perhaps not."

She saw his disappointment. "Hey, we can decide later. Right now, let's have lunch. And then—" She kissed him meaningfully.

"You, O'Hara, are oversexed."

"Complaining?"

"Nope, just stating fact."

ii　　　They sat watching the "Benny Hill Show" on television, laughing together at the titillating, broad-brush humor of the British comedian. It had been a pleasant day, warm and loving and relaxing. Rosie was grateful that Captain Sullivan hadn't called again, and there had been no talk at all of the demise of Jack Carmen. They had been out to their favorite neighborhood tavern in the Old Town for an early dinner, where they had chatted, with many corny jokes, about how they were going to spend the largess of the late K.C. Ballard. But there had been no more discussion about a trip to Tennessee.

They sat on the sofa now, Rosie snuggled in Casey's arms, giggling as Benny Hill chased a scantily clad nubile blonde around an English garden, stepping on rakes, tumbling over wheelbarrows, and getting soaked with water from a hose wielded by a cross-eyed gardener.

The doorbell rang.

Ballard groaned, looking at his watch. "After ten—who in the hell would that be?"

"There's one way to find out." Rosie pushed herself up from the sofa, hurrying to the door, fearful it might be Marty Sullivan. She put her eye to the security peep-hole. "Oh, Jesus!" she muttered. *It was worse than Marty Sullivan.* She was looking at the sober face of Police Commissioner Paul Stiles, distorted by the peep-hole glass. She took a deep breath as she undid the doorchain and turned the bolt lock, swinging the door open wide, presenting a smiling face to the unwelcome visitor.

"Well, Commissioner, what a surprise," she said gaily, loudly enough so that Casey would hear her in the living room.

"I really must apologize, Rosalie, for this intrusion . . . " He sighed deeply. "But there are no hours in this job."

"I can appreciate that," she said lightly, gesturing him into the living room.

He was a tall, slim man, well-dressed, distinguished in appearance. Most thought him very handsome.

"Good evening, Paul," Casey said evenly, not bothering to get up from the sofa. He did that deliberately; he resented bringing into his home what he knew the commissioner meant to discuss.

Stiles glanced at the TV picture. "I see you're boning up on culture."

"With a capital *K*." In other circumstances the minor banter would have been humorous. It wasn't now.

"May I get you something, Commissioner?" Rosie asked as she turned off the television.

"Would it be an imposition to ask for a cup of tea?"

"Not at all." She left to go into the kitchen.

"Look, Casey," Stiles said at he sat on the edge of an easy chair opposite this sofa, "I'm forced to come here under very trying circumstances . . . " He was speaking hurriedly. "And I'd like to suggest that we have our discussion . . . uh . . . without upsetting Mrs. Ballard."

Casey didn't try to hide his sarcasm. "Mrs. Ballard lives here, too."

"Yes, of course . . . " The commissioner coughed nervously. "But I don't wish to distress her."

"She's a big girl."

Rosie reentered the living room, carrying the makings of tea on a small tray, putting it down on an end table next the Stiles' chair.

"Thank you, Rosalie."

She sat down again on the sofa. Casey put his arm around her protectively. "Paul has suggested," he said, "that you might be distressed by what he has to say."

"I've been a cop's wife long enough, Commissioner," she commented, "not to be easily distressed."

"Yes, we policemen seldom give our wives enough credit for the roles they play in our hectic lives."

As Stiles busied himself with pouring the hot water over the tea bag and adding two cubes of sugar, Casey thought of all the years he had known him. He had been a working policeman himself, putting in a decade on the force before going into politics and getting elected to the state senate. When the mayor, a member of the same party, came to City Hall, Paul Stiles was appointed police commissioner. That had been six years earlier. As far as Casey was concerned, Stiles was a reasonably good commissioner, although perhaps a bit *too* political. There was talk Stiles fancied himself in the mayor's office some day; some even said he had his eye on the governorship.

The visitor took an appreciative sip of the tea, leaning back in the easy chair. "Casey, I've just come from a meeting with the mayor. Marty Sullivan was there, too, of course . . . " Ballard nodded. "And I think you can appreciate what ramifications this Carmen shooting has had."

"I didn't think the mayor would be concerned because a cop shooter got blown away."

"Yes, well—it's a bit more than the mayor's feelings that matter here. It's the perception of the department that's at stake. You know Chicago's police got a terrible black eye during the 1968 Democratic convention, with all of those charges about a police riot, and the attendant 'the whole world is watching' crap . . . "

"Uh huh."

" . . . but since that time great strides have been made in setting right the image of the Chicago police officer. The days of the 'cowboy' are gone—forever, if I have anything to do with it. New procedures, new rules, new hiring practices, have made the Chicago Police Department one of the best in the nation. It requires vigilance to keep it that way."

The commissioner paused briefly, taking another sip of tea. "I would be something less than candid, Casey, if I didn't tell you I found the Jack Carmen shooting . . . uh . . . appalling. Your methods were abhorrent. You were a vigilante, not a cop—"

"Damn it, Paul," Casey interrupted, his emotions on the surface for the first time, "you don't know! You weren't there!"

"No, I wasn't there," Stiles said slowly, "but I had the occasion tonight to interview an eyewitness—"

"Wait a minute—there weren't any eyewitnesses. I had the attendant clear out that men's room before there was any shooting."

"Except for at least one fellow in another toilet stall."

Ballard groaned, remembering the feet he had seen under several stall doors.

"There *was* a fellow in one of those stalls who could see you through the space between the door and the doorframe. You know—maybe a half-inch or a quarter-inch of space . . . "

19

"Yeah."

"And he could see you moving along, a shotgun in your hand, and he saw you kick open the door—" He let the sentence trail off, glancing apologetically at Rosie, who was squeezing Casey's hand. Hard.

"And that citizen came forward?"

Stiles nodded affirmatively. "He went to see the mayor. He's a sometimes golf partner of His Honor and a contributor to the mayor's campaigns. What he reported was . . . well, *damning*. He said you never identified yourself as a police officer and you didn't properly identify the occupant of that toilet stall before you kicked in the door and fired. The mayor was most agitated about that point. 'Suppose he had been wrong?' he said to me. 'Suppose there had been an innocent citizen sitting on that toilet?' I didn't have any answers, Casey."

"What that eyewitness didn't know," Ballard said angrily, "and what you and the mayor seem to choose to ignore, is that Jack Carmen was a wanted man—for shooting a cop, for Christ sake!—and armed, too. I saw the gun in his hand while I was chasing him. And that weapon was recovered. You can yell all you want about the use of deadly force, but the reality was, in that men's room, it was either my ass or Carmen's. And it wasn't going to be mine!"

"That was your intent from the beginning, wasn't it?"

"What?"

"What struck me about the eyewitness account," Stiles went on, "was that you never said a single word. Nothing. I find that very strange, Casey. Look, I hold no brief for the Jack Carmens of the world, but we can't permit our police officers to operate on Carmen's level. You made errors, Casey. More than one. And the mayor, when the meeting began tonight, was determined to have criminal charges filed against you."

Rosie gasped.

"I realized then that I was in a position of a damage-control officer. I had to find a way to cut our losses on this thing. It took a while—and the rhetoric was bitter—but I finally convinced the mayor that bringing criminal charges against a veteran, and often honored, Chicago police officer would only make it worse. That it would keep alive any hue and cry over the sloppy methods employed in the attempt to apprehend Jack Carmen, leading to his violent, and perhaps unnecessary, death. We struck a deal."

Commissioner Stiles held up a hand, the thumb tucked into the palm. "There are four parts to it. First, the shooting review board, under the chairmanship of Captain Sullivan, will meet in the morning and reach a decision that the Carmen shooting was righteous. Second, because of that decision, there will be no criminal prosecution. Third, you will resign—tonight . . . "

Rosalie began to cry.

" . . . being permitted to file your retirement papers. And fourth, in meeting with the press tomorrow the mayor will issue an appropriate statement in which your strong record of twenty-nine years will be stressed." The commissioner shrugged. "There's also a fifth provision implied. You'll make no statements to the press, no public breast beating on your part."

Casey stared at him for a long time. "Resign?" The word was barely audible.

"Yes, tonight. The mayor's waiting now to hear from me. And I've brought the retirement forms for you to sign."

Ballard looked at his wife, the question to her unspoken.

She brushed the tears from her cheeks. "I love you, Casey." And she kissed him. With joy, it seemed.

"Okay, Paul," he said, "you've got a deal."

Stiles went immediately to the telephone, dialing a familiar number. When someone on the other end answered, he said, "This is Stiles. It's agreed."

iii   For nearly an hour they tried to sleep, Casey holding Rosie in his arms. There had been no talk at all after Commissioner Stiles left the apartment. They had been like automatons in preparing for bed, each seeming to be lost in thought.

21

"Rosie? You asleep?" he whispered now.

"No."

"Want to talk?"

"Uh huh."

"I always thought my last day on the force would be a happy one," Casey said. "Which shows you how wrong a fellow can be."

"Hmmm. You know what I think?"

"What?"

"I think Paul Stiles has a shit job."

"He does," Casey chuckled, "and he's the perfect man for it."

"But I think he was very fair, you know," she said soberly. "It would have been easier for him to just go along with the mayor."

"I suppose."

"You know what else I think?"

"No, what?"

"I think it would be a very bright idea if you went down to Tennessee to look at your property."

"You're a witch, O'Hara, reading my mind. We could make plane reservations right now."

"No, just one reservation. I don't really see myself hob-nobbing with hillbillies." She giggled. "So why don't you just go down there, satisfy your curiosity about Mountain County and the Ballard clan, and collect your inheritance from the lawyer."

"You wouldn't mind if I go without you?"

"Of course not, darling. Why should I mind? You'll be coming back with forty grand, won't you?"

3

i   Casey Ballard had read somewhere that mountains have always filled Man with a sense of the supernatural. That he could look up from the mountaintop and feel the closeness of God. That mountains were holy places.

It wasn't a concept he fully appreciated until he was on Interstate 40, driving south through Mountain County. Because it was wintertime, the oak and the maple and the linden and the birch were without their leaves. And yet the place was largely green. Densely so. Giant pines (the valuable loblolly mostly, he was to learn) towered above both sides of the wide highway, touching the heavens. As a midwesterner, used to flat plains stretching out endlessly to a distant horizon, Casey found the mountains awesome. Made more so by the realization that what he was driving through now might be regarded as only the foothills of the Great Smokies, the highest mountain range in the eastern United States.

His father's words about the beauty of his birthplace came back to him. But Abel Ballard had been a pragmatic man, unable to express himself in lyrical terms, and what he had told his son, Casey understood at this moment, had been woefully inadequate.

Ballard had come to Tennessee on the morning flight from Chicago, to be met at the Knoxville airport by attorney Winston Marshall, who tried once again to get from him an agreement to sell his grandfather's property to the tenant family named Staley. And once again, Casey had the nagging feeling in his gut that all was not well with his inheritance.

"Those tenants," Casey had asked the lawyer, "might they be a little resentful of my having inherited almost everything from the old man?"

"Oh, not at all," Marshall said hurriedly. "Indeed, the generous offer for the property indicates . . . uh . . . they have accepted the reality of Mr. Ballard's will rather well, I'd say."

"What can you tell me about them?"

"Mrs. Lulubelle Staley is the mother. A middle-aged woman, I'd guess, although it's a bit difficult to tell; she's rather . . . uh . . . obese. A widow, I'm led to believe, and the mother of five grown sons. All of the sons are involved with their mother in the continuing operation of your grandfather's business."

"Farming?"

The question seemed to surprise the lawyer. "No, no. Old Mr. Ballard ran a tavern. What we call in these parts a *roadhouse.*"

"Profitably?"

"Well . . . uh . . . in the sense that it supported Mr. Ballard . . . " Casey sensed an evasiveness. "And enabled him to employ the Staleys."

"I see. Then the inheritance isn't just twenty-three acres, a house and a barn, is it, Mr. Marshall? It also includes an ongoing business."

Marshall laughed. "Not in the sense of a business we might know in Knoxville or Chicago. As I understand it, it was more of a . . . uh . . . cottage industry. Very small, you know."

"But a business nevertheless?"

"Yes."

24

"One that has had to file tax returns?"

"Yes."

"And to file proper tax returns, books had to be kept, right?"

The lawyer was very uncomfortable. "That's the usual procedure, yes."

"Can you show me those books, Mr. Marshall?" Casey was boring in, his words hard, accusatory.

"Really, Mr. Ballard, I believe you're misinterpreting your grandfather's venture. It's been rural, very small—hardly a business at all, really."

The Chicagoan set his chin. "The books, Mr. Marshall."

Nervously, the attorney replied, "I don't have them."

"Have you ever seen them?"

"No."

"Have you ever seen the physical property?"

Winston Marshall actually groaned. "No . . . but Mr. Ballard, you have to understand that this was to be a simple probate of the will and I—"

"Then how could you suggest to me the offering price for the property was 'reasonable'?"

"This is all very embarrassing. The . . . uh . . . evaluation of the property was made by Zeb Alderman."

"And who's he?"

"Zebulon is his full name. He runs the Mountain County Trust Company, the bank holding the mortgage on your grandfather's property. I believe, also, he may have handled old Mr. Ballard's financial interests. At least, that's my impression."

"Uh huh." Ballard glared at him.

Marshall smiled broadly, trying to defuse Casey's anger. "You'll like old Zeb. He's a . . . well, an *entertaining* old fellow, capable of telling you all kinds of hair-raising stories of Mountain County. Most of them, I suspect, you should take with a grain of salt."

"A warning that might have been given to me about you, too." Casey leaned closer to him. "Why is it, Marshall, that I still believe you're not telling me everything?"

The lawyer sighed. "Those mountains, Mr. Ballard, hide things from strangers. They often conceal matters best left alone."

"A warning, Counselor?"

"More of a simple word of caution, you might say."

Casey was thinking of that now now as he spotted the exit off I-40 leading to Hillside. The LED clock on the dashboard told him it was nearly three o'clock. In less than a mile he was in the center of the small town. It surprised him. While there were many old buildings, the community didn't have a time-worn, neglected look. He drove by a nearly new, handsome brick building, of attractive design, with a sign proclaiming it to be the ELMO RALSTON JR. COMMUNITY CENTER. Next to it was an expansive, carefully tended recreation field, with several baseball diamonds and a half dozen tennis courts.

Hillbillies playing tennis? He recognized the thought as an attitude best dismissed; he was going to have to approach Mountain County with an open mind.

Then he came upon the Hillside Inn, where attorney Marshall had reserved a room for him. He had visualized a rambling antebellum mansion with tall white pillars and pretty women in hoopskirts sitting lady-like on the veranda. Instead, the Hillside Inn was circa 1980s, of an architecture born of the Holiday Inn chain; six stories high and surrounded by a huge parking lot, now nearly empty.

Inside the motor-hotel the lobby was deserted and there was no one behind the registration desk. He waited impatiently at the desk, drumming his fingers on the counter, wondering whether the place was closed for some kind of afternoon siesta.

A young woman appeared from an office behind the desk, brunette hair piled high on her head, perhaps too much makeup on her attractive face. Her eyes opened wide, in a startled manner, when she saw him standing there.

"Oh, I'm sorry, sir," she said, the drawling accent soft and appealing. "I didn't know anyone was out here."

Ballard smiled at her. "That's okay, miss. My name is Ballard . . . Casey Ballard . . . "

Once more the eyes opened wide.

"And I believe a reservation has been made for me."

The clerk searched through a few reservation cards. "Oh, yes, Mr. Ballard, here it is. From Chicago?"

"That's right."

She began to fill out a room slip. Casey saw her write *K.C. Ballard*.

"Excuse me, miss, but the name is *Casey* Ballard—spelled out. C-a-s-e-y."

Without comment she crossed out the initials, correcting the name. The form was pushed across the counter to him, with a ballpoint pen. "Would you fill in the top part, Mr. Ballard?"

As he printed his address, he asked, "Did you know my grandfather?"

"Your grandfather?"

"Yes—K.C. Ballard. You started to write the name that way."

"Oh." She hesitated. "Well, I knew *of* him. I guess everybody around here knew who K.C. Ballard was."

"Famous, eh?" he chuckled.

"A lot of people knew him," she said in a flat tone, selecting a key from the rack behind her. "That will be room 316, Mr. Ballard." The girl thrust the key at him. Ballard had the distinct impression the young woman didn't want to talk about his grandfather.

"Could someone take my bag up to the room? I want to get to the Mountain County Trust Company before the end of business."

"Of course."

"Is the bank nearby?"

"Just a block down the street—at the next intersection. Opposite the courthouse."

As Casey headed for the lobby door he could see, out of the corner of his eye, the girl clerk hurrying into the office, the registration slip held high. Like a flag.

His arrival, it appeared, was of more than a little interest.

Zebulon Alderman was a reed-thin old man. In his seventies, certainly, but not aged. There was a youthful spring in his step as he came forward to shake Casey's hand. He wore an old-fashioned, gates-ajar winged collar, decorated with a black string tie; he was in his shirtsleeves, an unbuttoned vest covering most of the striped shirt. Granny glasses were perched precariously on his long, thin nose.

"Well, well," he said enthusiastically, "so you're ol' K.C.'s grandboy!"

"Yes."

"Don't favor him at all."

Ballard made no comment.

"Set, set," the banker said, gesturing to a chair in front of a huge oak desk. He retreated to a high-backed leather chair behind the desk, bouncing into it. "Welcome to Mountain County, Mr. Ballard."

"Thank you, sir. From what little I've seen of it so far it's a beautiful place."

"'Tain't nothin' now, you oughta see it in the spring."

"Perhaps I will."

"An' you'd be jest as welcome then, Mr. Ballard, as you are now." He glanced at a clock on the wall. "Past three-thirty so I guess I can offer you a mild libation."

"I think that might be a good idea."

A quart mason jar was produced from a deep desk drawer, along with two glasses. Alderman poured liberal amounts of a water-clear liquid into each. One of the glasses was offered to Casey.

"Local stuff?" the visitor asked.

"Nectar o' the gods," the old man laughed.

Casey took a swallow. The fiery liquid burned its way down his esophagus. "Wow!" His eyes were tearing.

Alderman roared with delight. "It's meant to be sippin' whiskey, Mr. Ballard."

"I can understand why." He took a cautious sip now. "It's made from corn, isn't it?"

"Could be, but not this batch. You can distill brew from

any number o' things. Tell you what—pour a couple o' drops into your palm, an' then rub your hands together real smart-like." He illustrated with his own hands.

Casey followed the instructions.

"Now, smell your hands. What do you smell?"

"Peaches!"

"Thet's right, this batch was made from peaches. Matter o' fact, thet's some of your granddaddy's stock."

"Really?"

"Yep. K.C. made the best moonshine in East Tennessee."

"You mean he was a bootlegger?"

"He was engaged in private enterprise, Mr. Ballard, in the best American tradition." That was said with a grin, but the face sobered quickly as he leaned back in his chair. "Most folks don't understand thet, you know. I always thought, if I was younger an' smarter, I'd be . . . what's thet word they use now? . . . an entrepreneur an' market this stuff for what it is. Pure! No additives an' no colorin' an' thet kinda stuff. No, sir! This stuff is . . . " He held up the glass and peered through it. "Pure an' simple *organic* liquor. Now, wouldn't thet be a pluperfect sellin' point these days, Mr. Ballard?"

"It makes sense to me," Casey grinned.

"Yes, sir . . . pluperfect." He took a slow sip of the moonshine. "Young Marshall tells me that you might have doubts 'bout sellin' to the Staleys."

The sudden switch of subject caught Ballard off guard for an instant. "Well . . . uh . . . I just wanted to see the property before I make my decision."

"Any chance you might not sell?"

"Probably not," Casey replied off-handedly, determined to go slowly with Alderman, recognizing he was dealing with a clever old man. "Maybe you can put it down as simple curiosity about the property. And the family. Now that I've retired, I have time to—"

"Retired from what, Mr. Ballard?"

Something prevented Casey from telling the whole truth. "The security business."

"Hmmm. Another one o' those strange businesses o' these modern days," he mused. "Have you been thinkin' 'bout retirin' to these parts?"

Casey laughed, understanding he was being interrogated. "My wife seems to prefer Arizona."

"I hear tell it's right pleasant out there. Sunshine an' all—"

"It's lovely here, too."

The banker nodded. "Mr. Ballard, you ever been in Mountain County before?"

There was that question again. "No," Casey replied.

"An' I gather you never met your granddaddy? Nor any of your Ballard kin?"

"No."

Alderman put his thin fingers together in a steeple formation, studying them. "The Ballards always were strange folks."

"Strange . . . how?"

"They always seemed to be involved in . . . well, in unfortunate killin's."

Ballard chuckled, remembering attorney Marshall's warning that Zeb Alderman's stories had to be taken with a grain of salt. "I have the distinct impression I'm about to have my leg pulled."

"No, sir—I tell the gospel truth! Take your aunts Sarah an' Esther, your daddy's older sisters. They took off one night with a couple o' drummers from Nashville an' they were found, with the drummers, in a roadside cabin near Hot Springs, jest over the Carolina border."

"Found?"

Alderman smiled slightly. "I guess thet's a nice way o' putting it. Sarah an' Esther were in bed together, an' the two . . . uh . . . gentlemen were on the floor, trussed up with bedsheets. None o' 'em had any clothes on, an' all four had neat bullet holes precisely between the eyes. Not too purty, I reckon. The law said the holes came from a thirty-ought-thirty. Seems they were caught in the act o' considerable sinnin'."

"And the murderers?"

"Never caught, not to this day. Sarah an' Esther, you see,

were married an' the authorities came lookin' for their husbands. Matter o' fact, it was ol' K.C. thet got the husbands off—claimin' his sons-in-law were with him at a cockfight out t' his place at the very time thet the girls musta been killed. Prob'ly a couple o' dozen of other folks at the cockfights woulda testified to the same thing if there'd been a trial. Never was, though."

Casey stared at the banker, his suspicions growing about Zeb's careless drawl. It was inconsistent, seeming to get heavier when the old man was trying to stress a point. Yet there were diplomas on the wall from both the University of Tennessee and the Vanderbilt University law school; the drawl, at times, belied a formal education.

"Yes, sir," Zeb went on with a shrug, "you might say thet misfortune had its way with the Ballards. Take King David Ballard—he was a bit older'n your daddy. King David was killed when somebody hacked him up with an axe."

"Good Lord!"

"Didn't su'prise nobody. King David wasn't exactly the lovable type an' there was a list of suspects more'n a mile long."

"Was the killer caught?"

"Nope." Alderman grinned. "I suspect the law didn't try too hard. Most folks jest figured good riddance."

"You paint a rather bleak picture of the Ballard family," Casey commented.

"Don't mean to. Jest tellin' the truth. I remember your daddy as a real good feller. We were 'bout the same age, give or take a year or two. An' we did a little hell raisin' together." The banker's eyes took on a faraway expression. "Even courted the same girl once."

"Oh?"

"Yep. Alice Ralston—Judge Ralston's daughter. Purtiest thing you ever did see. Your daddy left Mountain County when ... uh ... well, when Alice turned him down." The voice was deeply sad. "It was me who married her, you see. She's been gone nearly ten years now. There are days when I jest can't believe it. Alice was the sweetest thing ... ."

There was a long silence.

It was Casey who broke the somber mood, trying to move the storytelling along. "So that's when my father went to Chicago?"

"That was when. 'Course we didn't know it was Chicago at first. Truth is, we never did hear directly from him again. But there was a rumor he joined the law."

"Yes, he was on the Chicago police force."

"I'll bet he was a good one, too."

Ballard took a sip of the moonshine. "He was killed, Mr. Alderman, in a shoot-out in the robbery of a currency exchange."

"Misfortune," the old man sighed, reinforcing the point he had made earlier about the Ballard clan. "But . . . you didn't come here jest to hear my tales. You wanna know 'bout the property, right?"

"Yes." The conversation was back where it started.

"This bank holds the mortgage on ol' K.C.'s Place—jest shy of fifteen thousand."

"So I understand. Attorney Marshall has told me I might clear forty thousand if I sell to the Staleys."

"Seems like."

"My problem with that, frankly," Casey said carefully, "is that I have no way to judge the validity of that offer until I see my grandfather's books."

Zeb's mouth dropped open. "His books?!" He began to laugh. "K.C. Ballard never kept a book in his whole goddamned life! Couldn't have, even if he wanted to. The ol' man couldn't read or write."

"Marshall has suggested you kept the books for him . . ."

Alderman shook his head negatively. Vigorously.

"That you counseled him on financial matters."

Still laughing, the banker snorted, "That young lawyer is a damned fool! Books? Financial matters? Jee-sus, thet's really funny."

Casey waited until the laughter ended. "I don't imagine the IRS thought it was so funny."

Alderman sighed deeply, leaning back in his chair. "Mr.

Ballard, lemme 'splain somethin' t' ya." The deep drawl returned. "Yer granddaddy, an' a whole lot of the hill folks, jest don't give a damn 'bout the IRS. Thet's federal gov'ment an' federal gov'ment people ain't never been welcome here. Goes back a long way, mostly havin' t' do with the alcohol tax people. The idea thet the gov'ment kin tell a free-born man he gotta pay tax on homemade brew jest don't make no sense to 'em. A lot o' good men, on both sides, died over thet disagreement. An' the IRS or the FBI or whatever are all the same as the alcohol tax people. They's rev-noo-ers," he stretched out the word, "an' there ain't no respect shown 'em, believe me."

"But—?"

"Years ago, Mr. Ballard," Zeb pressed on, "the IRS figured it was too costly to fight these hill folks over filin' tax returns. 'Course if a legitimate business, like this bank, tried thet, they'd get mighty upset. But with the hill folks . . . " He extended his bony hands in a gesture of resignation.

"That's hard to believe."

"It's fact. An' you've got to understand thet K.C. Ballard's business, if that's what you insist on callin' it . . . " (the heavy drawl was gone again; the device was beginning to annoy Casey) ". . . was strictly a cash-flow thing. He took in some money and he spent it for his own pleasures, which were many. Gave some of it away, too; he was what is known as a soft touch. As for my financial advice—hell, I had to nag at him over the years to put a few dollars in a savings account. As it was, he saved less than three thousand dollars and thet, as you probably know by now, goes to Lulubelle Staley."

Casey nodded. "Then you think forty thousand is a reasonable offer for the property?"

Alderman pondered for a moment. "Let me put it this way—I don't believe you're goin' t' get another offer."

"Why's that?"

"Well, sir, a lot of folks here 'bouts think the place should have gone to Lulubelle an' her boys."

"And they resent me because I inherited it?"

"Thet's 'bout the size of it."

"And your own view?"

"I was su'prised . . . " He paused for an instant. "No, I was *shocked* when K.C. willed it to a grandson he's never seen. But he always was a man who did as he damned pleased."

Zebulon Alderman came to his feet, indicating the interview was ended.

Casey stood, too. "Well, thank you, Mr. Alderman, for your candor." He extended his hand and the banker shook it. "I appreciate your hospitality, sir, and especially the peach . . . uh . . . brandy." He laughed.

"Weren't nothin'," Alderman grinned, exaggerating the mountain patois once again.

Ballard started for the door, then, remembering something, he turned back to the old man. "Say, didn't I also have an uncle named Moses?"

"I plumb forgot 'bout him," Zeb admitted. "Maybe thet's 'cause I barely knew him. Moses was K.C.'s first born. He was only 'bout fourteen or fifteen when he disappeared."

Casey's eyebrows shot up questioningly.

"The way the story's told, young Moses went out one mornin' to check a couple o' still locations for K.C. Took a rifle an' a couple o' hounds with him, figurin' to get in some coon huntin', too. Well, the hounds came back home, but Moses never did. Some folks say revenue agents killed him an' buried him out there in the woods somewhere. Could be, I suppose. It wouldn't have been the first time—or the last."

The Chicagoan shook his head. "What a roster—Sarah, Esther, King David, Moses, and Abel—all coming to a violent end."

"Thet's the sum of it," Alderman agreed soberly.

"My grandfather must have had a liking for Biblical names."

"I believe thet was Ellie's doin'."

"Ellie?"

"Eleanor Foster Ballard," the banker explained. "Your grandmother. She died in childbirth, havin' your daddy."

Casey exhaled deeply. "I think I'd better go before we exhume any more ghosts."

iii   Darkness was falling by the time Casey Ballard left the bank building. He had initially thought he might go to see the Staleys that evening, but he was weary from his trip—and the depressing tales of old Alderman—and, as he made his way back to the Hillside Inn, elected just to have an early dinner and go see his grandfather's property, his inheritance, in the morning.

As he approached the inn a Mercedes-Benz left the parking lot at a high rate of speed. At the wheel was the brunette who had checked him into the hotel earlier. *A hot set of wheels,* he thought, *for a hotel room clerk.*

Only three other tables in the inn's dining room were occupied when he walked in. As the hostess led him to a table, Casey commented, "It doesn't seem to be very busy this evening."

"Not at this time of the year," the woman informed him. "Summer is when we're busiest—when the tourists come to the mountains."

"Then you get a lot of tourists?"

"Well," she admitted, "not really that many. Gatlinburg gets most of them. And Pigeon Forge. The folks over there make a lot of fuss over tourists."

"And you don't?"

"There's not much here for tourists, I guess," she answered defensively, dropping a menu on the table and leaving him there.

But he had a good meal, an excellent steak, and he ate heartily. He hadn't had anything to eat since his breakfast at the Knoxville airport. He finished the steak, lit a cigarette, leaned back and signaled to the bosomy young waitress.

"Miss, I think I'll have a nightcap. A Scotch sour."

"I'm sorry, sir," the girl said blandly, "we don't serve liquor. Mountain County is dry."

"Dry?" The revelation was unexpected.

"Yes, sir. Are you a guest in the hotel?"

"Yes."

"Well, there's a private club on the roof for our guests. Just show your room key."

Casey took a final swallow of coffee, left money on the table for the check and tip, and made his way to the elevator, wondering whether the private club would be any busier than the restaurant.

Six stories up the elevator deposited him into a small foyer, where a uniformed guard stood in front of a large, dark double door. Casey showed his room key and the doors were swung open for him. A cacophony assaulted him: sounds of a loud country music band, laughing and boisterous conversation.

The large room was jammed. A dozen couples gyrated on a small dance floor. To his right he spotted a long bar at which four or five men sat. He made for it, depositing himself on a stool.

"How do, neighbor," an open-faced bartender greeted him. "What's your poison?"

"Scotch sour. And keep the vegetables." That was one of Casey's idiosyncrasies. At home he drank martinis; abroad he drank Scotch sours, believing no one could make a decent martini but Rosalie.

It was only seconds before the bartender placed the mixed drink in front of him, shoving a wicker basket filled with salted peanuts toward him.

"Busy night," Casey said.

"Every night."

"But someone told me Mountain County is dry."

"It is. This" (he made a sweeping gesture encompassing the club) "is an accommodation."

"And all these people are registered at the hotel?"

The bartender laughed. "Let's just say the guard at the door knows who is and who isn't."

"That's most convenient in a *dry* county."

"I'm pretty good at accents, mister," the barkeep said, "and I'll bet you're from the midwest. Chicago, maybe."

"Chicago," Ballard admitted.

"Don't miss very often. Your first time in Mountain County?"

"Yes. And you—are you a native?"

"Nope. From Nashville. Came here a few years back when the hotel opened."

"Hmmm. If you don't mind my asking, would you by any chance have known a man named K.C. Ballard?"

"Old K.C.? Oh, sure!" The bartender became animated. "Hell, I had a little deal with K.C." He dropped his voice conspiratorially. "He'd come in here every once in a while with some of his 'shine and I'd trade him a bottle of some taxed stuff for it. Just to have a little moonshine around for the tourists, you know. Want to try a shot of it?"

"No, thanks," Casey chuckled. "I was baptized a little earlier today. But this Ballard—did he come in here often?"

"A couple of times a month, maybe. And always with a different broad. Always young, you know."

"Are we talking about the same man? I understood Mr. Ballard was in his nineties."

"Yeah, he was. But that didn't stop him." He grinned wickedly. "When you checked in was there a girl at the desk?"

"Yes."

"Great pair of jugs, dark hair, piled way up?" He held a hand six inches above his head.

"Yes."

"That's Kathy Ringer. She lives here at the hotel—works here, lives here. Well, Kathy was one of K.C.'s favorites. He used to visit her all the time."

"You're putting me on!" But Casey was remembering how startled she had been when he had told her his name.

"I swear," the bartender said soberly, "it's true."

"But why in God's name would a young, attractive girl want to—?"

"Beats me." He shrugged. "I only know he was scoring with a lot of young ones." Again there was a malevolent grin. "Maybe he had a new way of doing it or something. Anyway, it didn't surprise me when I heard he died in the saddle."

"What?"

"The story is," he went on with enthusiasm, "that K.C. had a heart attack while he was humping one of those whores out at his place."

Casey wondered whether there was ever going to be an end to the revelations about his grandfather. "Whores?" he asked weakly.

"Sure thing. That place he ran out there on the interstate has the best-looking girls in all of East Tennessee." He went away to attend to others at the bar. When he came back to where Casey was seated, he added: "K.C. brought in new ones all the time from Kentucky and the Carolinas, and I've been told he tried them all out himself before putting them into service."

The visitor shook his head in disbelief. "I have the distinct impression you're exaggerating for the entertainment of strangers like myself."

"Lord, mister, I wish I had the imagination to invent stories like that, but I don't. K.C.'s Place is one of the best—maybe *the* best—roadhouse in the whole state." He paused. "You see, there's a lot of long-haul truckers running along I-40 who stop at K.C.'s pretty regular. I mean, they know that anything they want they can get there. Women—clean ones, too—and craps and high-stakes poker and slots and cockfights. Pit bulls every once in a while, too. And booze, of course."

"Drugs?"

The bartender frowned. "No, I don't think so. Not hard stuff, anyway. Maybe pills. Uppers and downers, you know. Stuff truckers might use."

"Hmmm. It sounds like a pretty lucrative operation."

"I'd say so! Except for the Ralston family—they own the lumber mills and a lot of real estate, including this hotel—I'd bet that K.C. was the richest man in Mountain County. Remember that Kathy Ringer I told you about? The desk clerk?"

"Yeah."

"Well, she's driving a Mercedes now, and I heard K.C. gave it to her for last Christmas. Just about a week before he cashed in."

Casey finished the Scotch sour. "Better give me another one."

The bartender complied quickly.

"Look, doesn't the law bother that roadhouse operation? I mean, how can it keep going so . . . openly?"

"Are you kidding?" the young man chortled. "The sheriff is a regular customer out there. On the cuff, of course. With a few . . . uh . . . contributions, if you know what I mean."

"But . . . this is the middle of the Eighties," Casey said, determined to tap this source for as much information as he could get, "and I find it damned hard to believe that such a place could operate as openly as it must without drawing some considerable . . . uh . . . law-enforcement interest. If the local law doesn't bother, then, certainly, the state authorities must show concern."

"Oh . . . in a way, yeah. There was a state's attorney a few years back who wanted to make some points—the story was he wanted to run for governor—by cleaning up Mountain County. K.C.'s Place isn't the only joint, you know. There are a lot of two-holers."

"And *what* is a two-holer?" Casey was visualizing outdoor privies.

"A joint with a jug of moonshine and two whores." The bartender laughed loudly at his witticism.

Casey did, too.

"Anyway . . . this state's attorney raised hell for a while, even sent a couple of bootleggers to jail and closed a few two-holers. But in the end, nobody seemed to give a damn. About the only real effect he had was to lower the quality of the whores for a few months."

"And this fellow, K.C.—he wasn't touched?"

"The guy never laid a glove on him," the bartender replied matter-of-factly.

"Why was that, do you think?" Casey asked.

There was a shrug. "The people around here just want to be left alone, you know."

"Uh huh." He took another sip of the Scotch sour. "Now that this Ballard is dead, what happens to his place?"

"A fat witch named Lulubelle Staley's running it right now and I guess she gets it. She was his . . . uh . . . manager for a long time. His madam, I guess you could say. And she's still there—and those boys of hers. A strange group, mister, a really strange group."

"Strange? How?"

"The Staley boys are stupid mean." He thought for a moment. "No, *crazy* mean! This club is off-limits to them, and the sheriff sees to it they stay out of here."

"Your sheriff seems to be very accommodating."

"Yeah . . . well . . . " Again the bartender went away from Casey's position to serve the other customers.

When he returned, Casey said to him: "If this K.C.'s Place is as colorful as you say, maybe I ought to go out there and see it before I finish my business here."

"You'll have your eyes opened, mister." He hesitated. "If you do go out there, do yourself a favor and ask for Trixie. She's just a kid, and a dummy, but the best damned lay—"

"Dummy?"

"Yeah, a deaf mute. But she makes up for that with what she can do in bed. Believe you me!"

4

i   Casey had slept fitfully, and when he awoke the residual effects of a nightmare disturbed him. He couldn't recall it fully once he was awake, but he knew the dream sequence had dealt in some manner with the violent deaths that plagued the Ballard family. No doubt his father had been in the nightmare, although he had no specific memory of it. Nevertheless, he was disquieted.

It was almost ten A.M. before he had showered, dressed, called Rosalie in Chicago and talked exclusively of the beauty of the place, breakfasted, and was ready to visit his grandfather's property, the roadhouse of which the bartender had painted such a lurid picture.

As he walked through the lobby, he detoured to the registration desk where a different girl was on duty. A small blonde, a mousy little girl.

"Excuse me, miss," he said, "is Kathy Ringer on duty this morning?"

She stared at him, her mouth open.

"Kathy Ringer—is she here?"

"No . . . uh . . . just a minute, I'll get the manager." She fled into the office.

It was only seconds before a young man appeared in a gray business suit. "Good morning, sir. I'm Bobby Reston, the day manager. How may I help you?" The manner was unctuous.

"I was inquiring about Kathy Ringer."

Reston smiled broadly. "You're Mr. Ballard, room 316, aren't you?"

"Yes." Casey was suddenly very ill-at-ease. "Are you clairvoyant, Mr. Reston?"

"Hardly." The young man laughed heartily. "There are so few guests in the hotel at this time of the year that one can make an educated guess, you know, and I've just made one, I suppose."

"You certainly have, Mr. Reston." Ballard was annoyed. "But I'm still looking for Kathy Ringer."

"Oh, dear . . . I'm afraid Miss Ringer is no longer with us."

"But she was here yesterday. Her departure was sudden, wasn't it?"

"Not at all, Mr. Ballard. She had given us notice and yesterday was her last day. She's on her way to her new position. In Memphis, as I understand it."

"I see."

"But can I be of some service to you, sir?"

"Oh . . . no, no." Casey affected embarrassment. "It's just that she was so kind yesterday when I checked in and I realized this morning I hadn't properly thanked her."

Bobby Reston smiled that smile again. "Miss Ringer *was* an exemplary employee and we're going to miss her."

"I'm sure you will." Casey started away from the desk and then turned back again to the day manager. "She went to Memphis, you say?"

"Yes."

"Where in Memphis—another hotel?"

"I believe so, Mr. Ballard, but I'm not sure."

"Uh huh. Well, you'll probably be hearing from her

again," Casey said nonchalantly, "and when you do please tell her I inquired about her . . . "

"I certainly shall."

"And tell her, 'Thank you for the information you gave me about my grandfather.' "

Reston's smile died on his face.

"You'll do that, won't you, Mr. Reston?"

"Yes . . . yes . . . certainly."

Casey turned and walked briskly through the lobby to the parking lot. The little exchange with the day manager had been interesting, but Casey had no idea what it meant. Yet Kathy Ringer, who the bartender had told him was one of his grandfather's young lovers, had made what seemed a hasty exit from Mountain County. Maybe it wasn't hasty; maybe she did have a new job in Memphis—but Ballard thought not. Somehow there was a connection between his arrival in Hillside and Miss Ringer's departure.

He could almost hear Rosie chastising him: *Casey, stop being a cop, will you?*

He grinned to himself.

ii   It was huge, a rambling Victorian-style house, a building of angles and corners and gingerbread cornices and wide shutters on the deep windows. It was the kind of house Casey had seen often in motion pictures, made gloomy and foreboding by movie lighting—always photographed at night—the background for murder and madness and ghostly apparitions. Yet this house, perched on a high knoll overlooking I-40, was inviting, the morning sun of this clear January day glinting off the windows, the old glass reflecting back tiny shards of color.

Casey wondered, as he approached it on the interstate, whether his grandfather had built this house. If he had, it suggested an affluence not previously perceived for a hillbilly moonshiner and whoremaster. Perhaps the bartender had been right; perhaps K.C. Ballard had been a man of wealth.

He slowed his car when he spotted a sign with the simple legend "K.C.'s" on it, an arrow pointing the way along a wide lane leading to the house.

Once he made the turn into the lane and had gone some thirty yards, he realized a large, graveled parking lot had been bulldozed out of the woods at the base of the knoll. Access to the house from there was by a long, steeply sloping wooden stairway of more than twenty steps, with a sturdy railing on each side. Nine or ten large tractor-trailer rigs were parked there, together with a scattering of pickup trucks and three cars.

Casey parked next to the stairway. As he got out of the rental car he found himself patting under his left arm to make certain his holstered gun was there. It was reflex action; he had been carrying the weapon for twenty-nine years. But it wasn't there this time. The gun, like the cop, had been retired.

He made his way up the steps and then along a brick path to the house. A wide, roofed porch went three-quarters of the way around the building, which he decided was in good repair. Indeed, the bright yellow paint job, with green accents on cornices, trims, and shutters, appeared to have been done in recent months. At the door he was instructed by a crudely printed sign, out of place with the neatness of the house; "KNOCK," it said. He did. And waited. He knocked again.

There was the sound of a bolt being thrown back and the door was opened by a huge woman, a green satin dressing gown gathered around her obese body, her hair hennaed red, an inordinate amount of makeup on her flabby face. She glared suspiciously at the stranger.

"Mrs. Staley?" Casey asked tentatively.

"Yeah."

"My name is Casey Ballard."

The glare turned to a broad grin, revealing a gold tooth in the center of the heavily rouged mouth. "Well, Ah'll be god-damned—ol' K.C.'s kin!"

"Yes, his grandson." It was a silly redundancy, perhaps, but he was taken aback by the sight and loudness of her.

"Thet lawyer feller in Knoxville told me t' 'spect ya." She held the door open wide. "Come on in, sweetie!"

She led the way into a large, high-ceilinged living room jammed with overstuffed furniture and overgrown potted plants and populated with a dozen women in various stages of undress. *The day shift,* Casey thought. To the police officer in him it was a cathouse scene from another time, one he had never really witnessed first hand—so old-fashioned and so much of a visual cliché it brought a smile.

In one corner there lounged a burly man dressed in dirty overalls and heavy clodhopper boots. Pulled down over his eyes was a baseball cap with the CAT logo on it. He seemed to have no interest at all in the arrival of Ballard.

"Alvin!" Mrs. Staley shouted at him, "go fetch the boys! We're havin' a meetin'!"

Surly faced at having been given the order, the man unwound himself from the chair, exiting the room with deliberate languor.

"Goddamned lazy—" the woman muttered.

She gestured Casey through the living room and into a side parlor that was lined on three walls with slot machines of varying denominations. None was being played at that hour. They went through a door at the far end of the parlor and Casey found himself in a spacious, old-fashioned kitchen, the centerpiece of which was a massive wooden table with eight chairs arrayed around it haphazardly. The remains of what must have been breakfast were still on the table.

"Sonofabitch!" Mrs. Staley cursed. She bellowed: "Martha!"

A skinny black woman rushed into the kitchen, her eyes wide in concern. "Yas, ma'am?"

"Clean up this here goddamned mess!"

"Yas, ma'am." She scurried about, swiftly removing the dirty dishes from the table and dumping them into a sink and then attacking the soiled table top with a wet dishrag.

"I hope I haven't come at a bad time," Casey said apologetically.

"Ain't no bad times at K.C.'s," Mrs. Staley grinned, the

gold tooth glinting. "It's jest thet ya cain't git no good niggah help no more."

Casey didn't respond.

The black woman, having completed her chores, fled the kitchen as hurriedly as she had arrived.

"Set down," the hostess said, nodding toward a chair. "Want some coffee? Or mebbe somethin' stronger?"

"Coffee will be fine." Casey sat at the table. "Mrs. Staley, I hope—"

"Name's Lulubelle," she corrected him. "Ev'rybody calls me thet."

"Of course." He smiled. "Lulubelle, I hope—"

"An' yer K.C. Ah'd like to call ya thet 'cause it'd make me feel good."

"It's not really 'K.C.,' with initials," he explained. "My father named me Casey . . . uh . . . like Casey at the bat."

"Okay." She shrugged. It was evident the allusion to the baseball legend meant nothing to her.

Maybe I should have used Casey Jones, Ballard thought.

"Lulubelle," he started once again, "I hope you don't think I've come here to haggle about the price. I've been assured what you've offered is reasonable. But there are some things I'd—"

Again she cut him off. "We'll talk 'bout it when the boys git here." She put a cup of coffee in front of him.

Alvin sauntered into the kitchen at that point, dropping disjointedly into a chair across the table from Casey. "They's comin'," he reported to his mother.

"Thank ya, baby boy."

Casey fought back a smile. The endearment was so incompatible with the gross woman that he wondered whether Lulubelle was putting on an act for his benefit.

Two others came in. One was blond, slightly built, his face florid, as if he had been drinking heavily. He said nothing as he found a chair. The second was a giant—a balding redhead with powerful forearms, liberally tattooed. That one had two teeth missing in the center of the upper row; his face was scarred with several obvious knife cuts. *He must weigh two-eighty-*

five, Casey told himself. *The Chicago Bears might like to know about him.*

The woman made no effort to introduce them. There was an uneasy silence as they waited.

Finally, a younger version of Alvin entered the kitchen. He was burly and scowling.

"Thet damned hound bitch," he complained to no one in particular, "ain't tendin' her puppies."

"So let 'em die," Alvin laughed.

"Mama!" the last to arrive whined, child-like.

"Don't fret yerself, Birch," Lulubelle crooned. "Alvin were jest funnin'. Ah'll take of them puppies."

Birch beamed his appreciation.

His mother, shaking her head in exasperation, turned on Alvin. "Did ya tell Eddie Ah wanted 'im here?!" she screamed at him. Her disparate emotions—from cloying tenderness to sudden rage—suggested a kind of madness to the visitor.

The brutish Alvin was cowed. "Ah did, Mama, honest."

A head poked its way around the doorframe, the long, light-brown hair wildly tousled. Dark eyes in a pinched face revealed what Casey believed was genuine fright.

"It's all right, Eddie," Lulubelle assured him with great gentleness. "Ain't nobody gonna hurt ya. Jest come in an' set yerself, baby."

Alvin laughed meanly.

"An ya keep yer goddamned mouth shut!" the woman railed at him. The laugh died in Alvin's throat.

Hesitantly, the young man called Eddie, who was wearing military fatigues made of camouflage material, stepped into the kitchen, making a wide circle around the table until he reached a chair as far away from Ballard as he could get. He sat on the edge of it, poised to flee.

"Now!" Lulubelle announced gaily, "all mah boys is t'gether. Babies, this here is Mr. Casey Ballard, K.C.'s only livin' grandboy."

The faces around the table were sullen.

"An' Casey, Ah want ya t' meet all mah sweethearts." She

pointed. "Thet there is mah first borned—Alvin. January thirteen, 1945, it were."

The finger went to the man who had shown concern about the hound puppies. "An' thet's, Birch—October three, 1945. Figure thet Mr. Staley caught me in the foal heat." Lulubelle laughed raucously.

Alvin smirked.

Again the woman's emotions took a roller coaster ride. Her eyes teared. "Mr. Staley, God rest his soul, left us on New Year's Day of '46. Went to meet Jee-sus, he did, leavin' them baby boys with no poppa."

There was a sob, a shrug, and she got back to her introductions, moving the finger to the florid-faced blond. "An' thet's Chester." She stared at him for a moment. "Chester Richmond—November seventeen, 1947. Poor baby, he's jest like his daddy. Drunk mostly." As an afterthought: "But Ah dearly loved Mr. Richmond long as he stayed 'round."

Lulubelle pointed now to the behemoth with the tattooed arms and scarred face. "Thet's Daniel—December twenty-three, 1948. Mah Christmas present, he were." Her crooked grin suggested a measure of sinfulness. "'Course, Ah ain't real sure who left it. Got mah suspicions, but—" Yet another shrug. "He's Daniel *Staley*, though, legal-like."

She had come to the younger man in the camouflage fatigues. When the hand with the extended finger reached him, he flinched.

"An' this here's mah *real* baby—Edgar. January ten, 1950. Served in Vietnam, he did, an' got a lot o' medals." Pride was evident. "Eddie, ya oughta show them medals t' Casey."

Eddie's attention was fixed on the floor between his feet.

"Vietnam ain't done 'im no good," Lulubelle went on sadly, no longer seeming to be talking to any of them. "Ain't done 'im no good t'all. 'Course, mebbe thet's mah fault. Joined the Marines when he weren't but fifteen, an' Ah signed the papers sayin' he were eighteen." She sighed. "Po' baby."

Addressing Casey directly now, she asked, "Ya think he favors yer granddaddy?"

"I really can't say," Ballard admitted.

"Well, he oughta. He's ol' K.C.'s boy—Edgar Ballard. He's yer kin!" She caught the surprised look on Casey's face. "Thet's gospel! Eddie's yer uncle. Now, ain't thet somethin'?"

"It's certainly news I hadn't . . . uh . . . anticipated."

"Me an' K.C. talked 'bout marryin' a time or two," Lulubelle explained, "but we jest never seemed t' git 'round t' it."

Casey made no comment.

"Well . . . them's mah boys," the fat woman said, putting a period on the introductions. "Now, what were it ya wanted t' say 'bout the inheritance?"

Ballard was totally ill-at-ease in the strange company. He looked around the table. "What I was trying to say to your mother earlier is . . . uh . . . well, I have some questions about this place—" He made a small gesture which he meant as an indication of the entire roadhouse operation. "Frankly, it boils down to this. I have no way to know whether your offer for the property is reasonable without seeing some records of the business."

Alvin leaned forward menacingly.

"Records?" Lulubelle asked weakly.

"Yes. Books, ledgers, financial records, you know."

"There ain't no books," the woman told him sullenly.

"Mr. Alderman has told me that. But," Casey had the feeling he was on very shaky ground, "what kind of income is there—?"

"Thet ain't none of yer business," Alvin snarled.

"But it *is*, young man," Ballard said, trying to keep an even tone. "You see, under the terms of the will, it's *my* business now."

"Mama?" Alvin looked to his mother, startled by what the stranger had said.

Lulubelle set her flabby face into a stern mask. "Yer gonna git the property, an' we wanna buy it from ya. Do ya wanna sell or doncha?"

"I came here with the intention of selling. But first I must know what it is I'm selling."

" 'Bout twenty-two acres," she said, "this house, a barn—"

"And a business," Casey added.

"Thet ain't part o' it!"

"Of course it is, Mrs. Staley. Didn't K.C. Ballard run a business here for many years? Isn't the business being operated right now?" He waited for an answer.

"Yeah."

"Then . . . that business becomes part of what my grandfather left me in the will. It's part of his estate."

"Nope, cain't be."

Casey sighed deeply, determining to try one more time to get his point across. "Look, Mrs. Staley . . . and fellows . . . I realize you've been caring for my grandfather in his declining years—"

"An' it weren't no goddamned picnic," Alvin growled. "Thet crazy ol' fool—!"

"Shut yer stupid mouth!" Lulubelle bellowed.

Alvin leaned back in his chair, appearing to be suddenly disinterested.

"Perhaps, Mrs. Staley, it would be best if you discussed this with your lawyer."

"Thet shit ass!" she thundered. "He sez we just oughta offer ya a price fer the place an' you'd prob'ly sell. But now ya ain't! So what the hell does he know?"

"Talk it over with someone else, then. Maybe Zeb Alderman."

"Yeah . . . mebbe."

"I'll tell you what," Casey tried for a conciliatory tone, "let me go away for a few hours to give you time to discuss the terms of the will with Mr. Alderman. I'll come back later and we'll finish this, huh?"

"There's a lot o' damned ways t' finish things," Alvin mumbled threatingly.

This time Lulubelle didn't silence him.

iii   Rosie Ballard had spent an hour delicately balancing the need to support her husband and her own fears. She had wanted him to go to Tennessee because it seemed an ideal digression for him, something to relieve his mind of the trauma of having been summarily dismissed from the police force. In the public eye, of course, it was a retirement after twenty-nine years of exemplary service. But to Casey—indeed, to Rosalie, as well—he had been fired. In her innermost secret thoughts, the cop's wife was thankful. If she didn't have to say it out loud she could admit her husband had made a grievous error in the Jack Carmen incident. An error that, if he had stayed on the force, he might have compounded at a later date.

She had seen it happen to other veteran police officers; something so virulent it might have been classified as a disease. It was too complex to label, but it had to do with a growing hardness, coupled with a firm belief nothing could harm them. And in the final throes of it, the assumption of a god-like stance, a determination to act without any rules, any morals, save the ones in their own commandments. Rosalie was convinced Lieutenant Casey Ballard had been in the final fevered stage of the "disease" when he had gunned down Jack Carmen. A year earlier, a month earlier, maybe even a week earlier, he would have apprehended Carmen by the book and been exhilarated by it. Perhaps the fever reached its peak at that very moment the felon fled into the men's room at the Northwestern Station. He was doomed then because the malady had left Casey with no choice but to think of killing Carmen.

That was why Rosalie offered up a silent prayer of thanks when Commissioner Stiles had left their apartment with Casey's gun and shield in hand. And that was why she had encouraged him to go to Tennessee to conclude matters on his grandfather's inheritance. A brief stay in a new environment, she had reasoned, would be an antidote to the poison she could not name. And Casey would return home refreshed, at ease, and they could go on with their lives in happy, loving retirement.

Now she feared, however, that Mountain County was not going to provide the "cure." In a long telephone call with Casey she recognized the symptoms of "a case." Things were not right in Mountain County he told her. There were forces afoot suggesting to him a plot of some kind. Even though he had been there only twenty-four hours, he had come upon a conspiracy to hide the real worth of K.C. Ballard's estate.

"My grandfather was one of the wealthiest men in the county," he insisted. "My God, Rosie, this roadhouse operation here has *had* to be a goldmine. Gambling and illegal booze and whores—running wide open without police interference. Most likely with the acquiescence of the law, some kind of partnership, I'll bet. And at the end the old man had only a small savings account of three thousand dollars and twenty-two acres, a house and a barn for which I'm now being offered forty grand. It doesn't make any sense."

"Maybe your grandfather just blew it all with his profligate living," Rosie offered.

"They'd like me to believe that. There was this young girl at the hotel reservation desk—" Casey told her the story of Kathy Ringer and her affair with K.C. "And then, when I want to question her, they hustle her out of the county. To God knows where."

"People do get other job offers, you know."

"Hmmm. This one was too damned sudden."

Rosalie decided to change the subject. "Darling, I miss you."

"Yeah . . . me, too."

She laughed. "What a romantic devil you are, Casey. You really know how to sweet talk a girl. 'Me, too.' That's lovely."

"You know how much I love you, Rosie."

"Yeah, and I also know you haven't been off the reservation for a long time. And now you're down there where the woods are full of bosomy Daisy Maes and where the livin' is easy. Or so I'm led to believe."

"No Daisy Maes so far," he chuckled. "The one woman I've had any real contact with must weigh three hundred pounds, has four chins of flab, and sweats."

Rosie giggled. "You know what they say: the longer you're in the jungle the better the native broads look."

"Yeah, well . . . I'd rather take my turn in the barrel."

"Before you're forced to do that, darling, come on home." She flavored the line with a meaningful pause. "Better barrel."

"O'Hara, you're becoming positively pornographic in your advancing age."

"Uh huh. And aren't you glad?"

They were laughing together now; a normal mood had returned.

"Be back soon," he promised. "No more than a day or two."

As she hung up the phone, she murmured, "Dear God, don't let it be a case."

iv   By midafternoon, when Casey Ballard returned to K.C.'s, the parking lot was jammed, forcing him to find a place on a small grassy plot off the gravel, where a group of mud-spattered pickup trucks had been drawn up in a circle in the manner of an Old West wagon train positioned for an Indian attack.

As he got out of his car Casey was greeted by the sound of a rooster crowing. And another. And another. Wire cages in the beds of the trucks held chickens. And in the center of the circle there were as many as twenty men of varying ages engaged in noisy banter.

His curiosity drew him onto the fringes of the circle. Two older men, with birds held firmly in strong hands, were jabbing the heads of the fowl at each other. *Jab, jab, jab.* But the birds weren't being allowed to really become engaged. Simply put, the men were using them to feint jabs as might be done by prize fighters.

"Ain't never seen fightin' chickens, huh?"

Casey turned to find a smiling young man at his elbow, dressed in denim jeans and jacket and wearing a baseball cap on which the logo proclaimed: RUDY'S GARAGE. His question had been perceptive.

"No," Ballard admitted, "I haven't. But how did you know?"

There was a laugh. "Don't see many fellers 'round here wearin' a suit an' tie."

53

"No, I suppose not. But could you tell me what's going on here?"

"Mostly braggin'," the young man chuckled. "The fellers foolin' 'round there with them chickens is tryin' t' talk up their birds. An' set somebody up fer a bet fer t'night's fights."

"Large bets?"

"Ya might say thet. Last Friday night, Deacon Carter from the west end o' the county won ten grand. Leastways thet's what Ah heared tell." He looked around the circle. "Ah don't see 'im here yet, but ol' Deacon'll be back, believe ya me. An' mebbe lose the whole wad, too."

"Do you have . . . uh . . . . fighting chickens?"

"Naw. They's too damned much trouble. Got a garage 'bout four miles south on I-40." He stuck out his hand. "Name's Rudy Pitts."

The Chicagoan shook the hand. "Casey Ballard."

Rudy's eyebrows shot up. "Kin t' ol' K.C.?"

"Yes, his grandson."

"Well, Ah'll be damned! Word's been goin' 'round thet ya was here, but Ah didn't 'spect t' meet ya." He pumped Casey's hand once more. "Real pleasurable, Mr. Ballard."

"Thank you. Maybe later you can fill me in on the fine points of fighting chickens."

"Be pleased t'. Mighty pleased!"

Casey clapped the young man on the back, making for the house, feeling somewhat like a Mountain County celebrity.

At the door he knocked once and it opened immediately. Chester stood there, his face more florid than before. It was obvious Lulubelle's son had been waiting for him.

"This way," Chester grunted. Walking unsteadily, he led Casey along a hallway—a part of the house he hadn't seen on his first visit—ending in a barroom. A juke box blared a rock-abilly tune, a few couples were dancing, and several whores were seated at tables, drinking with their paramours of the moment.

He followed his drunken guide to a table near the long bar, where there were four chairs but only one occupant—a man of

Casey's age, dressed in a tan policeman's uniform, a silver badge on his chest.

"Here," Chester mumbled, stumbling away.

The man rose, smiling, offering his hand. "Mr. Ballard, I'm Sheriff Terry Foster." He was darkly handsome, broad-shouldered, self-confident.

"Pleased to meet you, Sheriff," Casey said, accepting the hand. Foster's grip was powerful. They sat down.

"Lulubelle tells me," Foster was still smiling, "that there's some hitch in the sale of K.C.'s Place to her."

So that's it! The power of the local law is being brought into this thing.

"Oh, I think that's a misunderstanding," Casey replied, maintaining a friendly manner. "It's not a 'hitch' so much as it's a desire on my part to get a proper evaluation of the property. Books, ledgers, perhaps tax records." He matched the sheriff's grin. "Then, too, I'm in no hurry to leave. I'm somewhat enamored of Mountain County."

"I can readily appreciate that. It's an exemplary place."

Casey hesitated, but he had to know. "Are you a native of Mountain County, Sheriff?"

Foster laughed heartily. "What you meant to ask was how is it I don't sound like a hill-country redneck?"

"Well—"

"My father, who was sheriff here for many years—as was *his* father before him—sent me to Vanderbilt University, where I graduated *cum laude.*" He was enjoying Ballard's unease. "When my father died, I ran in the special election to succeed him—successfully, as you can surmise."

"I see."

"You might also be interested to know, *Lieutenant* Ballard, that I majored in criminal justice."

Casey fought to keep his face immobile.

"It wasn't difficult to find out who you were," Foster continued. "One call to the Cook County sheriff's office gave me what I wanted to know: Lieutenant Casey Ballard, second in command of the vice squad of the Chicago Police Department. Twenty-nine years experience. Currently involved in an imbroglio over the shooting death of a felon named Jack Carmen. Son of Patrolman Abel Ballard, late of Mountain County, who was killed in the line of duty. Husband of Rosalie, née O'Hara. No children." He shrugged.

"Very efficient, Sheriff." Apparently his informant in Cook County hadn't yet heard of the forced retirement.

"Thank you."

"Now . . . may I ask," Casey said quietly, "why you thought it was necessary to know all that?"

"I become very interested in people when they seem to be hiding something, as you did when you chatted with Zeb Alderman yesterday. Really, Lieutenant, you might have been more imaginative in describing your occupation. *Security*, wasn't that what you said?" Again he laughed loudly.

Casey was on the defensive and he didn't like it. "What I do for a living has nothing at all to do with the reason for my visit to Mountain County."

"Perhaps not," Foster conceded, "but some of our folks might not take too kindly to the presence of a big city cop, and that might lead to trouble. You see, Lieutenant, I like being the sheriff of Mountain County. And I'm good at it because I know what's going on here every minute of the day. I head off a lot of difficulties that way. And the people here appreciate that because they feel as I do, that Mountain County is their preserve in which they can live their lives as they see fit."

"In places like this?" Casey swept his arm to encompass the roadhouse operation.

"If that's what they want."

"Whores and bootleg whiskey and gambling and cockfights?"

"Uh huh."

"And it doesn't bother you, Sheriff, that all of this is against the law?"

Foster smiled tolerantly. "The law is what the people want it to be. It has always been amazing to me what happens to a man who gets elected to public office. He quickly assumes he has been given the power to play God with the people's morals. I don't make that assumption. For instance, is it worse to get drunk on homemade moonshine than on bottled-in-bond, high-tax whiskey?"

"I wish I could see the law in such simplistic terms."

"Maybe in Chicago you can't," the sheriff replied, "because most of the time you're dealing with people you don't know. Virtual strangers. Now here, it's much more simple. You might say we can tailor the law to fit the people involved, because we know the people intimately."

"Tailoring the law, as you put, is *not* what it's all about, Sheriff." Casey's words were harder now. "You can't pick and choose the laws you want to enforce and not enforce."

"Maybe in Chicago—"

"Don't give me that shit, Foster! Murder in Chicago is the same as murder in Mountain County. Prostitution is prostitution wherever it occurs. Illegal whiskey is illegal whiskey in both places. The law is not a matter of geography!"

Foster studied Casey's angry face for a moment. "I'm sure we could carry on this fascinating dissertation for hours. But let's get to why I asked to see you. As I understand it from Lulubelle's rather . . . uh . . . colorful outburst, you'd like to see some documentation of the worth of your grandfather's estate."

"Yes."

"You know, of course, that K.C. Ballard was an illiterate, unschooled old redneck."

"So I've been told."

"Then it must be obvious to you that there are no documents, no files, no books, no ledgers—" Sheriff Foster sighed. "Your grandfather, Lieutenant, was a free spirit. A woman-chasing old scoundrel whose only sense of money was that it was to be spent. And believe me, he spent it—with both hands!"

"Hmmm."

"I hate to fall back on a cliché, but what you see is what you get: acreage, house, barn—worth about what the Staleys are offering you. So, I ask you, Ballard, what are your intentions?"

"Well, I have several options—"

"Excuse me, Lieutenant, but I respectfully suggest, as a courtesy of one police officer to another, that you don't have *options*. Why don't you just sell the place to Lulubelle and forget it?"

"An ultimatum?"

"Ultimatum is such a harsh word. I'd prefer the phrase 'friendly advice.'"

"I'll bet you would," Casey responded sarcastically.

"And the sum of that friendly advice is as follows: sell the property to Lulubelle and her baby boys . . . " He grinned. "Allow the kind folks of Mountain County to show you a good time for a few days, as a kin of old K.C., and then take that plane, on which you already have an open reservation, back to Chicago. Shall we say by Sunday afternoon?"

"How did—? You searched my hotel room!"

Sheriff Foster sat silently, not bothering to deny Casey's accusation.

"Damn you, Foster!"

The Mountain County lawman waited for Casey's anger to subside somewhat. "I've suggested to Lulubelle that, to bring this matter to an amicable conclusion, she and the boys sweeten the pot. She's accepted my suggestion. They're offering ten thousand more."

Ballard forced a grin. "You really want to get rid of me, don't you?"

"I want what's best for Mountain County."

Casey slumped back in his chair. His back was paining him again, sharp spasms making him want to cry out. He glanced toward the bar.

"Drink, Lieutenant?" Foster asked perceptively.

"I think this might be the time for one."

The sheriff signaled toward the bar and within a few moments a Scotch sour, without the fruit garnishes, was placed on the table by a waitress. Ballard stared at it.

"That's your drink, isn't it?"

"So you talked to the bartender at the inn, too?"

"You said yourself I was efficient." Foster reached over to a vacant chair to pick up a file folder he had placed there. "I figured you wouldn't approve of our . . . well, our methods here, and I thought I might have to give you a graphic illustration of the worth of the selective justice of Mountain County. I went back into my father's old files to find the details of a February 1933 killing. In this very place, as a matter of fact. It had to do with the death of one King David Ballard, age nineteen, a son of the departed K.C. Now, King David was a hellraiser of some note in those days—my father had more than one run-in with him, if I am to believe the records."

Casey was remembering the story told to him by banker Zebulon Alderman.

Sheriff Foster opened the file folder. "On that particular February day—Thursday, February sixteenth, to be exact—King David Ballard, mean drunk, got into a family dispute with a younger brother, Abel Ballard, age eighteen. They fought. In the course of that fight, which was going badly for Abel, he picked up an axe from a convenient woodpile and struck King David on the left temple, apparently killing him instantly. Then, in his rage, Abel fell on the dead body and continued to hack at it, inflicting," he looked down at the papers inside the folder, "fourteen additional wounds."

The Chicagoan gasped.

"There were two eyewitnesses to the fight," Foster went on unemotionally, "and the subsequent axe incident: a sister, Sarah, and a patron of K.C.'s Place, one Barney Daniels. Both told essentially the same story, with only inconsequential varying elements of detail."

The sheriff took a deep breath. "Abel, though, had taken off. What was apparently persistent questioning by my father elicited from sister Sarah the admission that Abel, driving a stolen Model A, was heading for Chicago. My father must have pondered what to do. His thoughts, sad to say, are not written down, but the decision he reached is noted: *Case Closed,* he wrote, and he put his signature underneath it."

Foster slowly closed the file folder, tossing to across the table to Casey. "So, you see, my father had options. He might have reasoned the world was a better place without the likes of King David Ballard, that young Abel Ballard wasn't really an evil individual, and that if he reached Chicago, he might prosper in the new environment. Was my father wrong? Was that poor law enforcement? I don't think so. Do you?"

The sheriff got to his feet. "Think it over, Lieutenant. Have a good meal; they've got a pretty good cook here. Relax a bit, take in the cockfights tonight, and . . . well, my suggestion is, if I may be redundant, that you accept Lulubelle's latest generous offer."

Casey nodded. "I'll think about it."

"Good, good. Keep the file, Ballard. That's only a photocopy." He paused. "I still have the original if it ever becomes necessary to reopen that case again." Foster took a step or two away from the table, before turning again to the visitor. "It has just occurred to me that, while the sins of the father cannot properly be visited on the son, it might be damned inconvenient, while you're answering the charges on that Jack Carmen killing, to have the accusations against your father made public."

Clapping a broad-brimmed hat on his head, Sheriff Terry Foster strode away. Grinning broadly.

Casey nursed his Scotch sour, deep in thought. What had just transpired didn't make a lot of sense to him. The sheriff had gone to great and unusual lengths, he believed, to bring to a conclusion a simple real estate deal. A damned *modest* real estate deal.

Why? Why does Foster think it's necessary to threaten, to try to blackmail me, really? What's behind it? It certainly isn't the solution of a fifty-two-year-old murder case. It's deeper that that. My presence here is a threat to him in some way. There's something else he doesn't want me to know. But what the hell is it?

Ballard's stomach rumbled and he decided to accept at least one of the sheriff's recommendations. He summoned the waitress, ordering dinner.

5

i   Strong spotlights, stabbing their beams through the cloud-like haze of dust and smoke hanging over the ring, illuminated the ancient rituals of the cockfight. Boisterous male voices, with a smattering of female shrieks in counterpoint to the guttural basses, ricocheted off the high oaken beams of the big barn at K.C.'s Place.

Casey Ballard's place now.

For that had been his decision. A half hour earlier he had told the gross Lulubelle Staley he meant to retain ownership of his inheritance, although he was ready to lease the property to her (and to her "boys") in perpetuity, as it were, for a modest stipend. He had suggested one hundred dollars a month. "Only a token," he had told her. She had been furious.

He stood now, one of more than two hundred beings in the barn, thinking not of Lulubelle's anger, nor of the "friendly advice" or implied threats of Sheriff Foster, nor even of the razor-sharp steel spurs, the torn flesh, and the broken wings: the terrible, sickening ingredients of the cockfights. His thoughts were zeroed in on what he was going to tell Rosalie O'Hara Ballard about the decision he had reached.

She's going to think I'm insane! And maybe—? Questions without answers held him there in a vise-like grip. *Rosie's going to want me to be rational about all this and there's nothing rational in what I've just done.* He could leave Mountain County right then fifty thousand dollars richer. And yet—

"Ya bettin', Mr. Ballard?" a voice shouted over the din.

Casey turned to find the young man from Rudy's Garage smiling at him.

"No, Mr. Pitts, I really don't understand anything of what's going on here."

"See that big feller over there?" Rudy inclined his head to the right, indicating a bearded giant who held an orange-red rooster in his hands. "Thet's Clarence Bimstock an' thet chicken he's got there is the best here t'night. 'Course, most of the rednecks hereabouts don't know thet yet, so the odds are gonna be against him. A good bet now could earn ya some real money, believe me."

"Operating on inside information, Mr. Pitts?" Casey chuckled.

"Well . . . Ah never bet less'n Ah got some solid reason t' do it. Bimstock's rooster is mah reason t'night. Take mah word fer it, Mr. Ballard, an' git some money down."

"Uh . . . I'm not familiar with the methods—"

"Ah'll be happy to place the bet fer ya."

Casey shrugged. "Hell, why not?" He had just taken a much bigger gamble in turning down the offer for K.C.'s Place. Reaching into his pocket, he came out with a twenty-dollar bill.

Disappointment showed on young Pitts' face. "Is thet all? Ah figure yer gonna git five-t'-one, mebbe as much as eight-t'-one. Seems a shame jest t' bet twenty in thet case. Ah'm puttin' up a thousand."

Ballard was astonished. "No, no, Mr. Pitts," he said soberly, "I'm not that big a sport, I'm afraid."

"A hundred? It's a lock, Ah tell ya."

"It is, eh? Well, Mr. Pitts, I might as well."

Quickly, Casey counted out eighty dollars more, handing the money to the open-faced garage mechanic.

"Ya won't be sorry, Mr. Ballard. Gotta go now an' git this down." He hurried away.

Casey almost immediately dismissed the hundred. Rosie's angry face showed in his mind's eye once more. Trying to clear himself of that image, he strolled along the back fringes of the crowd, studying the faces. He spotted Alvin Staley tight against the ring rope, screaming obscenities at a bird flopping in the dust, near death, as the opposition cock raked it with the cruel spurs.

He turned away from it, fully understanding for the first time why the exhibitions were outlawed. In front of him, as he turned, he saw the figure of Edgar Ballard huddled on a bale of hay, the same dreadful fright in his eyes Casey had observed earlier in the day. Smiling in a friendly manner, Casey moved toward him; Eddie's feet went to the barn floor, prepared to escape.

Very slowly, Casey sat down on the hay bale as Eddie inched away from him.

"Eddie, since we're kin, maybe we ought to be friends." Casey extended his hand. The younger man just stared at him, seeming not to comprehend what was expected of him. Casey kept the hand extended and, after a few moments, Eddie reached out touching the alien hand lightly.

God, that must have taken courage!

"I've got to admit," Ballard chuckled, "that I never expected to have an uncle who was younger than I was."

Eddie stared.

"How old are you, Eddie?"

He stared some more. Then: "Thirty-five—last week." The answer was barely heard in the noisy barn.

Encouraged by that response, Casey went on. "Your mother said you were in Vietnam?"

The shaggy head shook affirmatively.

"Rough, huh?"

Another affirmative nod.

"Where were you, Eddie?"

It seemed the eyes opened wider in fright. Thirty seconds went by. A minute. "Hue," he said sadly. There was another long silence. "An' Quang Tri."

"Jesus Christ!"

"Ah came out March twenty-nine, '73."

"The last day?"

"Yeah." He swallowed hard, tears starting down his cheeks. "In mah company Ah were the on'y one—" The emotions of his memories overwhelmed him; no more words needed to be said.

Ballard could only look at him sympathetically, seeing in that one man all of the brutalities, the senselessness, of the Vietnam war.

Suddenly, with no warning, Eddie leapt to his feet, racing away.

Startled, Casey looked around to see what might have occasioned the flight. Sheriff Foster was approaching the hay bale. He sat down next to Ballard.

"Lulubelle tells me you're not going to sell."

"That's right."

"A mistake, Lieutenant." Terry's previously friendly attitude had vanished.

"Oh, why?"

"I didn't think I'd have to spell it out for you," the sheriff answered disparagingly. "You're not welcome here, Ballard."

"But I won't be here."

"Your *presence* will, because you'll own the place."

"I'm flattered that you'll be thinking of me."

"Cut the shit, Lieutenant!"

Casey got to his feet. "Excuse me, Sheriff, but I want to find Eddie."

"You can't help him. His life is finished. But you *can* still help yourself."

"By selling the property to the Staleys?"

"Exactly."

"I'm sorry, I can't do that. I don't think my rental proposal is unreasonable—"

"Lulubelle *deserves* this place."

"Apparently my grandfather didn't think so."

"Your grandfather was a senile old fool!"

They were interrupted as Rudy Pitts rushed up, wildly waving a stack of bills. "What'd Ah tell ya, Mr. Ballard. We won! At seven-t'-one!" He started to count out Casey's profits.

The sheriff watched for a brief moment. "You've been betting on the cockfights?"

"When in Rome—" Casey laughed.

"Don't you know that gambling is illegal in Mountain County?"

"Then you'll just have to arrest me, won't you?" Ballard held out his hands, wrists together, pantomiming his readiness for handcuffs.

"There are other ways, Lieutenant!" Foster stalked off.

Pitts was perplexed. "What the hell were all thet 'bout?"

"The sheriff and I have a little difference of opinion on a business deal, Mr. Pitts."

Rudy dropped his voice, leaning closer to Casey. "Don't mess with 'im, Mr. Ballard. He kin be a mean sonofabitch."

"Thank you for your advice, Mr. Pitts. I gather it's as accurate as your advice on fighting cocks."

"It is," the garage mechanic answered firmly. "Believe ya me, it *is.*" He shook Casey's hand and melted into the crowd.

Ballard went looking for the distressed Eddie. He didn't know what he could do for him, but he was impelled by the feeling he ought to try something. Almost anything. Eddie had earned some concern. He circled the cockfight ring without spotting the frightened man. Then he left the barn to search outside. After fifteen minutes, he gave up the frustrating hunt. There were just too many places in which Eddie might be hiding from his terrors.

Idly, without knowing why, Casey returned to the barn. He was moving around the ring, studying the faces once more, when the sound of a shotgun blast stopped him in his tracks. Dust and minor bits of debris fluttered down from the high ceiling indicating the shot had been fired in the air. He also recognized that both barrels had been fired simultaneously.

Casey's mind conjured up the body of Jack Carmen smashing against the wall of the Chicago men's room. He felt ill again. Instinctively, he reached for the gun he no longer carried.

How long am I going to keep doing that?

The din in the barn had subsided to a few nervous whispers.

In the center of the ring stood three men, their faces hidden behind ski masks. Two of them held shotguns; one was reloading his. The third, the tallest of them, held a .45 pistol leveled at the spectators directly in front of him.

"Don't nobody git nervous!" the tall one bellowed. "Pure an' simple, git yer money out—an' fast!"

His shotgun-toting companions, each with a burlap sack, began moving through the crowd collecting wads of bills. Casey guessed the haul would be considerable.

The leader turned his head slowly, the pistol muzzle following the movement of the head. His eyes stopped on Casey. "You!" he shouted, gesturing with the gun.

"You speaking to me?" Ballard asked.

"Ya goddamned right! Git yer ass over here!"

Then, a loud metallic click, the ominous sound of a weapon being cocked.

From out of the crowd came a blood-curdling cry as a body hurtled at the tall man. *Edgar!* A shot. Two shots. Three.

Lightning struck Casey Ballard on the left temple. As he crumpled in the dust, his blood mingled with that of the defeated cocks.

ii   His head pained him. A searing, roaring pain. Worse than anything he had ever known before. He moaned.

"Well, Mr. Ballard, Ah'm pleased t' see thet yer comin' 'round." It was a male voice.

Casey opened his eyes. He was in a double bed in a room he guessed was in K.C.'s Victorian roadhouse. Bending over him was an elderly man, his hair snowy white. He was smiling.

"Ah'm Doc Willson—Amos Willson. An' Ah tell ya, Mr. Ballard, ya had a mighty close call. Mighty close, indeed."

Casey stared at him dumbly.

"Ya don't remember?"

"Not much," he replied weakly.

"Three men held up the cockfights. One of 'em shot ya. Or shot *at* ya. Eddie jumped 'im an'—"

It came clear now. "Eddie! Is he okay?"

"Well, now," the doctor said sadly, "he took a .45 full in the chest. Ah'm jest a country doctor, but Ah've seen mah share o' gunshot wounds, an' that'n wasn't good. He's in the Gatlinburg hospital. Last Ah heard he was critical."

"Oh, good Lord—"

"Mighta been critical for ya, too. The bullet grazed yer left temple. Left a mighty deep furrow there. A millimeter or two closer an'—" He shrugged. "Gave yer head a purty good whack, though, an' Ah know ya got a concussion o' some sort. Ah also know ya got five stitches in the temple—put 'em there mahself."

Casey started to nod his understanding, but excruciating pain stopped the movement.

"Yer mighty lucky, Mr. Ballard."

"Yeah."

"Yer gonna have a hurtin' head fer a bit, but after a li'l rest Ah think ya'll be all right."

Ballard thought of Rosie. "What day is it, Doctor?"

"Saturday." He checked his watch. " 'Bout one A.M. Ya've been out for more'n three hours."

The patient groaned. *How in the hell am I going to explain this to Rosie? She must have been frantic when I didn't call her last night.*

"Now, Ah wanna give ya a sedative," Dr. Willson said, "but the sheriff's been waitin' fer ya to come to, an' Ah figured t' hold off on the shot 'til he could talk to ya. He's out in the hallway. Ya wanna talk t' him?"

Casey sighed. "Yes, as a matter of fact, I do."

The old doctor went to the bedroom door, opened it, and gestured. Sheriff Foster entered, going to the bed and looking down at Ballard.

"You had a close call," he said.

"Not close enough for you, I'll bet."

Sudden anger showed in the lawman's eyes. "What the hell does that mean?"

"Look, Foster, I know a setup when I see one. That damned robbery was just a cover to get me!" It pained him to speak with such vehemence, but he wanted to have this confrontation with the sheriff.

Dr. Willson, sensing he was in the wrong place, started for the door.

"No, Doctor, you stay," Casey called to him. "I may need a competent witness."

The sheriff modulated his voice. "Lieutenant, I can understand that you're upset, but it was a robbery and nothing more. It's unfortunate that Eddie was crazy enough to—"

"You sonofabitch! Eddie saved my life. That prick with the .45 was gunning for me. He came in there to shoot me!"

Foster shrugged. "I was hoping you'd be rational enough to give us some kind of leg up on who those fellows might have been, but—"

"Oh, I'm rational, Sheriff. I'll know that bastard with the .45 if I see him again."

"You will?"

"Absolutely."

"But the other eyewitnesses all say the three gunmen wore ski masks."

"Then you weren't in the barn at the time?"

"No," Foster said firmly, "I had just driven away."

"Convenient."

The sheriff waited for a moment. "I'm going to ignore the sarcasm, Lieutenant, because your wound is obviously affecting your thinking . . ."

"It's not."

"But how will you know the man with the pistol?"

"He had only three fingers on the hand with which he held the gun."

Foster sucked in a deep breath.

"You know him?"

"No. He's probably from out of the county."

Casey laughed and it send shards of pain through his head. "I'm sure he is, Sheriff, because as close as you are to your people you'd certainly know a man with three fingers."

"I would, yes. And I don't know of any such individual. But your description, if accurate, ought to make it easier to find him."

"Hmmm."

"Anything else?" the sheriff asked.

"No." He closed his eyes and then opened them again quickly. "But I do want to know about Eddie."

"I'll keep you informed."

When the sheriff left the bedroom, Dr. Willson brought a hypodermic syringe and gave Casey a shot in his right arm. "Thet'll let ya get a li'l sleep—an' kill some pain—an' Ah'll check with ya later."

"Thanks, Doc."

Willson busied himself with the contents of his medical bag. "Mebbe Ah oughta stay out o' this, but—" He hesitated.

"What is it, Doctor?"

"Ah know a man with three fingers."

"What?!"

"Yeah. Feller named Willie Young. Lost the fingers in some farm machinery. Matter o' fact, Ah did the operation on his hand."

"Does he live in Mountain County?"

"Nope, over the Carolina border three or four miles."

"Does Sheriff Foster know him?"

"Cain't say. Don't know why he would. Willie's a hard-scrabble farmer. Nobody special, ya know. 'Cept he had three fingers."

"On his right hand?"

"Yep."

"Do me a favor, Doctor. Let's keep this three-fingered man confidential between us. Okay?"

"Glad t'. Ah don't wanna . . . well, ruffle Terry Foster's feathers." The elderly man closed his bag. "Thet sedative will work purty soon now. It'll let ya rest."

He left the room, turning off the lights as he did.

Casey closed his eyes. And slept. Dreaming of the warmth of Rosie next to him.

iii   Tears ran down the fat cheeks, making tiny furrows in the overabundance of makeup. Lulubelle Staley had done nothing but cry for hours. Now, at ten o'clock on that Saturday morning, it seemed impossible there were any more tears left to shed.

She dabbed at her ravaged face with an elaborately embroidered handkerchief, wailing once more: "Mah deah li'l baby, Eddie. Oh, sweet Jee-sus, save 'im!"

Alvin Staley, lounging in a chair next to her, looked at his mother in disgust. "Mama, cain't ya hush up fer a minute? All thet noise ain't helpin' 'im, ya know."

Her loud lamenting stopped, but the deep sobbing was anything but quiet.

Birch was there, too. And Chester, taking numerous pulls on a small jug of moonshine he had brought along. And Daniel, spending the time contemplating the colorful tattoos on his forearms, making them come alive with small, jerking motions of his muscles.

The Staleys sat in a waiting room at the Gatlinburg hospital. They had been there since just before midnight of the previous evening, for all of those long hours Edgar Ballard had been on an operating table and then in intensive care, as doctors tried to save his life.

It was ten minutes after ten when a surgeon, still wearing his gray-green surgical gown, entered the waiting room. His face was drawn with fatigue.

"Mrs. Staley?" he asked of the fat woman.

"Yeah," she sobbed.

"I'm sorry, ma'm, but your son has died. The damage was just too severe to—"

Lulubelle's screams of anguish cut him off.

"Mama, for Christ sake!" Alvin yelled at her.

The bitter wailing only grew louder.

"Birch! Take 'er the hell outta here!" the elder brother commanded.

His arm around the obese woman, the muscular Birch guided her firmly out of the waiting room. Her screaming could be heard until her son had her out of the building.

"She were most partial t' Eddie," Alvin tried to explain to the doctor.

"It's always difficult to accept—"

"Now—what the hell went wrong, Doc?" There was no mistaking Alvin's accusatory tone.

"The bullet, fired at close range," the surgeon began quietly, "entered the left side of your brother, coursing upward and toward the back." He indicated on his own body the path traveled by the bullet. "Both lungs were involved and the heart was nicked. We have reason to believe the slug was scored in some manner, because it literally disintegrated. Quite honestly, I'm not really sure how many fragments there were. But there was no exit wound and the internal damage was severe."

Alvin stared at him, trying to comprehend what he had been told. "Ya mean a dum-dum—?"

"Something like that," the doctor sighed. "Ballistics experts may be able to be more specific after an autopsy. But I do know the individual fragments of the slug . . . well, raised havoc within the chest cavity."

"Jee-sus Christ!" Alvin's face reddened in rage. "Thet sonofabitch Ballard! It's his doin'—an' Ah'll git thet bastard if'n it's the last thing Ah do!"

6

i   Maybe it was a slight movement that awakened him. Or maybe it was an exterior noise. Or maybe it was the light forcing its way through the curtains on the windows. But Casey Ballard came awake suddenly, instinctively trying to sit up. Even that slight exertion, though, was painful. His head ached mightily.

"Oh, God—!" That was aloud, followed by a moan.

Someone put a hand on his brow. Tenderly. And there was the faint odor of . . . what? Lilacs?

Casey forced open his eyes to see her sitting there beside him on the big bed, the blankets covering her only to near the waist. She was naked.

She seemed an illusion to him, a specter. But a beautiful one. Black hair, tumbling attractively to her white shoulders, framed a child-like face, from which startlingly violet eyes studied him with concern. Her skin was smooth, with the healthy luster of youth. Her breasts, perfectly proportioned to her slim body, were firm, the areola encircling the nipples a deep rose-red. The stomach was flat. And the smell of lilacs clung to her.

In his pained state, not trusting his senses, Casey spoke to the lovely apparition. "Who are you?" It seemed such an inane question, totally inadequate to the moment.

She made signs to him with her fingers. Smiling.

"You can't talk?"

She shook her head negatively.

They came back to him now, the words of the bartender at the Hillside Inn: *If you do go out there, do yourself a favor and ask for Trixie. She's just a kid, and a dummy, but the best damned lay—*

"Are you Trixie?" He mouthed the words carefully.

She beamed, delighted he knew her name.

"But—?" His face reflected his lack of understanding.

Still beaming, she got out of the bed, skipping to a bureau and picking up a small pad of paper and a pencil. In an instant she was back in the bed, writing on the pad, holding it up to him.

My room, she had written.

He took the pad from her. *Were you here all—* He stopped, glancing at the clock on the bedside table, noting it was ten-fifteen. In the morning, quite obviously. The last time he remembered was one A.M., when Dr. Willson had been there. Casey finished the note, writing, *night?*

She nodded gaily.

In bed with me?

Another nod, with a sweet shyness.

He thought for a moment, and then he wrote: *Did Lulu—*

Trixie stopped his hand, seizing the pad. *Myself. Wanted to be with you.*

She returned the pad to him.

Thank you. You're beautiful.

She lowered her gaze, again with that extraordinary shyness. Casey had never seen a prostitute before with such . . . innocence. In his job on the vice squad he had known a lot of whores, some of them as young as twelve, but all had a hardness about them. Trixie had none of that.

The girl took control of the pad. *You rest.*

Gently, she pushed him back onto the pillows, fluffing them, and getting out of the bed to smooth out the sheets and blankets. She put on a filmy wrapper; if it was meant to hide her figure, it failed. She left the bedroom, returning in only a few minutes with a basin of cool water, with which she bathed his throbbing head.

Trixie was just ending her tender ministrations when Dr. Willson arrived.

"Well, Mr. Ballard," he said pleasantly, "Ah see ya got the best nurse in Mountain County."

"Yes, she's wonderful."

She had read his lips and grinned.

The doctor removed the bandage from Casey's head, studying the crease left by the bullet. "Reasonable," he muttered. "Ya still got a headache?"

"No worse than a hangover," Ballard lied.

"Hmmm." Dr. Willson took a thermometer from his bag, shook down the mercury, and stuck it in Casey's mouth. He counted the pulse as they waited, and then removed the thermometer. "Jest a hair 'bove normal. Thet's good—Ah was afraid there might be some infection. But seems not."

"Good, then I can get out of here," Casey said.

"If ya wanna be a fool," the old doctor said sternly. "At the very least ya oughta spend another day in bed."

"But I can't continue to stay here . . ."

"Most men would want to," the old man grinned.

"How about letting me go back to the inn—to my room there?"

"Ah suppose thet would be all right. Let's see how ya negotiate."

With both the doctor and Trixie supporting him then, Casey got to his feet. The room spun crazily and he felt nauseous, but he willed himself to walk several times the length of the bedroom, feeling his sense of balance returning. There remained, however, the lightning strikes of pain behind his eyes.

Trixie fluttered around him, concern on her pretty face, trying to position herself to catch him should he fall.

"Seems okay, Doc," he lied once more.

Willson's face showed his doubt. "Well, suppose ya jest rest here another hour or so 'fore ya strike out fer the hotel." He laughed. "Hell, jest let this li'l gal pamper ya fer a while longer. Thet shouldn't be hard t' take."

"Not hard at all, Doc," he grinned. But he was thinking of Rosie.

Casey had fallen asleep again, with Trixie perched on the edge of the bed holding his hand. It was eleven-thirty when Sheriff Terry Foster walked in noisily, his arrival bringing the patient awake.

"A cozy little domestic scene," Foster grunted, glaring at the young whore. "But you look a lot better, Lieutenant."

"I feel better." *There was that lie again.*

The sheriff sighed. "I have some bad news. Eddie Ballard has died."

"Oh, shit—!"

"Just about ten o'clock. From preliminary reports the .45 really ripped him up. One of the surgeons says he believes the slug was scored."

Casey winced.

"So much so that there was no exit wound, because the fragmenting just—" He stopped.

Trixie, finally comprehending what Foster was saying, burst into tears.

Casey took a deep breath. "Well, that means our three-fingered shooter is a murderer."

"Yes." The sheriff hesitated. "Yes," he repeated. "If you're up to it, Ballard, I'd like you to take a little drive with me."

"Why?"

Foster inclined his head toward the girl, nodding negatively, suggesting a need for some secrecy.

"Okay." Casey gestured toward his clothes hanging on a chair back and Trixie brought them to him, helping him dress.

When he was ready to leave, he took her notepad and wrote: *See you later. And thank you again.*

She didn't smile, scrawling one word in reply: *Careful.* And then she stood on her toes, kissing him full on the mouth.

As Ballard and Foster left the bedroom, the sheriff chuckled. "You seem to have made a conquest, Lieutenant."

"She's been kind."

"I've heard it called a lot of things, but not *kind.*"

"Damn you, Foster, just shut up about it!" He forced himself to put down his anger. "Now, what the hell are we doing?"

"That robbery at the cockfights," the sheriff said as they walked to his squad car, "netted our three gentlemen something in excess of a hundred thousand dollars."

"How do you know that?"

"We've recovered it."

"You've what?!"

"Recovered it," he said again. "There was a falling out among the thieves and . . . well, we recovered it."

They got into the squad car and Foster spun the wheels on the gravel as they sped away from K.C.'s Place. The siren was activated as they raced along I-40 for several miles, then took an exit to a county road, finally turning into a dirt lane. Only then did Foster reduce the speed, silencing the siren. Casey was grateful for that; his head ached terribly.

The lane narrowed, the woods becoming more dense. Then it was little more than a footpath as they inched ahead. Before them Casey could see another squad car. Foster pulled up behind it, killing the motor.

"We have to walk about twenty yards," the sheriff explained. "Are you up to it?"

"Sure."

As they got out of the car, Ballard could hear the bubbling of a brook. He was cold, uncomfortable, unsteady on his feet. Foster led the way through the underbrush and down a small incline toward the edge of the water, where one of his deputies stood.

"This is Lieutenant Ballard," Foster said easily. "And that's Deputy Randy Apple."

The deputy merely nodded, pulling aside some of the dense brush to reveal a body lying face down, half in the water and half out.

"That's one of the thieves," the sheriff said carelessly.

"Do you know who it is?" Casey asked.

By way of an answer, Foster motioned to his deputy, who reached down, grasped the arm of the corpse and turned the body over. *There was no face!* It had been obliterated by a shotgun blast. Ballard sucked in a deep breath against his nausea; as often as he had seen violent death, it still made him ill.

"There's another one over here," the sheriff said, leading the way around a huge pine, where a second body was slumped in a sitting position against the trunk. There was a neat hole in the center of the forehead, a gelatine-like trickle of blood having oozed from it. The open eyes glared at them in dead anger.

"This is the shooter, to use your Chicago vernacular, Lieutenant." Foster took hold of the right arm, lifting it up so that Casey could see there were only three fingers on the hand. "We don't know who *he* is, either. Not yet, anyway." He dropped the limp arm.

Casey shivered. Partly because of the dank January temperatures. But also partly because he was suddenly fearful. *This is all too pat. Too convenient. Is that the Willie Young Dr. Willson mentioned?* He debated with himself about whether he should bring up the name of Willie Young. He decided not to, not then. Instead: "What about the third man?"

"Gone," the sheriff answered flatly. "You see, this all started when my office received an anonymous tip this morning that the three of them were holed up in here. There used to be a moonshine still along this creek and there's an old shack about a hundred yards over that rise," he pointed to his left, "which you can't see from this vantage point. Our guess is that they argued over the split of the loot, and the third man must have . . . uh . . . prevailed, you might say. Deputy Apple, following up on the tip, drove in here and surprised the survivor, maybe only a few minutes after he had killed his companions. He took off through the woods—Randy could hear him running—and in his panic he dropped the burlap sack he was carrying. It's in Randy's car now. As I said, there's more than a hundred thousand dollars."

"The deputy didn't pursue him?" Casey inquired, incredulous that the third man had been allowed to escape.

"No. I don't ask my men to be foolish, Lieutenant. Thrashing around in these woods after an armed man is a good way to come up dead. Randy did as I would have done. Once the money was recovered—" He shrugged.

Ballard only nodded.

"But we'll get him," Foster went on. "If not today, then tomorrow. If not tomorrow, the day after. The Mountain County people know we want this man. There'll be no place he can hide."

"I imagine not," Casey said quietly. He shivered again, seeing in his mind's eye the corpse of the third man. Silenced in death, unable to tell anyone what really happened in the cockfight barn. "I'd like to go back to the hotel, Sheriff," he said, touching his bandaged head. "I'm feeling a bit rocky."

"That's understandable." Foster instructed his deputy to call for help to remove the two bodies, and walked to his squad car with Ballard, offering his arm for support.

Very little was said as they drove to the Hillside Inn. Casey discouraged conversation by leaning back and closing his eyes. He needed the silence to run Foster's scenario through his throbbing brain. The more he thought of it, the more he became convinced the robbery of the cockfight patrons had been staged to cover what was meant to be his own murder. That the plot had been foiled when the brave Eddie Ballard gave his own life made it even more horrible.

They arrived at the hotel. "I think I'll follow Dr. Willson's advice," Casey said, "and just rest the remainder of the day."

"That's wise," the sheriff replied. "Say, is your car still at K.C.'s Place?"

"Oh, damn—"

"Don't worry about it. I'll have someone bring it over."

"The keys are right here—" He thrust a hand into his pocket.

Foster laughed. "No need, Lieutenant. Someone will still bring it over."

"That will be helpful," Casey said coldly. He started to get out of the squad car.

"Before you leave," the sheriff said emphatically, placing a restraining hand on Ballard's arm, "how do you propose to settle this matter with the Staleys about your grandfather's property?"

"I suppose I should sell."

"Yes, you should," Foster said quietly.

iii   It was one o'clock when Casey called Rosalie. She answered on the first ring.

"Hiya, O'Hara," he said nonchalantly.

"Where in the devil have you been?" she demanded. "I've called your hotel at least a dozen times."

"I know, I have your messages. I'm back at the hotel now . . . but last night I was . . . well, the Mountain County folks threw a bang-up party for ol' K.C.'s grandboy and I'm afraid I got taken seriously drunk."

"Oh, Casey—!"

"What the hell, I figured I might as well be sociable," he laughed. "But I didn't count on the wallop the local moonshine has." He moaned. "I've got a head the size of the Goodyear blimp."

"Serves you right! You're getting too old, lover, for that kind of exercise." But she laughed, too. "And where, my dear husband, did you spend the night?"

"You're not going to believe this," Casey continued light-heartedly, "but I woke up this morning with a beautiful young girl in my bed . . . long, black hair . . . gorgeous violet eyes . . . a body that wouldn't quit . . . and—"

"Don't you wish," Rosie giggled.

"Wait, you haven't heard the best of it. She couldn't talk."

"Are you trying to get me to believe that your prowess in bed left her speechless?"

"No, I have to be honest. She was a deaf mute. Did all her talking with her fingers . . ." He tried for a wicked tone, "And in that context she was multilingual."

"That moonshine booze has you hallucinating."

"That must be it," he said, feigning sadness, "but isn't it a great story?"

"Very entertaining, Mr. Ballard." Rosalie dropped the bantering. "Have you settled the matter of your grandfather's estate?"

"That's all taken care of." There was guilt about the answer; it *had* been taken care of, of course, but not in the manner Rosie had meant.

"I'm glad." She hesitated. "And when are you coming home?"

"Not before Monday night or Tuesday morning—"

"Oh?"

"Still have to sign some papers," he lied, "and I can't do that before sometime on Monday."

"And in the meantime, I suppose, you're going to learn sign language?"

"I've got to admit I've thought of it."

"Well, *stop* thinking of it." The easy manner had returned to her voice. "And stay away from that hill country tart."

"Yes, ma'am."

"Casey?"

"Yeah."

"Violet eyes?"

"Uh huh. And she smelled of lilacs."

"Sounds like a whole damned flower garden. And if my bee keeps buzzing around he's going to lose his stinger."

"Do I detect a threat in that, O'Hara?"

"No threat, sir," Rosalie giggled once more. "That's a guarantee!"

iv   There was the musty smell of old paper as Casey paged through the bound files of the weekly *Hillside Truth*, searching for answers to questions not fully perceived. He was mentally groping; he scarcely knew where to start. But he sought the truth—recognizing the irony of the newspaper's name—on two diverse killings: that of the tragic Eddie Ballard and, more than fifty years earlier, the death of an uncle he never knew, King David Ballard.

After his call to Rosalie, he had lain back on his bed at the Hillside Inn trying to organize his thoughts, trying to bring some reason to what had happened in Mountain County, now and a half-century earlier. Logic told him the murders of Eddie and King David were totally unrelated. Experience told him that logic rarely was a companion to murder.

One question nagged at him most: *Why should my reluctance to sell my grandfather's property be of such importance?* He believed if he had an answer to that, all the other questions and answers would fall into place, like pieces of a jigsaw puzzle. Yet the puzzle before him was without line or form, without features. It was simply black, absorbing all light, all truth, and reflecting nothing back to him.

What had happened to Eddie was not yet a matter of any written record. But the King David incident was: he had the file of Sheriff Billy Foster, Terry's father, and he could surmise there had been newspaper coverage. And that's where he had to start.

It was then Casey telephoned the amiable garage mechanic, Rudy Pitts, the one person in Mountain County he was prepared to trust.

"Do you happen to know the owner of the local newspaper?" Ballard asked.

"Hell, yes!" Rudy had replied enthusiastically. "Well . . . Ah know the editor, Charlie Sams, real good. We went t' high school t'gether 'fore Ah dropped out. His ol' man owns the paper, but Charlie's runnin' it now."

"I realize it's a Saturday afternoon," Casey went on, "but do you think you could prevail on your friend to let me into the newspaper office to do some research in the back issues?"

"Do mah best, Mr. Ballard. Call ya right back."

Rudy's intervention got Casey into the small office of the *Hillside Truth,* where Casey turned the pages, searching, while the garage mechanic and the young editor sat in an adjoining cubicle, laughing and drinking.

It was 1933 that initially interested the retired cop. The month was February, when one King David Ballard had been hacked to death with an axe. The *Hillside Truth* published every Thursday and there was no mention of King David's demise in the issue of Thursday, February 16. It was clear the newspaper had been printed before the killing had been revealed; most likely before it had occurred. But the issue of Thursday, February 23, was lavish in its coverage of the murder.

There were, however, startling differences between the newspaper account and what Casey had read in the file of the case given to him by Sheriff Foster. *The body was discovered,* the newspaper story said, *by Barney Daniels, of Uno, a patron of K.C.'s Place. Mr. Daniels told Sheriff Billy Foster he had come upon the crime scene when he left the roadhouse to go to the barn where his horse and rig had been left the night before.*

Dr. Amos Willson, Mountain County deputy coroner, said the victim had been struck on the head in the right temple region by a sharp, heavy instrument which penetrated the skull and severely damaged the brain. "Death must have been instantaneous," Dr. Willson told this reporter. Sheriff Foster said an axe, found discarded on a manure pile several yards from the body, may have been the murder weapon. "But the axe had been wiped clean of any blood," the sheriff added, "and we can assume that fingerprints were wiped away, too."

There was no suggestion at all that Daniels had been an eyewitness to the killing, nor that Sarah Ballard, the sister, had been on the scene, nor even that there had been a fight between the brothers King David and Abel! Nor, for that matter, that there had been any more than the single head wound inflicted on King David Ballard, rather than the multiple wounds mentioned in the case file. Almost nothing in the newspaper account matched with what the late Sheriff Foster had written in his report, save that King David had been murdered.

Perplexed, Casey paged ahead to the issue of Thursday,

March 2, 1933, where he found a simple report on the funeral of King David, with a repeat of the same information about his death. This time his father, Abel Ballard, was mentioned, but only in the context of being a surviving brother of the victim.

Very carefully, the Chicagoan went through every subsequent 1933 issue of the *Hillside Truth,* looking for additional stories on the murder. It was never mentioned again. Nor was there any mention of Abel Ballard having left Mountain County for Chicago or any other destination.

What he did find of interest was a social note, reporting that Miss Alice Ralston and Mr. Zebulon Alderman had announced their engagement at a Christmas ball at the home of Judge Elmo Ralston. *A spring wedding is planned,* the article said.

Casey closed the bound copy of the 1933 issues, sitting in thought. *Why the elaborate drama about King David's murder in Sheriff Billy Foster's file? If the newspaper account is factual, then Billy doctored his case file. Or maybe Terry Foster doctored it for my benefit—to put additional pressure on me to sell K.C.'s Place. No, that doesn't ring true. How could Terry have known, before the fact, that I wasn't going to sell? Hell, I didn't know it myself. Anyway, doctoring the file in such elaborate detail would have taken longer than Terry had. Also, the file seems genuine. Only handwriting analysis would tell me whether Billy Foster wrote it, but the phrasing of the sentences is old-fashioned. From another era. That kind of thing is more difficult to fake than handwriting.*

Ballard drummed his fingers nervously. *Does Terry know his father's old file is in conflict with the newspaper account? Maybe he doesn't. That's it—he really doesn't! He believes the file to be true. He's too intelligent to use the file for pressure if he knew it could be so easily refuted by simply consulting the newspaper of the time of the murder.*

Casey shook his head. "Then why?" he said aloud to himself. He ran a hand wearily over his eyes, wishing the pains in his head would subside. When he got to his feet to put the volume back on its shelf he was suddenly dizzy. And then he was seeing two of everything; the double vision made him nauseous. He leaned against the shelves for a moment, breathing deeply, telling himself to be calm. The double vision dissipated and Ballard walked slowly into the adjoining office where editor Charlie Sams and Rudy Pitts were laughing over some remembered incident of their high school days.

"Find what you wanted, Mr. Ballard?" Sams asked.

"Yes, thank you."

"Say, if you have another minute," the newspaperman went on, "could you give me your version of what happened at the cockfights last night?"

"Well, I don't remember too much," Casey said, giving him a brief, unemotional report, not mentioning the three-fingered gunman nor his own belief that he himself was the intended target.

"Must have been scary as hell," Sams said.

"It wasn't too comfortable." He forced a smile.

The editor made no mention of the recovery of the money nor of the sheriff's men finding two of the thieves dead in the woods. *Terry must be playing that one close to the vest.*

As he left the newspaper office with Pitts, Casey asked, "Did you ever hear of a fellow named Barney Daniels?"

"Sure thing. Lives over at Uno. He's a woodcarver. Mostly birds, ya know. Sells a lot of 'em t' tourists comin' through." Rudy laughed. "Funny ol' feller."

"Funny? How?"

"He lives kinda like a hermit. Got a beard damned near down t' his waist. Ah don't think he's all there—kinda tetched, ya know."

"Is Uno far?"

"Naw. Twenty miles mebbe. Want me t' drive ya there?"

"No, not now," Casey replied. "Truthfully, I'm not feeling too well. And I expect Doc Willson to come by the hotel later. Maybe we can go to see this Daniels tomorrow?"

"Sure. Ah ain't got no plans."

V   It was six-thirty before Amos Willson rapped on his hotel room door. Casey, concerned now, told him of his continuing severe headache and the episode of double vision in the newspaper office.

"Ah'd feel a lot better, Mr. Ballard," the physician said, "if ya'd let me drive you over to Gatlinburg and check ya in over there fer some tests."

"And short of that?"

"Short of thet, Ah don't know. Ah can't honestly tell ya how severe a concussion ya mighta had."

"Hmmm. Could we think about it again in the morning?" Casey asked.

"Sure, but it's not somethin' ya oughta fool 'round with Mr. Ballard."

"Maybe some pain pills to get me through the night? Maybe if I just got another good night's sleep?"

Willson shook his head in doubt. "Be best if ya go to the hospital, Mr. Ballard."

"Okay, if I don't feel any better in the morning, I will."

"Fine. Ah'll jest give ya another sedative for t'night."

"Before you do," Casey said slowly, "I'd like to ask you to think back to 1933—February, 1933. You were the deputy coroner then, as I understand it, when my uncle, King David Ballard, was murdered."

"Yeah, messy thing."

Casey picked up the file folder given to him by the sheriff. "Would you mind reading this, Doc, and giving me your thoughts on it?"

Willson took it from him, sat down on the bed and started to read it. As he read, his eyebrows flickered up and down. Finally, he closed the folder and thrust it back at Ballard.

"Complete bullshit!" the old man said angrily. "There was no such thing as fourteen wounds, for Christ sake! He was hit once in the temple . . . left side, Ah guess . . . an' thet killed 'im right off. An' yer daddy wasn't there either. He was in Chicago by thet time."

"Oh?"

"Yep, he left fer Chicago on the mornin' of February third, 1933."

"How can you be so sure of the date?"

" 'Cause February second was mah birthday," Dr. Willson said firmly, "an' me an' Abel celebrated thet an' his leavin'. He had a cartage job waitin' fer 'im in Chicago. Anyway, we had this party out t' K.C.'s Place . . . I wasn't married then . . . an' we had the free run o' the place, 'cause he was K.C.'s boy an' all. Got drunk an' got laid an' had a helluva time." The old man smiled. "Yes, sir, had one helluva time."

"So by February sixteenth, when King David was killed, my father was in Chicago?"

"Yep, thet's the size of it."

Casey gestured with the file folder. "Why this fiction then?"

" 'Cause Billy Foster was—" He stopped for an instant. " 'Cause Billy Foster was the biggest goddamned liar on two feet. He'd tell a lie when the truth was a better story."

Casey wondered about that one hesitation in Doc Willson's story. Did it mean anything? He decided it didn't, taking the sedative shot and looking forward to a good night's sleep.

vi   Amos Willson walked slowly through the lobby of the Hillside Inn, pausing by the bank of pay telephones. He stared at them for a moment and then went to one of them, dropping a coin and dialing a number.

But before there was a ring on the other end, he hung up the phone.

"T' hell with ya," he mumbled to himself. "Ah've done all Ah'm gonna do fer ya."

7

i   Casey didn't have a lot of experience with woodcarvers. In truth, he didn't have any; the denizens with whom he dealt on the streets of Chicago had other uses for knives. Thus, Barney Daniels was a revelation. A throwback to a time when the wilderness of the Great Smokies was the western frontier of a burgeoning nation, when the white men who first came to live in the vast mountains survived on their wits and their peculiar skills and their courage.

The visitor could imagine Barney as one of those. His small log cabin had one room only, a utilitarian enclosed space at once a living room, dining room, bedroom, and kitchen. Yet it was comfortable and inviting, smelling of a variety of woods and collections of herbs hung to dry in tiny bunches from the ceiling beams. And everywhere blocks of rough-hewn wood (oak and cedar and maple and pine), the raw material for Barney's native talent.

Ballard wasn't there but a moment or two before he recognized Daniels as a superb craftsman. His bird carvings were so exact and so beautiful, one believed every feather, every color, had been precisely recreated. But in the cabin Casey saw no pictures of birds, no photographs. There were no books of any kind. The models for his art were in the thick woods surrounding the cabin, living and free.

As Rudy Pitts had suggested, Barney's most distinctive feature was his long beard, falling straight, without a curl in the hair, to his waist. Wood chips lodged in it as seemingly permanent adornment. But for Casey the most impressive thing about the woodcarver was his size. *Monstrous* came to mind. He was maybe six-foot-six; his weight must have been in excess of three hundred pounds. Everything about him was out-sized. And the hands! They were huge, ham-like extensions of massive forearms. It was almost impossible to believe those hands had carved the delicate birds scattered in haphazard disarray about the cabin.

Daniels was not a man of words. Rudy's introduction of Ballard brought only a grunt of recognition as he went back to his carving at a large table, on which rested a disinterested tame raccoon.

Casey spent a half hour studying the bird carvings, thinking he ought to take one of them back to Rosie. He finally selected a cardinal, fashioned from the fragrant heart of a cedar log. As he reached to take it into his hands he feared it would fly away.

"How much is this, Mr. Daniels?" he asked.

"Twenty-five," the woodcarver grunted.

Ballard began to count out the money.

Rudy chuckled. "Ah bet, Barney, ya ain't never had a customer like this before."

Daniels smiled, but said nothing.

"Have I done something wrong?" Casey wanted to know.

"Well, Mr. Ballard," Pitts answered, genuinely amused, "ya ain't never supposed t' pay the first price. Here in the hills yer supposed t' haggle."

"Oh, I see." Casey, laughing at himself, turned to the old man. "Is it too late to haggle, Mr. Daniels?"

"Yep . . . too late."

"Well, this beautiful thing is worth twenty-five dollars,

sir. Anyway, I don't think I'd be very good at haggling."

"Prob'ly not."

Casey handed him the money. "Are you a native of Mountain County, Mr. Daniels?"

"Yep. Been here ev'ry day of mah life," Barney replied laconically. " 'Cept a weekend in Gatlinburg. Back in thirty-four, it were. Didn't like it."

"Then you must have known a lot of my relatives. I'm a grandson of K.C. Ballard."

"Ah figured. Favor 'im some."

"You probably knew my father—Abel Ballard."

"Yep."

"And my aunts and uncles—Esther and Sarah and Moses and King David?"

"Yep, knew 'em all."

Casey pressed on. "I understand that King David was murdered."

"Yep."

"I read a police report that he was killed with an axe."

"Yep."

"And that you were an eyewitness to it."

Barney Daniels thought for a moment before answering. "Don't rightly recollect that. It were a long time ago."

"Then you don't remember my uncle, King David, and my father fighting?"

The woodcarver shook his head negatively.

"And there was a girl there—"

"No, no girl!"

Casey thought he saw a hint of fright in the old man's eyes. "My Aunt Sarah may have been there."

"Don't recollect."

"Hmmm." The Chicagoan grinned. "Well, I'm probably wrong," he said in an offhand manner. "Maybe it was another girl."

It was a shot in the dark, but Ballard was certain he had hit the mark. The woodcarver's face told him that; he had flushed, a startled look in his eyes. Daniels' attention went to the carving on which he was working.

"Then I'm wrong, Mr. Daniels?"

"Most likely. But . . . it were a long time ago." Casey sensed a pleading tone in the reply, one asking that the conversation be ended.

"Well, it's been pleasant meeting you, Mr. Daniels, and I thank you for creating this beautiful cardinal."

When they left the cabin, Rudy Pitts said, "Yer full o' su'prises, Mr. Ballard."

"I suppose I am." He got into his rental car on the passenger side; his lightheadedness, his throbbing brain, dictated that young Pitts should drive. "I haven't been entirely honest with you, Rudy. I'm a police officer, a member of the Chicago police force." A sigh. "At least I was until a few days ago."

"Hell, Ah knew ya was a cop."

"You did? How long have you known?"

"Since Friday night, jest 'fore the shootin'." He paused to organize his thoughts. "Ya 'member when Ah came up t' ya an' Foster with the winnin's on Clarence Bimstock's rooster—?"

"Uh huh."

"Well, it weren't more'n a minute or two later that one o' Terry's deputies came up t' me an' warned me not t' cotton up t' ya. Thet ya was a trouble-makin' Chicago cop an' that Terry might not take kindly t' me befriendin' ya. Things like thet, ya know. An' then the shootin' came an'—" He hesitated. "Ah kinda figured they was after ya, Mr. Ballard, but Ah couldn't reckon why."

Casey stared at the perceptive young man for a moment. "That deputy may have given you good advice, Rudy."

"Yeah, well—" Pitts shrugged. "Ah don't need Terry Foster t' tell me what t' do. Ah kin figure out who's square mahself. An' Ah think yer a square feller."

"I appreciate the vote of confidence."

"Ain't nothin'."

As they drove away from Barney Daniels' cabin retreat Ballard very carefully detailed the story of his association, only days old, with Mountain County. He told the garage mechanic *everything,* starting with the initial receipt of the letter about his grandfather's death and will. When he got to the part about being shown the body of the three-fingered gunman, Rudy interrupted him.

"Ya mean they killed Willie Young?" There was disgust reflected in the question.

"You knew Willie Young?"

"Sure. He were a good ol' boy from 'cross the border in Carolina. Ah useta work on his Ford tractor."

"And would Sheriff Foster have known him?"

Rudy laughed sarcastically. "Be damned funny if'n he didn't. He's bin bangin' Willie's daughter."

Casey's reaction was to suck in a deep breath.

"They call 'er Yolanda—ain't thet a crazy name? She's 'bout nineteen an' got a body like a brick shithouse. Yolanda's Terry's latest."

"Isn't he married?"

"What's that got t' do with it? Ev'rybody knows—includin' his ol' lady, Ah reckon—thet he's the biggest pussy-chaser in the county. It ain't hard t' git laid, ya know, when ya got a badge." Rudy looked over at Ballard. "Ah didn't mean y'all, Mr. Ballard."

"That's okay. A badge does offer certain advantages."

"Anyway, Ah figure he's gonna wear thet tool out one o' these days. Gits all them freebies out t' K.C.'s Place, too. 'Cept one, of course."

"Oh?"

"Yeah, thet sweet li'l punkin, Trixie."

Casey felt a knot growing in the pit of his stomach.

"The story is thet Terry wanted thet gal real bad, but thet she always turned 'im down. An' when he got mean 'bout it, ol' K.C. protected 'er. He were kinda daddy t' 'er. No tellin' what'll happen t' 'er now."

Ballard groaned disconsolately.

" 'Course, mebbe Ah'm overstatin' it some. Mebbe she'll jest let 'im dip his wick now that K.C.'s gone. But if she don't . . ." Rudy paused meaningfully. "Ah don't know. He might git rough with 'er, or he might jest throw 'er in jail. She *is* a whore, ya know."

"He's capable of that, isn't he?" It was meant to be a rhetorical question.

Pitts, however, saw a need to answer it. "Terry Foster's capable o' anythin'. Ya take all the mean low-life things ya kin think o', an' then double 'em, an' thet's the sheriff."

Casey clapped his hands together; he had reached a decision. "Take me back to the hotel, Rudy, and we'll call it quits. I have no right to involve you in my problems. And I certainly don't want Sheriff Foster to come down on you."

There was a silence. Then: "Mr. Ballard, ya cain't chase me. Ah figure thet Terry's gonna git his, an' Ah wanna be there when he does."

ii   "Do you know that Ballard has been out to see Barney Daniels?" the voice on the telephone asked.

"Uh huh." Sheriff Terry Foster grinned broadly. "And Barney didn't tell him anything."

"How can you be sure? Hell, Barney was just here to see me and he was shaking. That damned cop asked too many questions that indicated he knew what really happened."

"Look, old friend," the sheriff said easily, "you know how unstable Barney is. Some days he remembers, but most days he doesn't. And those times he remembers, it scares the hell out of him. Of course, he's an old man, and if you have doubts about him, you know that old men tend to be accident prone—"

"No!" The voice on the other end of the line was vehement. "Jesus Christ, haven't you done enough with Willie Young and those others? What is it with you?! Can't you think of any solution but killing?!"

Foster's voice also turned ugly. "You bastard! I gave you the perfect solution for all this from the beginning. Don't probate the will, I said. Burn it and tell the court there was no will, I said. But no, you had to do it *legally*. Probate the will, find the heir. And even when I told you he was a cop, you *insisted* on

94

going through with it. Don't worry, you said, he'll sell to the Staleys and leave. Well, you were wrong about that! From now on, I'll handle it my own way and you keep your goddamned mouth shut!"

"You're forgetting who's paying you, Sheriff!"

"Okay, stop paying me. That would be fine with me." Foster was speaking calmly again. "I'd prefer to sit back and let Lieutenant Casey Ballard run his course. It'll be more fun that way. And no skin off my butt. I didn't bribe an elected official to falsify the records of a capital crime. Your old man did that. Why, shit, I don't even know the King David file is a phony. How would I? I wasn't even around then. So I'll just wait until Ballard turns it over and plead my genuine innocence. Is that what you want?"

There was a pause on the telephone. "Do you think he'll find her?"

"He's a damned good cop."

Another pause. "We can't risk that, and you understand why."

"Perfectly." Sheriff Foster laughed. "We're both concerned about the well-being of Mountain County, aren't we?"

"That's my concern, certainly."

"And we're both liars. Now, you want this ended and so do I. The difference between us is that I know how to do it. So don't come crying to me again."

Terry slammed the phone into its cradle. There would be no further debate on what needed to be done.

iii   Layton Sams was not at all what Casey had expected. The founder and publisher of the *Hillside Truth* was a bird-like little man, but there was a unique presence about him belying his physical appearance. Here was a *gentleman:* from his modishly styled hair to his expensive velvet smoking jacket to his gleaming patent leather loafers. It seemed unlikely he would be of Mountain County.

Ballard had prevailed on Rudy Pitts to take him to see the elder Sams. Because what Casey needed now was information, background—in wholesale lots. Thus, when Rudy had mentioned Layton Sams was writing a history of Mountain County, the meeting became a necessity.

It was late Sunday afternoon when the publisher greeted Ballard at the door of his imposing home—circa 1930s, Casey guessed—and led him into a spacious den. The room had a cathedral ceiling and there were books everywhere; even a quick glance at some of the titles indicated the catholic nature of Layton's literary tastes: from O. Henry to Laura Lee Hope, from Tocqueville to Bruce Catton, from Shakespeare to Tennessee Williams, from Rudyard Kipling to Wallace Stevens, and autobiographical offerings from Winston Churchill to Johnny Cash. Casey couldn't help but wonder whether all of those books had been read.

There was a studied disorder about the den, and Sams laughed about it: "Since my wife died, my daughter-in-law has been coming in every once in a while trying to organize me. She's waging a futile battle, though."

Rudy was moving slowly along the shelves of books, idly studying the titles, as Casey was offered a leather easy chair next to a large oak desk, piled high with books and file folders that very nearly buried a Radio Shack personal computer.

"This mess," Sams said complacently, "is supposed to be the makings of a definitive history of Mountain County, Tennessee. I've even added the computer, the word processor, to make all of this appear legitimate . . ." He chuckled. "But I'm afraid I may not have the discipline needed to complete the task. I rationalize it every day. Who in the hell would want to read a history of Mountain County? But it's fun to dabble with it."

He dropped into the chair behind the desk. "Now . . . I understand you're looking into the background of the Ballard family. You're K.C.'s grandson, right?"

"Yes," Casey answered. "But I'm really most interested in a specific incident in the Ballard history. And I hope that doesn't make it sound too important. I'm not sure it is."

"Well, the Ballards have left a very distinct mark on Mountain County. Very distinct, indeed. What specifically are you seeking?"

"The murder of King David Ballard," Casey told him.

"Hmmm? What about it?"

"To be candid, sir, I'm a . . . uh . . . retired Chicago police officer, a deputy commander of the vice squad."

His host's face didn't register any surprise.

"When I came to Mountain County earlier in the week to settle my grandfather's estate I was shown an old case file from the sheriff's office in which it was alleged King David, my uncle, was killed in a fight with his brother, Abel, later to become my father. Now, when one's father is revealed as a murderer, it causes more than a little interest."

Sams smiled. "That's understandable."

"So I went into the bound copies of your newspaper yesterday—your son was kind enough to permit it—to verify, or contradict, the sheriff's file. What you wrote about the killing, Mr. Sams . . . and I'm assuming you were the writer . . . and what Sheriff Billy Foster had in his report simply don't match."

Casey laid the photocopy of the case file before the newspaper owner. "I wonder whether you would be good enough to take the time to read this file and compare it with your own recollections?"

Layton Sams flipped open the file, reading it as Casey watched his face for reactions. There was nothing he could conclude from the publisher's expression.

"Quite lurid," Sams commented as he finished his reading. "And it could very well be correct."

"Oh?"

"You see," the older man sighed, "I have to make a confession about my method of operation as publisher and editor of the *Hillside Truth*. Please bear with me; this may take longer than you bargained for." He grinned.

"My father, Charles Sams—my only son is named for him—was an original partner in what is known today as the Ralston Company. He and old Elmo Ralston pooled their capital to begin a lumbering company, a vastly successful operation

97

from the start. It quickly became the leading employer in the county. Mountain Countians who previously had nothing to look forward to except hardscrabble farming or bootlegging could now find honest employment here. But somewhere along the line Charlie Sams and Elmo Ralston, once close friends, had a falling out, the upshot of which was the dissolution of their partnership. Elmo bought out my father for the then astounding figure of a half million dollars. Thus, my family was affluent and my father, when I reached the proper years, insisted I should have an Eastern education."

He smiled at the recollection. "So it was off to Princeton University for me. By the skin of my teeth I managed to graduate and, believing a newspaper career was what I wanted, and waving my brand-new liberal arts diploma, I secured a job on the *Nashville Tennessean,* a proud publication then and now. But there was no great compulsion to succeed there. In less than a year I was back in Mountain County, some of my father's wealth enabling me to begin the *Hillside Truth.* It was an idyllic arrangement for a spoiled young man, believe me. Putting out a small newspaper only once a week allowed for plenty of time to indulge my true passions: hunting and fishing. I soon fell into a pattern of work, if you could call it that . . . my father never did . . . of being engaged with the newspaper Monday through Thursday, spending Friday, Saturday, and Sunday in the woods, hunting and fishing. And occasionally enjoying the company of a young lady on my . . . well, my sylvan treks.

"It was my routine, then, to contact the county authorities on Mondays and Tuesdays about what had transpired during my long weekends. I printed what they told me. Quite honestly, Mr. Ballard, I have no recollection of the specifics of your uncle's murder. I certainly didn't do any investigation of it. Most likely I wrote what Billy Foster told me of it. If he elected not to give me all the details, and this file would indicate he did not . . ." He tapped the folder. "Well . . ."

There was an apologetic shrug. "I'm sorry, Mr. Ballard, that my . . . uh . . . profligate lifestyle as a journalist was such that I can't be of much help to you."

Greatly disappointed, Casey tried to salvage something.

"Do you think it's possible, Mr. Sams, the report Billy Foster wrote on King David's murder was a phony?"

"Heavens, yes!" Sams roared with laughter. "Billy was a *dedicated* prevaricator. He should have been a novelist; he might have become one of our greatest Southern writers." He continued to chuckle. "Billy was a genuine character, Mr. Ballard. I remember how he used to handle a lot of his business on the telephone, calling up fellows suspected of being engaged in wrongdoing and ordering them to come in to be arrested. Most did, too."

Sams noted the incredulous look on Casey's face. "It's a fact, sir. Billy Foster was a domineering presence. There weren't many who dared oppose him. And he never carried a gun. Of course, he was liberal in the use of a big blackjack he always had in his hip pocket. That weapon, and his fists, were enough to establish his credentials in Mountain County."

"It seems Billy and his son established a dynasty," Ballard commented.

"Indeed. But it was more than just Billy and Terry. There's been a Foster as sheriff every day of this century so far. Did you know that?"

"Not really."

"It's true. Ben Foster, Terry's grandfather, was first elected sheriff in 1900. Only twice since that time has anyone challenged the Fosters at the polls. Ben was a brute of a man, mentally as well as physically. I guess you can say he was a personification of the Southern propensity for violence, on having a penchant for militancy. The Southern male, generally speaking, has always had a well-defined sense of *machismo*, to use a contemporary word. Cross a Southerner and expect a fight, most often taken to the ultimate limit. It was true two hundred years ago and it's true today.

"I suspect the Sheriffs Foster, if we are to be honest, did a great deal in Mountain County to legitimize violence."

He rummaged through the piles of papers on his desk, finally coming up with a lined, yellow sheet torn from a legal pad. It was filled with statistics.

"For example," Sams continued, "in 1976 there were

twenty homicides in this county, with ninety-seven felonious assaults. That's a devil of a lot of violence in a community of less than twenty-five thousand population."

His eyes glanced down at the paper. "Going back to 1950, we find there were *more* homicides officially reported than there were felonious assaults. Think of the implications of that! One conclusion to be reached, of course, is that what assaults were initiated most often led to death. The other implication is that violence was so accepted by Billy Foster—he was the sheriff then—that most of what would have been called felonious assaults weren't even recorded. And we can only speculate about how many actual deaths weren't officially reported, either."

The publisher smiled wanly. "Yet this belligerence has served Tennessee well down through its history. There were more Tennesseans at the Alamo, for instance, than representatives of any other state. The Mexican War could not have been waged successfully if it had not been for the thousands of eager Tennessee volunteers. And we must not forget that Tennesseans have had a well-defined sense of patriotism. Mountain County, you should know, sided with the Union during the Civil War, and its sons fought hard and well to preserve the United States of America."

There was a brief lull, Ballard not commenting.

"There's a distinction made in these parts," the newspaperman went on, "between killings and murders. *Killing* is something inevitable visited upon a citizen with less than a savory reputation. The phrase, 'He deserved killin',' is commonplace. A *murder,* on the other hand, is a killing not thought to have been inevitable, or deserved."

Layton Sams had finished his explanation. Casey throught for a moment or two before he said, "It seems to me, sir, that a newspaper's coverage might perpetuate that attitude."

"A point well-taken, Mr. Ballard," Sams said sadly, "a point well-taken, indeed. The *Hillside Truth* may have been less than diligent down through the years."

"And that doesn't bother you?" Casey's question had an angry edge.

"Of course it does. That's one of the reasons I've undertaken to write this history of Mountain County." Sams extended his hands to encompass the clutter of research material in his desk. "And one of these days . . ."

Casey was thoroughly disgusted by Sams' dilettantism. He excused himself without further comment. He'd have to look elsewhere for the truth on the King David murder.

iv "Ya know, Mr. Ballard," Rudy Pitts announced, "Ah think we're bein' followed."

They had been on the road for only a few minutes after leaving the rural Sams home. Darkness was nearly upon them, that uncertain period of fading light. Casey was slumped on the passenger's side of the rental car, trying to ignore his throbbing head. He reached up and turned the rearview mirror so that he could see what was behind them.

"You mean that red pickup?"

"Yep. He pulled out o' a side road right behind us soonest we left Layton's place."

"Speed up," Casey ordered.

Rudy tromped on the accelerator. The truck kept pace, but remained six to eight car lengths behind.

"Well, well, you may be right, Rudy. How well do you know the county roads around here?"

"Like the back of mah hand," the young man bragged.

"In that case, see if you can shake him."

"You bet." Rudy looked over at his passenger. "Ya better use the seat belt, Mr. Ballard."

Casey complied.

"Comin' up jest ahead on the right. Ah'm gonna swing real fast like without a turn signal."

The turnoff road rushed at them; Rudy had the speedometer at sixty-five. He stomped on the brake, putting the car into a turning skid, and then straightened away on the narrow country road. He slowed down.

Casey was looking into the rearview mirror. The red pickup appeared. "I'll be damned, Rudy, here he comes!"

"Now what?"

"Get us back on the road to Hillside and then see if you can outrun him to the hotel."

"Done an' done," Rudy laughed. At the next rural intersection he turned left, and left again after a mile or two, and finally, after reaching the three-lane macadam road once more, he made a right turn toward Hillside. His foot was heavy on the gas pedal.

Sixty, sixty-five, seventy. The driver looked around him. They had just started up a long hill, heavy forests on both sides. It was almost as if they were driving through a tunnel. A *lonely*, darkened tunnel. Rudy turned on the car's headlights. The pickup truck followed suit.

"This ain't the best place to be, Mr. Ballard."

"How far to Hillside?"

"Seven, eight miles yet."

"It's your play," Casey said quietly.

Seventy-five, eighty. The car began to protest. "Damn rental cars," Pitts said under his breath. "Ain't worth a shit!" He repositioned the mirror. "He's got somethin' special under thet hood."

Suddenly, then, the red pickup, clearly with more power than the rental car, came alongside them. There was a quick turn of the wheel and the truck bumped them. Hard. Rudy struggled to keep the sedan on a straight path. Another sharp, sideswiping collision and the lighter car went up on two wheels. Only Rudy's skill brought it back down on the road. A third crash and the heavier truck prevailed. In what seemed to be slow motion, the car started to turn over toward the passenger's side, finally falling that way, metal tearing away as it careened along the blacktop. Then it rolled side over side toward the woods, coming to a sickening, thudding stop against a giant loblolly.

"Jee-sus!" Rudy screamed. He looked over at his passenger. "Mr. Ballard! Ya okay?!"

"I hear you," Casey said weakly. Every fiber in him ached.

His brain was trying to burst out of the skull.

"We gotta git the hell outta here!" Pitts was wrestling with the badly sprung door, banging at it, cursing it. Ten seconds. Fifteen. There was the distinct, ominous odor of intense heat. The door started to open, the thin metal making protesting tearing noises as the young man used all of the strength in him to open it fully. He hoisted himself out.

"Come on!" he shouted, reaching down inside the over-turned car.

Ballard grasped his hand and Pitts tugged at him. To no avail.

"The seat belt!"

Another few precious seconds went by as Casey struggled to free himself from the restraint of the belt. He did finally, and Pitts slowly pulled him from the wreckage. Casey had no resid-ual strength to help him.

Rudy took him under the arms, half-pulling, half-pushing him away from the rental car. He covered perhaps thirty feet before he collapsed, exhausted, under the weight of the older and heavier man.

"It were Daniel Staley in thet truck," he gasped.

"You sure?"

"Ain't no mistakin' thet ugly face."

There was a whoosh of flame, impelling Ballard and Pitts to scramble a few more yards farther along. And then an ear-shattering explosion tore the car apart, hurling hot, jagged pieces of it in all directions. The two men, flattened tightly against the earth, somehow escaped being hit. Some of the debris fell in the woods, setting the underbrush afire.

They crawled to the berm of the road, sprawling there, those two unlikely friends, watching the orange-red flames, with a plume of jet-black, oily smoke, consume the Chevrolet Caprice.

"Ya know somethin', Mr. Ballard," Rudy said, "Ah don't think thet Mr. Avis is gonna try harder 'fer ya anymore."

They laughed. Together.

They laughed for the sheer joy of being alive.

8

i   The face of the handsome man in the wheelchair was twisted in anger.

"Damn you, Terry, can't you get it through your thick skull," he was shouting, "that your precipitous violence is only making matters worse!"

Sheriff Foster lounged insolently on a sofa opposite the wheelchair, grinning at the distraught older man. He hated him; hated everything he stood for. Even though he was confined to a wheelchair, his useless legs hidden under a multicolored quilt, the lawman had no sympathy for him; he still represented to the sheriff all of the things wrong in Mountain County. To Terry's way of thinking the Ralstons had been in power too long, and the Fosters—grandfather, father, and son—had been doing their bidding for too many years. He was resentful although mindful that Elmo Ralston, Jr., was the end of a line. He had sired no children; neither had the other instrument of power in the family, Elmo's brother-in-law, banker Zeb Alderman.

Both men were in their mid-seventies, their days numbered. It was a matter of great satisfaction to Terry Foster to consider he would outlive both of them, leaving the Fosters as the survivors of a unique two-family patriarchy that had controlled Mountain County for every minute of the twentieth century. It had always been the same: the Ralstons (Elmo Senior and Junior, and Zeb Alderman) with fiscal dominance, and the Fosters (Sheriffs Ben, Billy, and Terry) doing the dirty work. But that had to end. Soon, Terry believed. Time was his ally; he was only forty-eight years old. And there was Malcolm Foster, now in college, at age twenty being groomed to carry on.

Thus, the sheriff no longer cared about Elmo Jr.'s tirades, even though they galled him. *Let him shout. What the hell difference does it make?*

"Don't you understand," Elmo Jr. was going on, "that the so-called automobile accident only exacerbates the situation? It'll only make that Chicago police officer more determined to dig into our business."

Terry shrugged, showing his lack of concern. "He's not really a cop anymore. My source in Chicago says they've forced him out because he shot a pimp in cold blood." He laughed. "Big-city police departments put a great emphasis on proper procedure. But anyway, his fangs have been pulled. Believe me, Junior, he'll sell to the Staleys, and your precious secret will be safe."

Ralston groaned. "What a fool you are, Terry, to think his retirement as a police officer is going to take him out of our lives. Your stupidity has made it certain he *has* to stay!"

"Listen, Junior—"

"And that's enough of your insolence!" the old man exploded. "I'll not sit here and listen to your ill-mannered attempt to denigrate me by referring to me as 'Junior'!"

"Okay . . . *Mister* Ralston," Terry chuckled, knowing how much Elmo disliked the diminutive appellation. "But just understand this: I'm not the ass kisser my old man was."

"You may characterize it as you wish, but Billy Foster appreciated the need for preserving the . . . uh . . . integrity of what was important in Mountain County."

"Ah, yes," the sheriff said sarcastically, "the sainted Miss Alice—"

"You have no right to even breathe her name!"

The black butler entered the drawing room, coughing discreetly to attract his employer's attention. " 'Scuse me, Mistah Elmo, but there's a phone call fer the sheriff. Dep'ty Apple, he said."

"Take it there," Ralston grunted, gesturing toward the telephone on the desk.

Terry left the sofa to pick up the instrument. "Yeah . . . what do you have, Randy?" He listened. "When?" There was another pause as Deputy Apple reported. "Uh huh, I see. Well, have him bailed and make sure he's got his story straight." He hung up the phone, standing at the desk in thought.

"Well—?" Elmo asked demandingly.

"The state police have arrested Daniel on a complaint by Rudy Pitts. The charge is attempted vehicular homicide."

"Oh, good Lord!"

"Don't sweat it, Elmo. There are half-a-dozen good citizens of Mountain County who will swear Daniel Staley was getting drunk at K.C.'s Place at the very moment Ballard and Pitts were being forced off the road by *someone* driving a red pickup."

"And what about the truck being identified?"

"It's burned beyond recognition on a dump over in North Carolina. The situation is in hand."

Ralston sighed deeply. "No man was ever so deceived by another as by himself."

"Well, well," Terry grinned, "now we're quoting Fulke Greville." He was genuinely amused. "There's no need to try to impress me. I went to school, too, you know." The voice hardened. "You see, I'm not terribly impressed with the whole damned Ralston clan, and that includes your whacky sister, whose name I daren't breathe."

"Get out!" Elmo's face was livid.

"Gladly. And don't worry, *Junior*. The secrets of the sordid past are safe with me."

"Out! Damn you—get out!" His ire triggered a paroxysm

of coughing, doubling him over in the wheelchair.

Sheriff Foster swaggered out of the drawing room, encountering the butler in the foyer. "Boy . . . I think your master may need some help."

ii   Casey Ballard felt a kind of desperation as he poked disinterestedly at the room-service breakfast. It was a despair brought on by the certain knowledge he had made a calamitous mess of his visit to Mountain County, Tennessee. And all because of his decision to keep K.C.'s Place. It would have been so simple just to profit from his inheritance and be grateful for it; that had been Rosie's wish.

Rosalie?

He had lied to her again the night before, calling her from the Gatlinburg hospital emergency room to tell her he had been in a "minor auto accident," assuring her he was all right and would be "home in a day or two." In a way, that was a bigger lie than the one told about the automobile mishap. He had intervened in a community he would probably never fully understand and it was too late for him to walk away from it.

Twice in three days someone had tried to kill him. Even worse, Eddie Ballard had paid with his life because of Casey's folly. So, too, had the three-fingered Willie Young and his companion *(My God, I don't even know his name!)* in the cockfights robbery. And he had risked Rudy Pitts' life, as well. And for what? For a misplaced sense that only he could bring justice to Mountain County?

Rosie, weeping and angry, had accused him of that in their telephone conversation. "You can't play God down there, Casey! This isn't one of your police cases! This time it's different—this time it's *not* your job and you can't explain it away by saying, 'But, Rosie, that's what they pay me for.' "

He had chuckled. She had imitated his inflections perfectly.

108

"And don't laugh about it! There's no humor in it." All of her long-repressed emotions were on the surface. "There's been no humor in it for years. Worrying about whether some subhuman is going to put a bullet in your brain, or a knife in your heart—" Her sobbing halted the words.

"Yeah, yeah . . . I know," he sighed.

"You don't know! You've *never* known! I was a cop's wife and I knew my role. I accepted that when I married you. But this . . . this . . . *thing* you're doing down there isn't in my script, Casey."

"O'Hara, I'm sorry," Casey said softly. "Okay, I'll wrap it up and be home Tuesday after—"

"Why not tomorrow?" she interrupted vehemently.

"Because Eddie Ballard's funeral is on Tuesday and I have to be there."

"To bring him back from the dead?!"

"Jesus, Rosie, be fair. I'd be dead myself if it hadn't been for that man."

There had been a long pause on the Chicago end of the line. Finally, "All right, Tuesday then."

"I love you, O'Hara."

"Tuesday," she replied coldly, breaking the connection.

Ballard had been released from the emergency room after the intern's examination had revealed only a few minor contusions. He and Rudy Pitts were delivered back to Hillside in the same community ambulance that had taken them to Gatlinburg.

Casey hadn't slept well. His head ached, for one thing. For another, the knowledge that Tuesday and Eddie's funeral wouldn't end matters in Mountain County kept him awake. Endlessly, the details of what he knew about the county and the Ballards were replayed in his mind, serving only to keep him awake. Through the half-drawn blinds of the hotel room he had seen the sun begin a new day and this new day—this Monday morning—brought him no answers.

There was a knock at the door.

"Yeah, who is it?" Casey called.

"Rudy."

Wearily, Ballard pushed himself up from the room service table and went to the door to admit the young garage mechanic.

"Well, the state cops arrested Daniel," Pitts reported, "charged him, and he's out already."

"What?

"Yep. Lulubelle was waitin' right there to bail him."

"What kind of bail?"

Rudy laughed. "The J.P. set it at a thousand. He's gonna git away with this, ya know."

"I *don't* know that, Rudy."

"Well, he is. Daniel claims he were at K.C.'s Place when we was run off the road. Says he got a bunch o' witnesses what'll swear t' it."

Casey grimaced. "All very neat, huh?"

"Yep."

"And what did the good sheriff have to say about all this?"

"He weren't there," Rudy answered. "Nobody from the sheriff's was there. Jest two state cops an' me."

Ballard sank down on the bed with a small groan of disgust.

"Say, ya gonna eat thet breakfast?" Pitts asked, eyeing the table.

"No. Eat it if you want."

The young man attacked the country ham and eggs. "Damn, Mr. Ballard," he chortled, "this business o' nearly gettin' killed makes a fellow hungry."

iii   Charlie Sams, the editor of the *Hillside Truth*, was sickened by the sight of the torn body, half hidden in the underbrush. He had been called to the scene in the deep woods some ten miles from the county seat, summoned by Sheriff Terry Foster to be witness to the final act of the drama of the holdup of the cockfight patrons at K.C.'s Place four days earlier.

110

"It must have been bears," the sheriff said nonchalantly.

"Bears? In January?" Sams challenged him. "Bears are in hibernation now."

"Yeah, but if he got too close to one of their dens, and disturbed them, they would have been pretty damned mean."

"Hmmm, unlikely. It could have been dogs, of course." His mind conjured up the pack of tracking dogs maintained by the sheriff's department. Mean brutes, kept mean by rough handling and denial of food when sent tracking.

"Dogs?" Foster seemed to be considering that possibility. "Could be, I guess. There are a couple of wild packs in these woods. We try to kill them off, but . . ." He shrugged.

Charlie stared at the corpse. The flesh of the face had been half torn away; he could see only one eye. Most of the clothes had been shredded and there was blood everywhere. A piece of intestine poked through a hole in the abdomen. If his father had taught him anything it was the lore of the woods. And he had *never* seen a bear that didn't run at the sight of man. If cornered, they'd stand and fight. But attack a man like this—never! His story was going to say it was dogs. Whose dogs he'd leave to conjecture.

"Whatever it was," the sheriff continued, "it ends that damned story, doesn't it?" He gestured toward the body. "That's Cleon Bolton."

"How can you tell?"

"Found his wallet nearby—driver's license and all. Which means we can be sure of one of the others, too. Cleon didn't go anywhere without Raleigh Turner. We'll know soon enough from fingerprint records, but I'm sure the one blown apart by the shotgun was Turner. I should have thought of those two bastards right from the beginning."

"And the three-fingered man?" the newspaperman asked.

Terry Foster sighed deeply. "Identified him last night. A Carolina farmer, Willie Young. His daughter I.D.'d him. Real shaken up, too."

"Would that be Yolanda Young?" Sams had heard rumors of the sheriff's liaison with the young woman.

"Yes. I felt badly about putting her through that, but she

111

told me her father was missing and I took a chance he might be one of them." He sighed again. "What I can't figure out is what the hell Willie was doing with two sonofabitches like Turner and Bolton."

Charlie just shook his head.

The sheriff clapped him on the back. "Well, that wraps it up for you, Charlie. It'll give you a hell of a story for Thursday, won't it?"

"Yes." He hesitated. "Anything on that highway . . . uh . . . incident involving Rudy Pitts and Casey Ballard?"

"That's a state police matter," Foster explained. "But I hear Daniel Staley has an iron-clad alibi for the time of the accident. The way it's told to me, Daniel was at K.C.'s and has a bunch of witnesses who will swear to it."

"Hmmm. I was at the J.P. hearing. But does it ring true to you, Terry?"

"Why wouldn't it?"

The newspaper editor smiled. "I love interviews where I get questions in answer to questions."

Foster's face clouded momentarily, but then he laughed. "Yeah, I guess that is a pain in the ass. So—yes, Daniel's story rings true to me."

"Uh huh. Has there been any effort to trace the red pickup?"

"Effort, yes. Success, no. There are a lot of red pickups in Mountain County. But you may say the sheriff's office is cooperating with the state police in trying to find that one specific red pickup."

Sams scrawled in his notebook.

"But do you know what I think, Charlie?"

"What?"

"I think Ballard has poisoned Rudy's mind about the incident. I mean, Rudy knows Daniel has a red pickup, he mentions it to Ballard, and Ballard convinces him to say that Daniel was behind the wheel."

"But what motive would Ballard have for that?"

"All the motive in the world," the sheriff insisted. "The best motive there is: money! Lulubelle and her boys offered him forty thousand for K.C.'s Place, but he wanted more. So they offered him ten grand additional. Ballard turns that down, too. He's just like all those big-city pricks."

Sams shook his head in doubt. "My impression, after meeting him the other day, was that he was a pretty decent fellow."

"Which shows you how wrong first impressions can be." Foster dropped his voice into a confidential tone. "If you check with your newspaper sources in Chicago, Charlie, you'll find that Ballard was booted off the police force last Wednesday for killing a man in cold blood. Oh, they permitted him to retire— to save the departmental face, you know—but that doesn't change the fact. He gunned down a man while he was sitting on a toilet, for Christ sake!"

Sam's face showed his disbelief.

"And if you want more, Charlie, I can tell you Ballard's old man was a fugitive from Mountain County on a charge of murdering his own brother. It's an old case, but it's also factual. The sheriff's files are a matter of public record, you know. So if you want to see that particular file, just stop by the office."

The editor closed his notebook. "I'll probably do that later today."

"It's a hell of a story, Charlie. Yes sir, a hell of a story. And I can tell you . . . and you may quote me . . . that I spotted the bastard as a foul ball the first day he walked into the county."

9

i   It was high up on a flattened mountaintop. If it hadn't been a cemetery—as it had been for more than a century-and-a-half—the location would have stirred the creative juices of any real estate developer. The view in all directions was spectacular: the sky wide and light blue in the midmorning sun, lesser mountains arrayed below in dress of somber winter colors, but always with the dominant greenness of the pines, and a few fleecy white clouds racing along with an underpinning of dark gray, as if suggesting the weather was about to change to something more ominous.

As Casey Ballard left the borrowed Hillside Inn station wagon, he pulled his light topcoat tighter about him against the stiff, cold breeze blowing across the cemetery's carefully tended acres. He was early for the burial of United States Marine Sergeant Edgar Ballard; the funeral cortege had not yet made an appearance. But he wanted to be early. He hadn't wanted to make an "entrance." Casey reasoned it would be much better if he was simply there when the others arrived, drawing less attention to his presence.

Idly he walked between the neatly spaced aisles of graves, glancing at the names on the stones and monuments, recognizing the cumulative stories of those resting there would make a valid history of Mountain County. He was surprised by the large numbers of Civil War dead buried there, most of them members of the Union army, but a few epitaphs boasting Confederate service. Similarity of names on some of those graves served to emphasize again the tragic reality of brother against brother in the bloody conflict.

And then he came upon the name BALLARD. In multiples. All were etched on wide, flat, highly polished marble slabs in which were reflected the clouds sailing above him. The names were familiar to him now: *Sarah, Esther, Moses* (was that grave empty?), *King David.* And *Eleanor Foster Ballard,* his grandmother. He stared at it, making a connection for the first time with the Sheriffs Foster. Was it possible his grandmother was kin to *those* Fosters? He dismissed the thought; certainly someone would have mentioned it to him had that been true.

Next to his grandmother was the newest stone: *K.C. Ballard, 1892–1985.* Casey gazed down on it, wondering why it was the old reprobate had selected him as his heir. Had it just been senility, as Terry Foster had suggested? Or had his grandfather meant to draw him to Mountain County to sort out the facts and fictions of the Ballard family? To solve the "mysteries" of the Ballards?

He sensed someone standing near him, turning to find a little man, an ancient, leaning heavily on a hickory cane. He was skinny with age but smartly dressed in a dark gray suit, a white shirt with a tastefully striped tie, shiny black shoes, and a well-tailored black overcoat. Clear blue eyes looked at Casey through thick wire-rimmed glasses.

"Ya know ol' K.C.?" the man asked.

"Not really, but I'm his grandson."

"Oh?" There was a momentary hesitation. "Then ya must be this Casey feller Ah been hearin' 'bout. From Chicago, ain't ya?"

"Yes."

The man held out his hand, smiling for the first time.

"Ah'm Herman Armstrong, the cemetery superintendent." Casey shook the hand. "Been thet fer some seventy-five years."

"The place is beautifully cared for, sir."

"Thank ya. 'Preciate thet. Most folks don't seem t' notice. Ya here fer the Eddie Ballard funeral?"

"I am, yes."

"Hmmm. Heard 'bout what happened, too. Ya must feel strong 'bout Eddie."

"I do," Casey said firmly. "Edgar Ballard saved my life."

"Some folks say ya was . . . to blame fer Eddie gettin' killed," Armstrong said with startling frankness. "But Ah figured it weren't nothin' but some kinda scheme by the sheriff."

"Why do you say that, Mr. Armstrong?"

" 'Cause Ah know the Fosters. Knew all o' 'em—Ben, Billy, an' now Terry. Weren't none o' 'em worth a pinch o' owl shit!"

Casey laughed. "A colorful evaluation, sir."

"True, though," the cemetery keeper replied soberly. "An' Ah hope ya ain't gonna mess with Terry, Mr. Ballard. He's jest plain, cussed mean."

The younger man nodded agreement. "In light of your strong opinions on the Fosters, I'm almost afraid to ask a question which has just come to mind."

"What's thet?"

"My grandmother," Casey said, pointing toward the gravesite, "was Eleanor *Foster* Ballard. Could she have been related in any way to the lawmen?"

"Sheriff Ben's sister."

"So, there's Foster blood running in my veins," Casey said wryly.

"Yep, but don't let it fret ya, Mr. Ballard. She were the on'y decent one in the family. Fine Christian lady. Died havin' yer papa."

"So I've been told."

The old man sighed deeply. "Sometimes the way o' the Lord is mighty puzzlin'. Ya cain't help but wonder why a sweet

117

lady like Ellie git taken, an' them other Fosters are . . . visited upon us, ya might say. Mebbe He jest wants t' give us a taste of hell here on earth t' make us 'preciate the heavenly home He promises."

Casey smiled. "That's a point. I wish I had met you earlier, Mr. Armstrong. You seem to be the most perceptive Mountain Countian I've come across."

"Know a lot, if thet's what ya mean," Armstrong said. Then a broad grin. "Ya see, most folks look at me like Ah'm an ol' fool, an' they say things in front o' me like Ah ain't there, ya know. Anybody gittin' to be ninety-two they think is a li'l foolish. Some is, but Ah *ain't,*" he added forcefully. "Reckon ah know more 'bout what's happenin' in Mountain County than any livin' soul."

The sounds of cars coming up the macadam road to the mountaintop came to them.

"Gotta go an' superintend now," the old man said.

"Mind if I tag along with you, Mr. Armstrong?"

"Be pleased at thet."

Casey followed the nonagenarian to the site of the freshly dug grave, where a tent over it snapped in the breeze. The first car had already stopped there and the Staleys were getting out of it. The sons first, all dressed in somber black suits. Ballard barely recognized Alvin, Birch, Chester, and Daniel. It occurred to him they looked almost normal. Lulubelle, all in black, with an incongruous wide black hat and veil, lifted her bulk out of the funeral director's limo.

From the second car came a tall, slim specter of a man, also all in black, with a stern, hawk-like face.

"Thet's Ashley Smith o' the Holiness Church," Armstrong whispered to Casey. "Call hisself a reverend, but Ah reckon he ain't had the schoolin'. Horse's ass, in mah thinkin'.'"

Casey allowed himself a smile.

As the cars of the cortege emptied out, his attention was drawn to a dark gray Lincoln town car, where there was much activity as a wheelchair was brought out and a frail, elderly man was lifted into it. A heavy lap robe was placed around his immobile legs and he was wheeled to a position very close to the grave.

Casey touched Armstrong's arm, nodding toward the wheelchair.

"Elmo Ralston," the cemetery superintendent said quietly. "Junior Ralston, owner of the Ralston Company. Got hurt thet way in a lumberin' accident. Tree fell on 'im." Feller behind 'im is Zeb Alderman—"

"Yes, I've met Mr. Alderman."

"Count yer fingers after ya shook hands with 'im?"

Ballard struggled not to laugh.

"Them Ralstons like t' think they's the first family o' Mountain County. An', if yer countin' dollars, Ah guess thet's so."

Up the hill, in silent cadence, came an eight-man United States Marine Corps honor guard in full-dress uniform. Edgar Ballard's brothers carried his flag-draped casket from the hearse, placing it on the webbing positioned over the hole in the ground. The funeral director and his aides hurriedly banked flowers around it. The scene was complete.

"Oh, Lord, hear our plea!" the Reverend Mr. Smith's voice boomed out. "Comin' your way, sweet Jee-sus, is a brave soul!"

Lulubelle's wail cut across the cemetery, echoing down the valley beyond. Alvin, standing next to her, grimaced.

Undeterred, the preacher never broke his verbal stride. "Oh, Lord, we ask that you fold Edgar Ballard to your sweet bosom an' nurture him in your love. For Eddie was a special man . . ."

As Reverend Smith's peroration continued, Ballard's eyes scanned the faces. For the first time he saw Terry Foster there, the sheriff glaring at him. Casey nodded to him and Terry mouthed some words the Chicagoan was unable to make out. He shrugged and Foster frowned angrily.

". . . And so, sweet Jee-sus, we send you another warrior for the army of God!" A pause. "Ashes to ashes, dust to dust . . ." The commitment words spoken, the minister added: "All of Eddie's friends should know there'll be a special memorial service, in conjunction with the Hillside American Legion Post, at the Holiness Church next Sunday morning. Everyone will be welcome." He drew a deep breath. "Amen and amen!"

Some others mumbled "amen" as well.

The Marine honor guard fired its traditional salute, and as the American flag was being folded for presentation to the distraught Lulubelle, *Taps* was played in echo by two trumpeters, the poignant notes drifting across the beauty of the Great Smokies.

The last note was still hanging in the air when Sheriff Foster roughly grabbed Casey's arm, propelling him away from the other mourners.

"You've got a lot of balls coming here, Ballard!"

Casey tried to keep his face expressionless, masking his own anger. "That young man saved my life," he said with studied calm. "At the very least, I owed him my presence at his funeral."

"You're really stupid!" Foster snarled. "If it weren't for me those crazy Staley boys would have finished you right here— this morning!"

"Daniel certainly gave it the old college try Sunday night."

Terry's vise-like grip tightened on the arm. "I'm not going to banter with you, Ballard. I told you once you had no options." He was spacing out the words, emphasizing each one. "And now I'm telling you again. Before this day is out you'll sign those sales papers, take your money, and get the hell out of here!"

"And if I don't?"

"I won't be able to continue to guarantee your safety."

Ballard laughed. He hadn't meant to, but the statement was so ludicrous, the laugh was involuntary. "I wasn't aware you were doing that, Sheriff."

"As I said, no more bantering. Today's the end of this shit!" Giving a final painful squeeze to Casey's arm, he whirled and stalked away.

Casey watched him go, understanding he had not been given an idle threat. Yet, he was somehow more at ease than he had been at any time since his arrival in Mountain County.

All pretense had been dropped. He was certain of the danger now and, being certain, he could deal with it.

He strolled slowly through the cemetery, studying the names on the stones once more. When he came back to Edgar's fresh grave, where two men were filling it in under Herman Armstrong's "superintending," the old man smiled at him.

"Have you ever wondered, Mr. Armstrong," Casey asked easily, "whether this," gesturing to the grave, "is really the final act of life?"

"Nope, never wondered," Herman answered without hesitation. "Since Ah been a small boy, Ah knew it weren't. Don't make no sense fer a feller to go through all he's gotta go through—the comin' out of the womb, an' the growin' up, an' the strugglin', an' the lovin', an' the marryin', an' the fatherin'—t' throw it all away on this. Nope, Ah always knew there were more t' life than dyin'."

"That's very wise."

"No, that's faith, Mr. Ballard."

Casey nodded, unsure his own faith was as hardy.

"Nearly finished here, Mr. Ballard. How 'bout a cup o' tea?"

"That would be welcome."

Armstrong gave his workmen their final instructions and led the way to a small stone cottage on the edge of the cemetery. Inside, there was a fire set against the chill of the January day. As the old man busied himself preparing the tea, he said: "Ah always been partial t' *Taps* played the way them Marine boys did it—ya know, one trumpet on the hillside an' one off a piece way, echoin' kinda."

"Yes, that's very moving."

"Yessuh, always been partial to thet."

He brought the tea to a small table, motioning for Casey to be seated. "This here's mah own herb tea. Grow the herbs mahself. Like t' think it's healthful."

"I'm sure it is." Casey took a sip; it was delicious. He said so.

"'Preciate thet."

"Mr. Armstrong, when I was walking through the cemetery, and I passed the gravesites of the Ralstons, I noticed there was no marker for Alice Ralston—Alice Alderman, wasn't she?"

"Yep, she were married t' Zeb." He put his fingers together, studying them for a moment. "Mebbe the reason ya didn't see Alice's grave is thet she ain't dead."

"What?"

"Least ways she ain't dead *here.* An' if she deceased somewheres else, Ah ain't heard of it. Ah reckon Ah would heard tell if she did—die somewheres else, thet is."

Casey was perplexed. "But Alderman very distinctly told me his wife—" He paused, trying to remember precisely what the banker had told him only a few days earlier. So much had happened in less than a week it seemed he had been involved with Mountain County for a much longer time. "Zeb told me," he continued slowly, "he lost his wife nearly ten years ago."

"Hmmm." The old man grinned at him. "Did he say she died?"

"No, I guess not." Once more Ballard paused. "I think he said it had been ten years since he lost her. No, wait—the phrase he used was more like 'ten years since she's been *gone.*' "

"Lost an' *gone* ain't dead, is it?" Armstrong asked.

"No."

"But Ah know thet's how people talk 'bout the deceased. They don't wanna say *dead,* so they use them other words. No, suh, Mr. Ballard, Ah ain't heard Alice Ralston Alderman is dead. 'Course, she *is* gone, no doubt of thet. But dead?" He shook his head in doubt. "Still, nothin' 'bout Alice would su'prise me."

"Why do you say that?"

" 'Cause Alice were a sure-fire scandal, even in Mountain County where we don't pay much mind to folks' . . . well, folks' fulsome livin', ya know. Mah late bride said she were a slut. Now, Ah don't know thet Ah'd go thet far mahself, but she were a caution, sure 'nuff."

"Would you tell me about it?"

Herman laughed loudly. "Ya'd have a helluva time, Mr. Ballard, stoppin' me now." He brought his laughter under control. "Ya see, the Ralstons mebbe had more money'n common sense. With the lumberin' company they took t' gatherin' in most o' the money there was hereabouts. Young Elmo Junior an' his sister, Alice, was both spoiled, but Alice . . . well, she were spoiled *rotten*. Ol' Elmo, he set 'er up like a princess."

Herman took a deep breath as he warmed to the story. "One o' the problems were thet she kinda . . . uh . . . matured faster'n most o' the girls o' 'er age. Ya shoulda seen 'er, Mr. Ballard—at thirteen she were a woman! Ah mean, she were the kind t' give a lot o' married men in the county wet dreams." He chuckled. "A pleasin', ripe beauty. Curly brown hair an' big hazel eyes—kinda innocent eyes, ya know. An' smooth skin the color o' buttermilk, an' a figure—Lord! She had a way o' walkin' thet were . . . well, suh, she were appealin' an' she knew it. She had a . . . uh . . . instinct, Ah guess ya'd say, thet gave 'er the advantage over any man what crossed 'er path."

Casey stayed silent, not wanting to intrude on the narrative.

"Thet's why it really didn't su'prise nobody much—'cept mebbe 'er daddy—when Alice set 'er cap fer Herschel Barnes. Now, Herschel were a good-lookin' young feller, mebbe twenty-one, jest outta college, when he come here as a gym teacher. Thet musta been . . . oh, 'bout twenny-seven. Ah'm sure a lot o' them young ladies at the high school thought Herschel Barnes were kinda excitin', but Alice, she knew what t' do 'bout it. If ya kin believe all the gossip—an' Ah didn't doubt it fer a minute—she seduced Herschel. Good an' proper, ya might say, 'cause the two of 'em run off one night an' got themselves married. Over in South Carolina.

" 'Course, ol' Judge Ralston weren't happy 'bout thet an'—"

"Excuse me," Casey cut in. *"Judge* Ralston? I also saw that mentioned in the *Hillside Truth.* What kind of judge?"

"Folks called 'im thet," the cemetery superintendent smiled. "Fact is he were a part-time justice o' the peace. An' the Ralstons always was inclined t' take themselves too serious."

"I see. Please go on."

"Well, ol' Elmo took to' havin' the marriage annulled an' Alice got packed off t' some fancy girls' boardin' school back

East. She were gone most o' four years, mebbe more, an' when she came back—now a *outstandin'* beauty—the story was thet she graduated from thet school. Ah heard one tale, though, thet they kicked er out fer foolin' 'round with a perfesser feller, jest like with Herschel Barnes, ya know. Anyway . . . she were back an' the ol' gossips had a field day. Anytime she were in ten feet o' any male, the stories started."

Casey interrupted again. "Zeb Alderman has told me my father, Abel Ballard, courted her. And she turned him down."

"Hmmm." Herman contemplated the contention for a moment. "Could be, but Ah doubt thet turnin'-down bit. Ah don't believe Alice ever did any turnin' down. But Ah recollect it were Abel's brother, King David, who were sweet on Alice. An' she returned the favor, as Ah 'member. Least ways, Ah heard tell."

"King David? He was murdered, wasn't he?"

"Yep. Got cold-cocked with a axe." Old Armstrong quickly returned to the subject of Alice Ralston. "Anyway, sometime in nineteen an' thirty-four, the Ralston family married Alice off t' young Zeb Alderman, who was runnin' the trust company—the Ralston bank, ya know."

"A successful marriage?"

"They tried t' make it 'pear so, they truly did." He grinned again. "But it were hard, ya know. Alice . . . well, she weren't too choosy most times. Even took to' beddin' down Sheriff Billy Foster fer a time or two. Mebbe more."

"Did Zeb know?"

"Hell, ev'rybody knew! But, ya know, there were somethin' strange 'bout it all," Herman mused. "Zeb seemed willin' t' share 'er, ya might say, jest t' have 'er 'round. Mebbe he loved 'er, Ah don't know. Then, she jest took off one day. There were one story thet she went to Europe, carryin' on with some Eyetalian count an'—" He stopped, shrugging.

"Didn't she ever return?"

"Nope."

"So she might be dead."

"She might," Armstrong admitted. "But, like Ah said, she ain't dead here."

"Uh huh." Casey was spinning the kernel of a scenario around in his brain. "Going back to the murder of King David, sir, would it surprise you if I told you there's an old sheriff's file in which my father is accused of having killed his brother?"

The old man's eyes opened wide. "Ain't possible. Ah knew thet youngster Abel Ballard an' he weren't the type t' kill, ya know. He were a straight-up young feller, Mr. Ballard."

"But perhaps the two brothers might have quarreled over the affections of Alice Ralston."

Herman pondered the suggestion. "Mebbe."

"But you don't think so?"

"No, Ah don't."

Casey's scenario, his theory, had grown into a tender seedling, not yet anywhere near full flower. And he decided not to try it out on the ancient cemetery superintendent. He appreciated Herman's openness, but he wasn't sure the old man wouldn't be just as voluble if Terry Foster came asking questions. Casey had no reason to believe Sheriff Foster would learn of his conversation with Herman Armstrong, but he couldn't know that for certain. For the moment, then, Ballard kept the incomplete theory to himself.

ii   Casey flipped the keys of the Hillside Inn's station wagon onto the registration desk. "Thank you, Mr. Reston," he said, smiling, "for the loan of the wagon. I appreciate your help."

Bobby Reston, the inn's day manager, nodded soberly, not his usual extroverted self. "Will you still be checking out this afternoon, Mr. Ballard?"

"Yes. Someone's picking me up at five o'clock to drive me to the Knoxville airport."

"In that case, I suppose it will be all right for a few hours."

"What will be all right, Mr. Reston?"

"I'm very distressed, sir," the young man answered in a scolding manner. "Your *friend,*" he made it sound like a dirty

125

word, "came rushing in here an hour ago, demanding to be let into your room. And he had with him one of those . . . uh . . . ladies from K.C.'s. He raised such a fuss I had little choice but to give him your key."

"You mean Rudy Pitts?"

"Yes, sir. And with that . . . *woman!*" He wrinkled his nose in disgust. "That deaf mute—"

"Trixie?" None of it was making any sense.

"I believe that's what they call her. You must understand, Mr. Ballard, we can't permit . . . uh . . . such people to use our hotel. She's a . . . *prostitute!*"

Suddenly, it was all very humorous to Casey. He laughed. "A first for the Hillside Inn, Mr. Reston?"

The day manager grimaced. "Admittedly, an occasional . . . uh . . . indiscretion does occur," he sputtered, "but we can't permit the Hillside Inn to become a roadhouse!"

"Don't worry about it, Bobby," Casey grinned. "I'll make sure Rudy and Trixie behave themselves while they're in your hotel." He hurried to the elevators.

At room 316 he knocked.

A male voice called from inside: "Who is it?"

"Casey."

The sound of the security chain being released came to Casey. Rudy threw open the door. "Gawd, Ah'm glad ya got here!"

"What the hell's going on!"

At that, Trixie rushed to him, throwing herself into his arms, holding him tightly, sobbing. There was a large, ugly purple bruise on her left cheek. Casey struggled to free himself from the distraught girl, guiding her gently to chair and putting her in it.

"Okay," he said to Rudy as he dropped wearily onto the bed, "let's have it."

"Well, last night," Rudy started, "Terry were at K.C.'s with Yolanda, drinkin' purty good . . ." The story poured out rapidly: of Terry and Yolanda Young getting into a loud, drunken argument in the barroom; of the sheriff leaving his girlfriend to go to Trixie's room, where he encountered another man, whom he beat severely; of Foster trying to force himself on Trixie; of Trixie resisting and getting beaten herself; and of the sheriff finally raping the young prostitute.

"This mornin'," Pitts reported, "one o' the other gals at K.C.'s brought a note t' me from Trixie an', while y'all was at Eddie's funeral, Ah went out there an' took 'er away. Ah brought 'er here, 'cause Ah didn't know what else t' do."

There were twinges of pain in Casey's back and his head throbbed again. "And now what, Rudy?"

"Ah figured we'd take 'er . . . well, someplace Terry couldn't find 'er."

"Give me a hint," Ballard demanded with some anger.

"Well . . . uh . . . Ah don't rightly—" He shook his head.

Casey groaned, looking at Trixie huddled in the chair, asking her rhetorically, "And you, young lady, where do you want to go?"

Trixie read his lips. Retrieving her notepad from a purse, she wrote one word, holding it out to Casey.

He took it. *Chicago,* it said.

"Oh, shit!" He rushed to the telephone, dialing his home number. Rosalie answered on the first ring. "Hiya, O'Hara," he said lightly.

"Are you on your way?" his wife asked coldly.

"Listen, Rosie, something has come up."

"Oh?"

"Yes, there's one more thing I have to do, so it'll have to be tomorrow."

There was silence on the other end of the line.

"Rosie?"

She broke the connection.

"Damn!" He sat holding the phone in his hand, staring at it.

"Listen, Mr. Ballard," Rudy said finally, "Ah got a aunt in Asheville an' mebbe—"

10

i   Asheville, North Carolina, was a revelation to the big-city boy in Casey Ballard. Even though the light of that Tuesday was fading as they drove into the town, it wasn't difficult to determine it was neat and clean, with streets of pleasant homes, not unlike the little play community Casey had had in his Christmas tree "yard" when he was a youngster.

Rudy bragged about the town when they entered Asheville on Route 19, paralleling the French Broad River. "This is 'bout the purtiest city in the southern highlands," he said. "Folks come from all 'round the states jest to spend their vacations here. Weather's near purfect, most times. It's called the eastern gateway t' the Great Smokies."

Their drive to Asheville in Rudy's pickup truck had been uneventful. Trixie had slept most of the way, huddled against Casey, a hand grasping tightly to his arm. The warmth of the young girl, coupled with her distinctive lilac fragrance, had been disconcerting to Ballard. There were erotic feelings conjured up about Trixie, followed by the mental picture of Rosalie's face, an angry face, and then tormenting doubts about the wisdom of his Mountain County adventure—all of these deepening his sense of guilt. Yet he was a prisoner of his conditioning as a cop, addicted to "the case" as surely as the mainliner was to heroin and the alcoholic to booze.

Before they had left Hillside, Casey had made two quick telephone calls. One was to the hotel office, to tell Bobby Reston he'd need to stay another day. "And don't worry," he had said with a chuckle, "my . . . uh . . . guests have already left."

"Thank you, sir," the day manager had replied. "I knew you'd understand our predicament."

"Perfectly. Rest easy, Bobby, the reputation of the Hillside Inn hasn't been compromised."

His second call was to Sheriff Foster, also couched in friendly tones. "I need a favor, Terry," he started. "I think it's better if I stay over another night."

"Now wait a damned minute," the lawman had shouted at him, "I said I wanted this shit cleaned up *today!*"

"I know, but I'm really exhausted, and my head is killing me," Casey explained evenly. "I'll cut off the phone and a good night's sleep will really set me up. If you'll arrange a meeting for ten o'clock tomorrow morning, I'll sign all the transfer papers then and still make the one o'clock Chicago flight from Knoxville."

Reluctantly, the sheriff had agreed to the postponement, and Ballard left the hotel by the rear entrance, as Rudy and Trixie had done minutes before, climbing into Rudy's pickup truck for the trip to Asheville. Casey hoped he had frozen Foster in place for a few hours.

Young Pitts turned now on to Haywood Road in Asheville, crossing the French Broad. "Mah Uncle Samuel an' Aunt Carrie ran a tourist boardin' house here fer years 'fore mah uncle died. An' then Aunt Carrie couldn't handle it all herself. Still lives in the big house, though." He drove slowly. "There it is . . ." Rudy was pointing.

It was a rambling frame house, with a big porch around three sides of it. Huge maple trees spread their branches across the entire expanse of the front yard. As they stopped in front of the house, the door opened and a woman stepped out.

"Thet's Aunt Carrie," Rudy announced.

They were welcomed effusively by the aunt, a woman in her seventies, white haired and almost a visual cliché of someone's favorite aunt, a woman Norman Rockwell would have painted.

In the spacious living room, furnished in an old-fashioned Thirties style, Rudy introduced Trixie to Aunt Carrie, using the girl's notepad to accomplish the task. Trixie was sober faced in these alien surroundings, trusting Casey Ballard but unsure of what would happen to her in the days ahead.

"Ya po' dahlin'," Aunt Carrie crooned to her, not fully understanding how to communicate with the deaf mute. She led Trixie away to the bedroom she had prepared for her.

"Let's git some coffee," Rudy said to Casey. In the gleaming kitchen, the young man poured two cups of black brew from an old cast-iron pot.

Casey looked at his watch. "We're going to have to leave right away. I want to try to be back in Hillside before the shit hits the fan when they find Trixie missing."

"Yeah . . . okay."

The Chicagoan groaned. "This is all so ridiculous! Why am I involved in this thing anyway? Why do I have to challenge that bastard Foster?"

" 'Cause it's the right thing t' do," Rudy replied quietly.

"Hmmm . . . maybe."

Rudy's aunt came into the kitchen. "Po' baby's puttin' her things away. Ain't got much in thet li'l bundle she brought along." She dropped her voice, whispering, "Is she really a . . . uh . . . prostitute, like Rudy said?"

"Yes," Ballard answered.

"Don't seem possible. She's so sweet. How old is she, anyway?"

"Eighteen, I believe."

"Deah me. What's this world comin' to?"

"Mrs. Pitts, I don't want to alarm you," Casey said sternly, "but you understand we've taken Trixie away from those who . . . well, controlled her. And they're not going to like that. I'm going to ask that you not let her go out of the house alone, and that neither one of you go out after dark. Rudy will keep in touch with you daily. I may call, too. But if anyone else calls asking about Trixie, don't tell them she's here. Lie about it, Mrs. Pitts."

"Ah ain't comfortable with lyin', Mr. Ballard," the elderly woman said.

"I can appreciate that. And you probably won't have to. It isn't likely that anything at all will happen here. I just wanted you to be aware there might be a small element of danger in this."

Aunt Carrie smiled. "Danger Ah don't mind. It's lyin' thet's sinful."

"Yes, well . . . thank you for helping out," Casey said with sincerity. "We'll relieve you of this responsibility just as soon as we can."

They left the Haywood Road home then, after being delayed for several moments while Trixie clung to Casey, not wanting to let him go. Rudy pointed the pickup northward for the return to Mountain County.

"Thet gal's in love with ya," Rudy said.

"Don't be stupid!"

"Mebbe Ah ain't very smart, but Ah do know a tad 'bout women. Ya got yerself a problem there, Mr. Ballard."

ii   The Westminister clock on the mantel chimed six o'-clock. Six P.M. on that January Tuesday.

Sighing deeply, Lulubelle Staley pushed herself up a re-cliner chair in her garishly decorated room. She had been sitting there for hours thinking of Edgar, and weeping about him, still wearing her black funeral dress. But now it was time to put all that behind her; there was K.C.'s Place to consider and she remained the manager of it.

There was still deep anger in her that old K.C. hadn't willed the property to her. From the time she had first come to the roadhouse in 1946, a widow with two baby boys, she had been the keeper of K.C. Ballard's enterprise. Lulubelle had been two hundred pounds lighter in those mid-Forties days and attractive in an earthy way. It was a matter of personal pride with her that she had *not* come to K.C.'s Place as a whore. While she was a woman with strong sexual appetites, dispensing her favors lavishly, she had never seen fit to accept money. In her own way she had loved every male with whom she had been intimate; all five of her sons were products of *love.* She was sure of that.

She could accept the betrayals of her love. Men were like that. Only women, she believed, could truly love. But it was difficult to accept the ultimate betrayal, the willing of K.C.'s Place to that damned grandson! Try as she might, she could find no reason for K.C.'s final cruel act. She recognized he was a man with the morals of an alley cat, but to deny her the place after all she had done—! Worse, their love-child was now dead. And K.C.'s grandson was responsible for that, too.

Sighing deeply, she removed the funeral dress, selecting a gold shantung evening gown from her big closet, the uneven texture of the weave of the cloth tending to make the gold shimmer a bit. It was one of her favorite gowns and, as were all of them, low-cut and revealing. She stood in front of a full-length mirror as she smoothed the gown with her beefy hands, admiring herself. The madam never thought of herself as fat; in self-descriptions she used the phrase *made fer lovin',* but never fat.

The mirror reflected back to her the damages done to her face by several days of crying and she sat down at her brightly lighted dressing table to make repairs. Lulubelle did that as she did everything: with abandon. While still sitting at the little table she slipped on a pair of gold pumps, grunting as she bent over.

And then she was ready to reassume her role as the mistress of K.C.'s Place. Walking slowly from her room she made her way to the stairway leading down to the large Victorian living room, standing for a moment at the head of the stairs to survey the early evening activities below. Then she descended the stairs, almost regally, making an entrance.

Her eyes swept the room and she bellowed: "Where's Trixie?"

Several of the whores looked at her blankly.

"Minnie! Go check 'er room!"

A bosomy blonde in a thin chemise raced up the stairs in response to the command. In only a few seconds she was running down the stairs again. "Ain't there, Lulu."

"Anybody see Trixie?"

There was no reply.

"Sonofabitch!" she muttered, striding toward the barroom. And she was mentally cursing Terry Foster, who had forced himself on the young girl the night before. Maybe the sheriff was important to her, but he had no right to—! By the time she entered the barroom, her ire was at full pitch. Her sons sat together at a table, drinking.

"Any o' ya see Trixie?!" she shouted.

They just stared at her.

"Alvin! Go lookin' fer 'er!"

"Oh, shit, Mama, why do Ah always got t'—?"

"All o' ya," Lulubelle screamed, "go find 'er!"

They scurried away, Chester stumbling in his perpetual drunkenness. The obese woman leaned on the bar, drumming her fingers impatiently. One by one the sons returned, each reporting Trixie was nowhere to be found.

Turning to the telephone on the bar, she dialed a familiar number. "Ah wanna talk t' the sheriff," she announced loudly when someone answered. Her massive bosom heaved as she waited for Foster to come on the line.

"Yes, Lulubelle?"

"Terry, ya bastard, Trixie's disappeared an' it's yer doin'!"

"Calm down, Lulu. I'll find her, for Christ sake."

"Ya better! 'Cause ya can't keep thet thing in yer pants, she's gone!"

At the sheriff's office, Foster hung up the phone, groaning. *That kid didn't take off on her own. Somebody helped her. Somebody . . . damn! Ballard!*

"Randy!" he called out.

The deputy came into the office. "Yeah?"

"Trixie's gone from K.C.'s. Put out an all-points for . . ." *Wait—Ballard doesn't have any wheels.* ". . . For Rudy Pitts' pickup. And if it's spotted, I don't want anybody to stop it. Just get in touch with me. Clear?"

"Any way you want it, Terry," Deputy Apple assured him.

iii   Sheriff Foster sat slumped in his personal car at the far end of the small parking lot at Rudy's Garage. A half hour earlier, Pitts' pickup truck had been spotted by a patrol car as it reentered Mountain County on Route 25. On the radio he had directed that Deputy Apple keep the pickup under surveillance and tail it at a discreet distance.

And he had learned that Casey Ballard was indeed traveling with young Pitts but that Trixie was not in the truck. *They've been to North Carolina, certainly, but where? Shit, I don't even know how long they've been gone. Quite a few hours apparently. They could have been to any one of a dozen places.*

Apple's voice was heard on the radio. "Terry, he's just dropped Ballard off at the hotel and we're on I-40 now, coming toward you."

"Okay, follow him in. And, for Christ sake, don't do anything to spook him!"

"Right."

Several minutes later: "Terry, he's turning off I-40 now."

Foster looked at his watch. It was almost midnight. He spotted the headlights of the truck, watching as it pulled directly up to the entrance of the garage. Rudy got out, quickly unlocked the front door, and disappeared inside. In a few seconds, Terry saw the lights come on in Rudy's apartment over the garage.

Deputy Apple's squad car, the headlights out, glided to a

stop next to Terry's car. Apple and his passenger, Daniel Staley, came to the driver's side of the sheriff's vehicle as Foster rolled down the window.

"Randy, you take this . . . *gentleman,*" Terry nodded toward Daniel, "and pay our friend a visit. I want to know where they've taken Trixie. And I don't give a damn how you find out."

Apple grinned. "Sure thing, Terry."

He and Staley walked to the door of Rudy's establishment.

"Open it," the deputy ordered.

Daniel lowered his massive shoulder, ramming it into the door, splintering the wood from the hinges. They raced up the stairs and Daniel once more approximated a battering ram at the door of the apartment.

Rudy, who was in the bathroom when he heard the first crash, had got only into the small living room when Apple and Staley burst in. "What the hell—!"

"Good evening," Apple said cheerily.

"Git the hell outta here!"

"Now, that's not neighborly at all," the deputy said, smiling. "Two fellows come to visit an old friend and he acts downright belligerent. Wouldn't you say so, Daniel?"

"Yeah." Staley advanced on Pitts, his huge hands balled into fists, clubbing the garage mechanic on the ear with his right. Rudy sprawled across the floor.

"Now, Rudy," Apple continued in a light-hearted manner, "suppose you just tell us where you took Trixie?"

"Go fuck yerself!"

"My, my . . ." the deputy sighed. To Daniel: "Pick him up."

With ease, Staley hoisted the slight Rudy from the floor, holding him in his muscular arms, the mechanic's arms pinioned to his sides.

Randy put his face close to Rudy's, whispering, "I don't believe you heard me right. I asked, where did you take Trixie?"

Pitts spat on him.

Apple drove a fist into Rudy's nose, the blood gushing

136

forth, the cartilage flattened. "I want an answer!"

Rudy was silent.

Another blow, this one to the mouth, split the lower lip. "Where did you take Trixie?"

"Trixie who?" Pitts answered defiantly.

Once more, Apple's fist crashed into Rudy's mouth and the victim could feel teeth break. "Where?"

Rudy shook his head negatively.

Slowly, expertly, Deputy Apple beat a tattoo on Rudy's face; on each ear, in each eye, on the nose and mouth again, pulping the face. But always careful not to render him unconscious.

"Now, again—where . . . did . . . you . . . take . . . Trixie?"

Through Rudy's rapidly closing eyes the figure of the deputy was only a blur. But he glared at him as best he could. His words were mumbled through swollen lips. "Is thet all ya got, ya sonofabitch?"

Apple buried a left into the pit of Rudy's stomach, the breath whooshing out, following with a right uppercut on the point of the chin. The mechanic's body went limp. Daniel dropped him to the floor, the head banging on the hard wood.

"What now?" the giant asked.

"Now we get Terry." Deputy Apple hurried down the stairs, signaling to his superior.

Nonchalantly, Sheriff Foster got out of his car, sauntering to his deputy. "What?"

"Nothin'."

"Shit!" Terry went up the stairs to Rudy's apartment, Randy in his wake. Inside, the sheriff paid no attention to the crumpled figure on the floor, but went instead to a small desk in the corner of the room, rummaging through the drawers, irritably tossing the contents in all directions. When he found a small address book he turned the pages slowly, carefully reading the names and addresses.

Finally: "Would you agree," he asked Apple, "that Asheville is an easy drive from here?"

"Yeah—three hours, maybe a little less."

Foster ripped a page from the book. "Five will get you ten

Trixie's in Asheville, with Rudy's aunt." He folded the page, jamming it into his hip pocket. "When we want her, we'll take a look there."

Rudy moaned, moving slightly.

"You guys are losing your touch," the sheriff laughed. He strode from the room.

The garage mechanic slowly rolled over on his back, the battered face a mask of pain.

"You heard what Terry said," Deputy Apple commented to Daniel Staley.

The giant stood over Pitts, looking disdainfully at him for a moment. Then he swung a booted foot into Rudy's kidney area. The scream was chilling. Again and again and again he kicked him—in the ribs, in the neck, in the head. With studied deliberateness he stomped on the young man's right forearm and the snap of the bone could be heard. The act was repeated on the left arm, with the same sickening result.

"Come on," Apple said quietly, "we've wasted enough time on that piece of crap."

Daniel grinned. "It weren't no waste."

11

i   There was a persistent loud pounding on his hotel room door, awakening Casey suddenly. He groaned, glancing at the clock as he put his feet on the floor. It was 7:30 A.M. The pounding continued.

"Okay! Okay!" he shouted, padding to the door. Through the peephole he could make out the distressed face of newspaper editor Charlie Sams.

"I'm sorry to get you out of bed," Sams said as Casey opened the door, "but something terrible has happened to Rudy."

"What?"

"He's been beaten up," the newspaperman said as he came into the room, throwing himself disconsolately into the one easy chair. "Damn near beaten to death! He's in the Gatlinburg Hospital now, listed as critical!

"Oh, good Lord—"

"A trucker who stopped at the garage early this morning for gas found the door leading up to his apartment standing open . . ." It seemed Sams was about to cry. "And when he

139

investigated, he found Rudy on the floor, beaten to a pulp. Jesus, Ballard, whoever did it meant to *kill* him, no doubt about it."

"Foster." Casey forced the word between clenched teeth.

"But why? Hell, Rudy wasn't the kind of guy to get himself in trouble with the sheriff."

"Until he befriended me," Ballard sighed. "Oh, shit . . . I've been so stupid . . . so *very* stupid."

"What happened?"

"Yesterday, when I came back from Edgar's funeral, I found Rudy here in the room with Trixie." He told Sams of the young whore being raped by Foster, of her sending a note to Rudy, and of the garage mechanic going to K.C.'s Place to take Trixie away from there. "So, to try to keep Trixie out of Terry's clutches, Rudy and I drove to Asheville late yesterday to take the girl to Rudy's aunt. Somehow, Foster put two and two together . . . he's no fool, you know . . . and obviously worked Rudy over to find out where Trixie had been taken."

"And do you think he told the sheriff where Trixie was?"

"Obviously, he didn't, not at first, anyway. But who knows what he might have said after they beat him?"

"They?"

"You can bet that Foster didn't do the dirty work himself. Maybe one of his deputies did it." He thought for a moment. "Or maybe one of those crazy Staley boys." He was thinking of Daniel Staley behind the wheel of the red pickup truck.

Charlie Sams shook his head. "I don't really understand what the hell's going on—"

"And you should," Ballard said quietly, "you should." In great detail, the Chicagoan told the newspaperman everything about his association with Mountain County, the whole improbable mess, as he had done earlier with Rudy Pitts. "And then there was last night, when we took Trixie to Rudy's aunt in Asheville."

"You mean all of that," Sams said incredulously, "was because you showed a reluctance to sell K.C.'s Place to the Staleys?"

"Yes."

140

"But that doesn't make any sense!"

"It didn't to me at first, either," Casey admitted. "But now I've developed a theory." He told Sams his theory, too.

"Christ! Do you really believe that's true?"

"I do."

The editor of the *Hillside Truth* was silent for a moment. "Then we'll just have to prove it, won't we?"

"No!" Ballard said vehemently. "Not *we!* Isn't it enough that Rudy may be dying because I involved him in my problems? I'm not going to involve you, too."

"If you had told me that a couple of days ago, Ballard, I might have walked away from this." Sams paused. "You see, I think I realized for the first time on Monday that the Sams men, father and son, have been coasting along for too many years, just playing at newspapering. That realization came when Terry showed me the body of one of those cockfight robbers, torn to pieces by some animal, or animals. The sheriff said it was a bear. But I didn't think so. I found myself visualizing Foster's pack of tracking dogs and—" He scowled. "And *now* they've done this to Rudy. He was my best friend, Mr. Ballard. I don't have a choice anymore. I'm in!"

"Are you *sure?*"

"I've never been more certain of anything in my life."

"Very well," Casey clapped his hands together sharply, "the first thing we have to do is—"

ii   "It's all going to come out. You know that, don't you?"

Elmo Ralston, Jr., sat across the breakfast table from his brother-in-law, the low winter sun flooding through the bowed French windows of the dining nook. The brightness of the light served only to accent the pallor of the two old faces.

Zeb Alderman shook his head resolutely. "No, Elmo, not if we don't panic. We've just got to be calm."

"Calm? How can we be calm when Terry keeps doing

things that keep this Casey Ballard in the county, poking around? This latest mess with young Pitts is—"

"That's just it, Elmo," Alderman interrupted. "Ballard's concerns are about the sheriff's idiocies. He's not likely to care about us. Why should he?"

"Because he knows about Alice."

"Don't be a fool!"

Ralston smiled wanly. "Fool? Have there ever been two bigger fools in the world, Zeb, than the two of us? We've spent a lifetime creating a myth about a woman who . . . who . . ."

"Who was a goddess!"

Elmo winced. "Why do we do this? Why do we keep insisting Alice Ralston was a paragon, when we both know what a bitch she was? What *evil* she was capable of."

"Because we loved her," Zeb said quietly. "And still do."

The two old men finished their breakfast in silence, each lost in his own reveries, each believing he was harboring a secret that couldn't have been known by the other.

iii   Alice spun around gaily, the delicate yellow dress swirling above her knees to reveal the tops of the new silk hose encasing her firm, young legs. She kicked up her feet to show off high-heeled pumps.

"Oh, Daddy!" she cried. "This is just wonderful!"

"The latest fashions from New York," her father said proudly.

"You're just the best daddy!" The young girl flung herself at the handsome man, her arms hugging him tightly around the neck, smothering his face with kisses, leaving some marks there from the first lipstick she wore. "Just the best damned daddy there is!"

"Alice!" Melanie Ralston screamed at her daughter. "There's no excuse for profanity!" She frowned darkly at her husband. "I wish you hadn't done this, Elmo."

He laughed. "Why not? My little girl is growing up. She deserves the latest fashions."

"Your little girl," his wife said angrily, "is only eleven years old today. Whatever possessed you to bring home these . . . these . . . decadent clothes?"

"For God sake, Melanie, don't make such a fuss. My little girl has become a young woman."

His wife screwed up her face in disapproval. She watched the giggling, dancing girl, recognizing that, even at eleven, her daughter *was* maturing. Alice moved easily to the long mirror in the corner, posturing in front of it, smoothing down the dress over her budding figure. Her face went pensive.

"Mommy," she said, turning away from the mirror, "don't you think I need a brassiere now?"

"Alice!"

"Well, don't I?" Looking into the mirror again, she touched her breasts, the tiny bulges visible under the sheer yellow cloth.

"Alice! A young lady does *not* behave in such a manner!" Melanie looked pleadingly at her husband.

"Your mother is right, Alice," Elmo Senior said finally. "There are some things a proper young lady just doesn't say in polite company." He grinned mischievously, looking at his son. "And most especially in front of her brother."

"Yes, Daddy," Alice said demurely. "I'm sorry, Mommy," she apologized. "It's just that I'm so excited about the new dress."

The family birthday dinner for Alice still reflected some of the strain of disagreement between husband and wife, but Elmo Senior worked hard to keep the conversation light and airy. The junior Ralston, three years older than his sister, followed his father's lead, concerned about the tension he felt.

His concern didn't end when the family retired for the night. Past experience had told him Melanie and Elmo would carry their disagreements into the bedroom; even in the well-constructed mansion the sounds of argument could be heard through the walls. Junior tried to force sleep, not wanting to hear it again. He failed.

Whatever possessed you, Elmo, to order those . . . those . . . flapper clothes for your daughter?

For God sake, Melanie, Junior heard his father say, *must you go on and on about this? It's 1925, woman. It's time you realized that.*

But I worry about Alice, Melanie insisted. *She seems so mature, so—*

There were no words for a few moments. Junior surmised his parents were engaged in some intimacy.

Then: *No, Elmo, I don't want to do that! It's not proper!*

Melanie, for Christ sake—!

I'm your wife, Elmo, not your whore!

The bed squeaked in a manner suggesting someone had got out of it. There were a few seconds of scuffling of feet and then his parents' bedroom door opened and closed. There were sounds of someone walking down the wide staircase to the living room, and sounds of someone stirring up the embers in the fireplace. Familiar sounds to young Elmo; he had heard them before when his father abandoned the bedroom.

Junior stared at the ceiling, wondering about the relationship between husbands and wives. Was it like this in other homes? Did other men make demands their wives would turn aside? And what does a man do with a whore that's improper to do with his wife?

Now, another sound came to him. Softer. But someone else was going down the stairway. His mother? Perhaps to apologize? Somehow, he thought not. If not his mother, then Alice. The thought frightened him. He believed he heard a tiny little giggle. His mind raced, trying to visualize what was happening. He was impelled to investigate.

Slowly, Junior inched opened his bedroom door, crawling on his hands and knees to the banister, where he could look down and see a portion of the living room. In part of his line of vision was the big leather chair in front of the fireplace. He focused his eyes to see Alice curled up in her father's lap, her face nestled in his neck. There was some whispered conversation and Junior tried to stop breathing so that he might make it out.

"Doesn't Mommy love you, Daddy?" Alice asked.

"Yes, in her way."

"But she doesn't love you like I do."

The father kissed her cheek. "The two loves are different, Alice. The love of a husband and wife, and the love children may feel for their parents, aren't meant to be alike."

"Why not?"

Elmo Senior sighed. "Well, the love of a husband and wife is . . . uh . . . physical. Intimate. Do you know what that means?"

"Yes."

He laughed lightly. "I'll bet you do, young lady. And I'm not sure you ought to yet."

"Does Mommy's love make you feel good?"

"It does."

There was a long silence.

"I could make you feel good, Daddy," Alice breathed.

In one quick move, her father lifted her off his lap and set her on her feet. "I think, young lady, it's time for you to go back to bed."

She stood staring down at him. "Am I pretty, Daddy?"

"I think you're the most beautiful thing God has ever created."

"More beautiful than Mommy?"

"That's enough!" he said sternly. "Off to bed!"

She didn't obey. Instead, she reached down slowly, grasped the hem of her nightgown and pulled it over her head, standing naked in front of her father. Junior, looking through the banister, forced back a gasp. She *was* beautiful!

"As beautiful as this?" Alice whispered.

Elmo Senior, transfixed, stared at her.

She moved to within inches of him. Boldly, she reached out, encircled his neck with her arms, imprisoning his face between her breasts. Time seemed to stop for a moment.

But her father shoved her away roughly, getting to his

feet. "Right now, young lady, to bed!" He pushed her toward the stairway. Unperturbed, Alice reached down, gathered up her nightgown, and raced up the stairs. Junior just barely managed to crab-crawl into his bedroom before she reached the second floor.

He sat with his back against the door, breathing heavily, wondering what it was he had seen. He knew it was wrong. And it nagged at him that perhaps his father had provoked it.

Junior slept fitfully that night and the next morning, after breakfast, he suggested to Alice that they go for a ride. A black groom saddled their horses and they rode into the woods. Once out of sight of the mansion, Elmo Junior stopped his horse, turning in the saddle to face his sister.

"I saw you last night," he said. "With Father."

She was unconcerned. "So?"

"What the hell were you trying to do?" he demanded.

Alice's reply came easily. "I was trying to seduce him."

Elmo wondered where she had learned that word. "Are you crazy? You can go to jail for that kind of thing!"

"For loving my father?" The question seemed so innocent.

"Don't you know that's called *incest*, for God sake?! It's against the law!"

His sister pondered that for a moment. "It shouldn't be." She slid off the horse, tying the reins to a sapling, strolling nonchalantly among the trees. After a moment, he followed her. They walked for many minutes in silence.

"Junior," she said eventually, "are you a virgin?"

"Yes."

"So am I," she said sadly. "I read some book that said losing your virginity should be the most special moment in your life. That it should be pure love."

"Yeah, I guess." He thought he ought to assume the role of the older, perhaps wiser, sibling. "But you're only eleven— you'll have plenty of time for that."

"In ancient Egypt, people got married that young. Pharaohs, and things like that. In India they still do."

"But not in Tennessee," Junior insisted.

"Oh, yeah, they do. I read in the paper the other day that a girl in Sevier County who was only ten had a baby."

"Not in nice families, though."

They turned back toward the horses.

"I don't think I'll ever love a man as much as I love Daddy," Alice went on. "That's why I want Daddy to take my virginity."

Her cold determination frightened him. "Alice, you shouldn't say things like that!"

"Why not? It's the truth."

"It's also silly," he said, trying for a lighter note. "You don't even know how to do it."

"When the time comes, Junior, I'll know how to do it."

In the months that followed the relationship of Melanie and Elmo Senior deteriorated rapidly. Arguments were more frequent, many of them precipitated by the senior Ralston's willingness to indulge any whim of his spoiled daughter. Bedroom scenes, heard through the walls, were more bitter, at times bordering on violence. The father began to drink more and to spend more time absented from the mansion. Junior heard gossip of his Daddy's dalliances; of nights spent with the whores at K.C.'s Place. He didn't know whether Alice also heard the gossip; he never tried to discuss it with her.

It was just two months after Alice's twelfth birthday that Melanie Ralston, dressed in a stylish riding habit, took off one morning on her favorite thoroughbred hunter. And didn't return. It was late afternoon before her body was found in the thick forest nearly five miles from the mansion, a part of her head blown away, her grandfather's Colt Peacemaker .45—the one with the cutaway trigger guard—by her right hand. The horse grazed peacefully nearby.

Mountain County was shocked by the suicide. All those stories about Elmo Senior's late-night escapades were replaced, in the "proper" households, by protestations of how much Melanie and Elmo had loved each other. *What could have possessed dear Melanie to do such a thing?* Hundreds came to the funeral, to witness Elmo Senior weeping by the grave and to excuse the fact that he was obviously drunk.

Junior wept, too. But not the self-assured Alice. Her beautiful face was impassive. Just as the casket was being lowered into the grave, she placed a hand lightly on her brother's arm, getting his attention.

"Junior," she whispered to him, "I'm not a virgin anymore."

"Shut up!" he snarled at her.

The young man tried not to think, tried to force his brain into a short-circuit, tried not to see the mental picture of his father and his sister in an intimate embrace, tried not to believe his mother killed herself because of her knowledge of the incest. It didn't work, but the terrible scenario was never put into words. Alice never spoke of it again.

For Elmo Junior it became a nightmare of nearly sixty years' duration. An awful secret.

iv   Zeb Alderman emptied his coffee cup, getting wearily to his feet. "Well," he said to his brother-in-law, "we just have to go on with our lives. I think maybe we're giving this Ballard fellow credit for more wisdom than he has. How's he going to find out?"

"Maybe you're right," Elmo Junior replied, wanting to believe the banker.

"What we know, by God," Alderman said, "we're going to keep to ourselves."

He left the mansion, forcing his thoughts to what he had to do at the bank that day. But he, too, had his secret. There was one other who knew, but——. Zeb groaned inwardly as a vision of her as he had known her so many years earlier intruded. And as he did every time he permitted himself a memory of her, he ached for her. As he had ached for her on that June night of 1927.

It had been a warm evening and a noisy one in the Ralston mansion, crowded with as many as fifty young people who had been brought together to celebrate Alice's thirteenth birthday.

The dance orchestra imported from Knoxville was playing *Ain't She Sweet* at an exaggerated up-tempo rhythm as Elmo Senior, the only adult on the scene, danced wildly with his daughter. The others circled the living room dance floor, applauding and shouting encouragement to the couple. Alice was laughing gaily at the gyrations of her drunken parent. And when the song was ended, Alice stood in an attitude of triumph in the middle of the floor, her arms reaching upwards, while her daddy feigned collapse and everyone cheered.

Zeb went to her as the orchestra struck up the ballad *Blue Skies*, extending his hands to her to dance, and she snuggled close to him.

"Isn't Daddy wonderful?" she bubbled.

"Yeah."

"There's no man like him in the whole world."

"No, Ah guess not." Zeb didn't know what else to say. He pulled her tight against him, feeling her firm breasts through the thin summer gown she wore.

He crooned into her ear. *Blue skies, smilin' at me, nothin' but blue skies do I see . . .*

"You have a nice voice, Zeb."

"Hmmm." He was pleased with the compliment. He was pleased with everything about her: the bobbed crown of golden brown hair, the startling hazel eyes, the smooth white skin, the smell of her. She was sweating from her animated dance with her father and there was a somehow musky odor that made her even more exciting. He kissed her on the cheek.

"Ah do declare, Mr. Alderman," she drawled teasingly.

He was emboldened. "You want to get some air?"

"Sure."

He led her into the garden, pulling at her hand until the music was just faint background and they were hidden by a tall growth of boxwood. And then he kissed her, and she responded passionately, open-mouthed, her tongue playing sensuous little games. Zeb put a hand on a breast and she strained against his touch. He sank slowly to the soft grass, pulling her down on top of him and all restraint seemed to evaporate. His hands roamed her body and she didn't resist him until he began

149

to explore under her dress, touching the inside of her thigh. Then she pulled back suddenly.

"I can't, Zeb," she whispered.

"Why not?"

There were several seconds of unbearable silence before she answered. "Are you my friend, Zeb?"

It seemed a strange question under the circumstances of the moment. "Of course."

"I mean, truly?" she demanded.

"Truly," he answered. "Ah'd do anything for you."

She sat up, smoothing out her dress. "Then I can tell you that I'm in love."

It was as if she had struck him in the face. "An' not with me," he said sadly.

"No."

"Who, then?"

She didn't reply.

"Someone here at the party?"

"No, but I can't tell you right now."

Young Alderman made an effort to salvage something. "Maybe you think, because Ah'm a senior Ah'm too old for you."

Alice laughed, getting to her feet and extending a hand to help him rise. "Believe me, Zeb, that's not the reason. But, if you're really my friend, you'll help me. Just as soon as the party is over would you drive me somewhere?"

"Where?"

"I'll have to tell you later. Just promise me you'll do it."

"Okay . . . sure," he agreed reluctantly.

Hand-in-hand they returned to the mansion. Another hour went by. An hour-and-a-half. Morosely, Zeb stayed on the scene, at one point helping Junior to put the passed-out elder Ralston to bed.

At midnight, the orchestra began to play *The Song Is Ended, But the Melody Lingers On,* and Alice came to him to dance the final dance.

"Remember what you promised me?" she asked.

"Yeah."

"Just as soon as everyone leaves, we'll go."

"This late?"

"Time doesn't mean anything when you're in love."

"Ah wouldn't know," he said sarcastically.

The final song was finished and party-goers began to drift away. It seemed to Zeb that Alice was pushing them out the door. She was a bundle of excited anticipation. Finally, everyone had left.

"Come on," she said, taking his hand.

"Maybe this isn't right."

Her face clouded. "Damn you, Zeb, you promised!"

"Okay . . . okay." He had driven to the Ralstons in his father's Model T and they hurried to it. Alice hurried; Zeb followed. When he started the motor, he asked: "Where?"

"Hillside. The Griner Apartments."

Zeb tried to remember who it was who lived in the small apartment building. There were only six apartments and he thought he knew all the tenants. None of them fitted with Alice.

"Who lives there?" he asked.

"Can't you go any faster?"

"Ah said, who lives there?!"

She giggled. "Hersch."

Zeb was shocked. "You mean Mr. Barnes?!"

"Yes." She was radiant with the admission.

"Mr. Barnes—the gym teacher?!" It was hard to believe.

"Yes!"

"But he's an . . . an . . . ol' man!"

"He's twenty-one," she explained defensively, "and that's hardly old."

"But you're only thirteen!"

"I'm a woman," Alice said matter-of-factly.

Alderman brought the car to a sudden stop. "No, Ah'm not going to take you there."

"Then I'll walk," she said, starting to get out of the car.

"Stop it, damn it!" he shouted at her. "You can't go to Mr. Barnes. You'll get into all kinds of trouble. They'll kick you out of school."

"Let them. I'm going to marry him." Her jaw was set defiantly.

"Alice, you said you wanted me to be your friend," he pleaded with her. "Well, Ah will be your friend by taking you back home." He started the Model T again, making a wide U-turn. "Ah'm not going to let you do this."

"You sonofabitch!" she shrieked at him. "You sonofa-bitching bastard!"

He let her rail at him, but he delivered her back to the Ralston mansion. Zeb didn't see her again until school began—his senior year—in September. Student gossip was rife with tales of Herschel Barnes, the handsome physical education in-structor, and Alice Ralston, who delighted in her role as the teenage temptress. Two weeks into the new school term, they eloped. They were gone for nearly a week before Sheriff Ben Foster tracked them down to a complex of roadside cabins in South Carolina and brought them back to Mountain County. Elmo Ralston, Sr., using his considerable influence, had the marriage annulled. Barnes was dismissed from his teaching position and Sheriff Foster made it plain to Herschel it would not be healthy for him to remain anywhere near Mountain County.

"If I see your ugly face just once after today," Ben told him, "I'll have you in jail for statutory rape."

Barnes believed him.

Alice was also removed from the Mountain County envi-rons, her father enrolling her in a girls' boarding school in Vermont. The gossip of the scandal began to die.

It was mid-October when Zeb Alderman got a phone call.

"It's Alice," a teary voice said. "Are you still my friend?"

He wanted to say *no,* but he said, "Yes."

"I need your help. I'm pregnant."

"Jesus Christ! What are you going to do?"

"I'm going to have the baby," she said with her old deter-mination. "But I need to find Hersch. I want you to find Herschel for me."

"How can Ah do that? Ah have no idea where he might be."

"He's from Austin, Texas. Maybe he went back there."
She began to weep. "Please, Zeb, I have no one else to turn to."

For four weeks, while he tried to keep up with his high
school classes and to hold down a part-time clerk's job at the
bank, young Alderman searched for Alice's lover. There was
phone call after phone call, starting with the Austin school
system and then branching out. Some of the phone calls were
made from the bank; those he made from his home were explained to his parents as being for "research" he was doing on
an American history paper on Texas for school. Finally, at a
place called Elgin, he found Herschel Barnes, teaching school
again. Zeb delivered his message; Barnes expressed his gratitude.

At Thanksgiving time, Junior Ralston invited his friend
Zeb to have turkey at the mansion.

They were halfway through the meal when Zeb asked:
"Have you heard from Alice?"

"Yes, as a matter of fact," the senior Ralston answered,
smiling broadly. "I think it's all working out very well. Alice
asked to transfer to a better school in Boston and I agreed. I
have nothing but glowing reports on her progress."

"That's good," Zeb said.

"Yes, I think that sad episode is behind us." Elmo Sr.
sighed. "You know, Zeb, I always thought you were sweet on
Alice."

"Well, Ah—"

"Maybe someday, when she's finished with her education,
she'll be ready to settle down here, and you might—if you'll
pardon an old-fashioned phrase—want to court her."

"Oh, Ah doubt Alice would be interested in me."

Elmo Sr. grinned at him. "I want you to know, young man,
that I'd be pleased to have you as a son-in-law."

Late in May of '28, as Zeb prepared to graduate from high
school, a letter arrived in the mail from Alice: *If you're going to take
a little vacation after you graduate, why not visit us for a few days? Hersch
and I would like to see you face-to-face and thank you. Maybe you will be
here when my son is born.*

Her son? That was just like Alice, always self-assured,

always determined to have things turn out the way she wanted.

Thus, in June Alderman traveled to Boston to spend three days with Alice and Herschel. And to find a brand new baby *boy*, named Max. They seemed happy.

"Does your father know yet about the baby?" Zeb asked.

"No. I'm going to finish school and then we'll decide what we're going to do. I don't imagine I'll ever go back to Mountain County."

There was the exchange of a few letters after that, and then nothing. Zeb, caught up in making his way at the bank and trying to further his education at the same time, thought less and less of Alice. The years passed quickly: 1929, 1930, 1931. Two days before Christmas of '32, he looked up from his teller's position to see Alice entering the bank. She was no less beautiful than he remembered her.

"Did Herschel come with you?" he asked.

She put a finger to her lips. "I don't want to talk here," she said. "Will you have time to have lunch with me?"

"Sure."

At lunch, Alice asked for a table in the corner, away from the other diners. When they had given their order to the waiter, she reached across the table and took Zeb's hand.

"Friends?" she asked.

"Always."

"Hersch has left me," she reported unemotionally. "I suppose it couldn't last forever."

"And Max?"

"Hersch wanted custody and I agreed. They've gone to Texas."

"Then you've been divorced?"

"We were never married, not after that first time in South Carolina, anyway."

Zeb was perplexed. "But what the hell happened?"

"Does it matter?" she shrugged.

"If, by that, you mean it's none of my business, Ah'll accept that."

"My sweet Zeb." She squeezed his hand tenderly, dropping her voice into a whisper. "Daddy doesn't know about Hersch. Or Max. He thinks Boston was just school."

Alderman raised an eyebrow, the depth of her deception appalling to him.

"Could that be our very own secret, Zeb?"

"If that's what you want."

"You *are* a friend. A *dear* friend." She smiled sweetly at him. "I have so much to make up to you, darling. So very much."

12

i   Mountain County had become a trap for Casey Ballard, a cruel snare. He was inextricably enmeshed now with people he hadn't even heard of six days earlier. There was a nightmare quality to it all as he stood beside a hospital bed in Gatlinburg, looking down at an immobile Rudy Pitts lying in an oxygen tent, his head bandaged mummy-like, both arms in casts and elevated somehow away from his body, tubes and electrodes connecting him with fluids and monitoring devices. Alive, Casey had been told, but just barely. Rudy was comatose, his condition grave.

The old country physician, Amos Willson, was there, too, his face drained of color, a white mask of agony.

"Ah don't know thet Ah've ever seen anythin' worse," Dr. Willson said quietly, "an' there still bein' life. The surgeons don't know how much brain damage there might be. There's three skull fractures." He shook his head disconsolately. "The right lung was punctured twice by broken ribs. There's been liver damage, mebbe caused by multiple kicks, or mebbe by blows from somethin' like a baseball bat. An', as ya know, both arms have been broken. An' God knows what else. If he lives there's gonna have t' be more operative procedures."

There was a long pause. "But Ah ain't figurin' he's gonna live."

"Jesus," Casey muttered.

"If yer a man o' faith, Mr. Ballard, Jesus is the one t' call on."

Before driving to Gatlinburg with Dr. Willson, Casey had ordered his cop's mind, making several hard decisions. For one thing, he had called Zeb Alderman's office to cancel the meeting at which he had planned to sign the final sales papers on K.C.'s Place.

"Circumstances have made the sale impossible," he had told the banker.

Alderman had repeated the statement to others in his office and Casey could hear Sheriff Foster cursing in the background.

Then, steeling himself against the ordeal, Ballard had called Rosalie in Chicago, having rehearsed in his mind what he was going to say when she answered. He wanted her to suspend judgment on what he was doing in Mountain County; as a matter of fact, he asked her to suspend the time—to wipe it out—between the day he left for Mountain County and the day he would return.

"What happens here, O'Hara," he had said, "is not going to change my love for you. If you'll let it, this can be regarded as only a minor diversion. We can pick up where we were before I left and never consider it again when I get back."

His wife was silent.

"Rosie?" he said pleadingly.

"You mean wipe it out of my memory?"

"Yes."

"I'll try." The voice was cold.

"That's all I can ask." He tried for a lighter tone. "It won't be long, O'Hara, before we'll be house-hunting in Arizona."

"We'll see." She broke the connection.

Casey had to accept that. On the drive to Gatlinburg, and now on the return again, he was making a mental list of what he knew and didn't know, what he would have to learn to solve the mysteries of Mountain County. He wondered how newspaper editor Charlie Sams was making out with his plea to state police authorities to intercede in the county, to supersede the elected sheriff and attempt to bring some order.

"They're not going to automatically agree, you know," Sams had said. "Mountain County has always been an anathema to them. On earlier occasions when the state police were called in on one killing or another they ran into a wall of silence. No one would talk. It got so that it was easier for the state cops to just let Mountain County exist as it wanted to. Maybe that's difficult for you to understand, Mr. Ballard, but it's a fact."

The Chicagoan dismissed that now, considering it to be Sams' problem, and let his mind arrange the other questions needing answers: *Why was Willie Young, an inoffensive farmer, involved in the cockfights robbery? Would his daughter, Yolanda, know? Why did the hotel desk clerk, Kathy Ringer, suddenly absent herself from Mountain County? Did she really go to a new job in Memphis? What am I going to do about Trixie? Is she safe with Rudy's aunt? Is Alice Ralston Alderman dead? If she is, or she isn't, does it have any meaning? And what about that woodcarver, Barney Daniels? What is it he knows about the murder of King David Ballard?*

Casey turned to Dr. Willson as they approached Hillside once more. "Amos, is there any doubt in your mind that my father went to Chicago *before* King David was killed?"

"Nope."

"Hmmm. You know, I think I found an interesting discrepancy between the newspaper account of King David's death and the sheriff's report—"

"Ah told ya Ben Foster's report was a phony," the physician interrupted.

"Yes, I know, but hear me out for a moment. In the sheriff's report it said King David was struck in the left temple, which means the murderer would have been right-handed, as my father was—"

"Yeah, but—"

"And in the newspaper story it said—quoting you—that King David was hit in the right temple, which would indicate the killer might have been left-handed."

Amos nodded agreement.

"Now, when we talked earlier about this you said you *guessed* King David had been hit in the left temple. Think about it again, will you?"

The old man wrinkled his brow. "Hell, Mr. Ballard, Ah jest don't recollect fer sure."

"Would you have any records in your personal files—a notebook perhaps?"

"Mebbe," Willson said slowly.

"Could we look for them now?" Casey pressed him.

The doctor shrugged. "If ya wanna, sure."

Instead of dropping Ballard off at the Hillside Inn, Dr. Willson drove him to his home, leading Casey into an old-fashioned doctor's office, disordered and musty and with medical journals scattered everywhere. He went to a wooden file cabinet, squinting at the legends on the drawers. He opened one marked "1933–34–35," riffling through the file folders jammed into it.

"My gawd, here it is," he said in surprise. "Ballard, King David."

He opened the folder, looking through several pages of papers, stopping to read one of them. "He was struck on the *right* temple, one blow with a sharp instrument," Willson announced.

"So the murderer had to be left-handed."

"Seems so," the old man agreed, "but Ah don't know what the hell it means now."

"Amos," Casey asked softly, "was Alice Ralston left-handed?"

"How the devil would Ah know?"

Ballard believed the question had frightened Willson. He shrugged. "You probably wouldn't, of course," he chuckled. "Put it down as a cop-type question, signifying nothing."

Dr. Willson seemed satisfied with the explanation.

ii   By the time Casey had been driven back to the Hillside Inn, Avis had delivered a new rental car for him. He told day manager Bobby Reston he would be staying "indefinitely," and went to his room, buoyed by the knowledge the murderer of his uncle had been a left-hander. Maybe it wouldn't mean anything to his investigation, but it was satisfying to know something he hadn't known before.

It led him to call a newspaper friend in Chicago, asking for some research he thought he needed.

"Is that *all* you want?" the reporter laughed.

"Yep."

"And you want it yesterday, I'll bet."

"That would help."

"Is there a story in this, Casey?" the friend asked soberly.

"A story? Well, if there is, I'll know who to give it to, right?"

Then he drove to the office of the *Hillside Truth,* to be told by Charlie Sams the state police, acceding to the editor's urging, would "look into" the aggravated assault on Rudy Pitts.

"But don't expect too much," Charlie warned. "They're going to have to get Rudy's story and who knows when that will be possible?"

They talked for another half hour, Ballard giving the young man his next assignment. He did it reluctantly, but he needed Sams' help. There were too many bases to cover alone.

Casey's next stop was at the home of Charlie's father, publisher Layton Sams, where he stayed for only a few minutes. It was after six o'clock when he left there, darkness having fallen. He headed the car toward K.C.'s Place.

Chester Richmond opened the door at the roadhouse, weaving unsteadily on drunken legs, contemplating Ballard through boozy eyes. "Hey, ya ain't s'posed t' be here!"

Smilingly broadly, Casey patted him on the shoulder. "Don't worry about it, Chester. I'm expected. Yolanda around?"

"In the bar." Doubt spread across the flushed face. But mebbe Ah oughta ask Mama—"

The visitor hooked his arm in Chester's. "No need to bother your mother. And since we're going to the bar, how about letting me buy you a drink?"

"Well, Ah—"

"One kin to another, huh? Just a friendly drink."

"Well . . . okay . . ." Chester agreed dumbly. He led the way through the long hallway into the barroom and right up to the mahogany bar.

"Give my . . . uh . . . cousin what he wants . . ." Ballard said in an outgoing manner.

" 'Shine," Chester mumbled.

"And I'll have the same."

Casey's eyes scanned the room, stopping on the figure of Yolanda Young sitting alone at a table, nursing a drink. His glass of water-clear moonshine in hand, he walked quickly to her. "A pretty girl shouldn't be drinking alone."

He had startled her. "Yeah . . . uh . . ." She recognized him then, and there was no mistaking the fright in her light blue eyes. She was voluptuous, pretty, without being beautiful. Somehow the accumulated attractive things about her added up to a sluttishness that made the total unattractive.

"I wanted to talk to you, Yolanda," Casey said familiarly, sitting down, "because I think we have something we *ought* to talk about."

"Ah ain't got nothin' t' talk 'bout with ya." She glanced about wildly, looking for someone to help her.

"Oh, I think you do, Yolanda. I think you ought to tell me about your daddy—and who killed him."

"One of them robbers killed 'im," she replied hurriedly.

Casey shook his head from side to side. "I don't think so, and neither do you, Yolanda. Terry killed him didn't he?" He knew his time was limited; he had to get to the raw flesh of his contention.

"No!" There was sheer panic in her eyes.

"Or he had him killed by one of the deputies. Randy Apple, more than likely."

"No!" Tears began.

He reached over to touch her hand gently. "Yolanda, I know you're scared to death, but you *can't* let your own father's murderer get away with it."

She was weeping profusely now.

"Let me tell you what I know," Ballard said. It wasn't what he really knew, but what he surmised. He spoke hurriedly. "Your daddy believed you were a good girl, Yolanda, and when he heard you had taken up with Terry, he came running to protect you. Terry laughed at him. Maybe you did, too. You were tried of being poor, and not having nice things, and you thought if you could get away from the farm, and from your old man, everything would be roses. Terry was your way out. So you weren't worried when Terry offered your father a deal: help out with a fake robbery at the cockfights and Terry would send you back home. Your daddy agreed. But you . . . you knew Terry was lying . . ."

"No!" She was screaming at him.

"He had no intention of letting you go, and you didn't want to go anyway. But if Willie Young was going to be an old fool, well . . . let him. But then it all went wrong, didn't it?"

Yolanda put her head down on the table, sobbing uncontrollably.

"Suddenly it was all a mess," Casey went on. "Eddie Ballard was shot and dying. Another man was wounded. Your father, badly frightened because he hadn't thought he'd be involved in a shooting, threatened to go to the state police and tell the truth of the whole thing. And that's when Terry—"

He stopped, hoping there would be some reaction. There wasn't any—there was nothing but her deep sobbing—and Ballard had to continue with his scenario, moving it forward so that he might find the touch-point to set her off, to get her talking.

"And now, after your father and those two other men are dead, you find that Terry doesn't want you anymore. He's tired of you, preferring the dummy, Trixie, to you. He wants to put you in Lulubelle's stable of whores, doesn't he?"

Only sobbing answered him.

"Doesn't he?!" Ballard insisted.

"Yeah." The reply was barely audible, muffled because she still had her head buried in her arms on the table.

"And you find yourself without anyone to protect you. Your daddy is gone and there's no one to care about you."

"Yeah."

"Well, I care about you, Yolanda. But I can't help you unless you help me." He drew a deep breath. "I need to *know* what you know about the cockfights robbery. You can only get back at Terry, Yolanda, if you tell me what you know. And right now!"

Without raising her head, she started: "Ah was there when Terry told Papa 'bout the robbery. But it weren't su'posed t' be like . . . Ah mean Papa weren't su'posed t' shoot ya. He were jest gonna fire a shot . . . to scare ya, kinda. An'—" Her head came up, the tear-filled blue eyes looking directly into Casey's. "Hones' t' God, he weren't su'posed t' shoot ya!"

Suddenly, terror came into her eyes, a hand going to her mouth as she stared over his shoulder. "Oh, Jee-sus—!"

There was a laugh as Casey turned to see Terry Foster standing in the doorway of the bar, Deputy Apple by his side.

"Well, Lieutenant," the sheriff said loudly, drawing everyone's attention to him, "are you planning to kidnap another whore?"

Carefully, Casey slid back his chair, getting to his feet, turning to face Foster squarely. The familiar nausea was in his gut. "Miss Young and I were having a pleasant conversation," he said, forcing a grin.

"I'll just bet," Terry responded sarcastically. "But I'm afraid you've overstepped yourself this time. This time, Lieutenant, you're under arrest!"

Ballard's grin grew broader. "Even you, Terry, need more than a conversation in a bar to effect an arrest. What charge are you planning to bring?"

Foster shrugged. "Oh, any number of them. Suspicion of kidnapping, for one. Yeah . . . that'll do for now." He started forward, reaching for his gun.

Deputy Apple moved quickly, clamping a strong hand on

Terry's, preventing him from drawing a weapon.

"What the fuck are you doing?" Terry snarled at his subordinate.

"I'm trying to keep you from making a mistake," Randy told him quietly. "This isn't the time, Terry. Not this way."

The sheriff thought for a moment. The hand on the gun in the holster relaxed. "Okay, but get him the hell out of here!" He strode angrily from the barroom.

"You heard the man," Apple said, gesturing toward the exit.

Casey reached his hand to Yolanda. She hesitated, then got up from the table and took the hand.

"Not the girl, Ballard!"

"Why don't you try to stop me, Deputy?" Pulling at Yolanda, Ballard walked quickly from the bar, down the long hallway, through the busy living room with its scattering of partially clothed prostitutes, and out into the night air.

"We've got to hurry," he said. They left the broad porch of the Victorian roadhouse, moved along the walkway to the wooden stairs, and then down them to the crowded parking lot under the knoll. Only ten yards from the rental car, their way was blocked by Alvin and Daniel Staley, who stepped out from behind a pickup truck.

"Ya goin' someplace?" Alvin asked with a cruel laugh.

"We're leaving," Casey replied without emotion.

"Not with thet whore, ya ain't!"

"*Both* of us are leaving."

As though by predetermination, Daniel hurled his bulk at Ballard, who sidestepped adroitly, smashing a fist into the giant's face, bringing blood gushing from his nose. Almost simultaneously, he drew a revolver from his belt (a weapon borrowed earlier on his visit to Layton Sams), pointing it directly at Alvin's head.

"Hold it right there!" Ballard shouted. "Unless you want your brains scattered!"

Alvin retreated, his hands held above his head. Daniel was leaning against the pickup, a hand to his nose, the blood running between his fingers.

165

Keeping the gun trained on the brothers, Casey looked around for Yolanda, not seeing her. "Yolanda!" he called. There was no answer.

"Yer whore done skipped," Alvin chortled.

"Shut your damned mouth!" Holding the Staleys at bay with the pointed revolver, he edged his way to the car. As he sped away from K.C.'s Place, the wheels spinning wildly on the gravel, Casey moaned. He had fouled up again. And now he might have lost the only witness who could testify to Sheriff Foster's conspiracy with the deadly cockfights robbery.

He hoped the editor of the *Hillside Truth* was going to be more successful on that evening.

iii   Charlie Sams turned his car onto Haywood Road in Asheville, North Carolina, looking for the address of Rudy Pitts' aunt. He passed a parked green Ford sedan, behind the wheel of which slouched a man, a felt hat pulled low over his eyes. His stomach muscles tightened. Ballard had warned him Sheriff Foster might have the aunt's house under surveillance, that Rudy might have talked during the severe beating. *Is that what that guy's doing there? Keeping an eye on Mrs. Pitts and Trixie?*

He spotted the proper address, the porch light lit, and pulled to the curb. When he got out of the car he walked slowly to the house; if he was being watched he didn't want to give the impression there was anything urgent about his visit.

The door opened before he could ring the doorbell, an older woman standing there.

"Mrs. Pitts?" he asked.

"Yes," she answered cautiously.

"I'm Charles Sams from Hillside. I think Casey Ballard called you."

"Come in, come in," she said nervously. The door was locked behind him when he stepped into the living room. Trixie, who had been watching television, rose and came toward him, smiling in recognition.

"Mrs. Pitts," Sams said, "that car parked down the block, does it belong there?"

"No." She frowned. "It's been there since late yesterday. I think they're watching the house."

"Probably so. Are you ready to leave?"

"Yes. Mr. Ballard told us only to take a small bag." She pointed to it sitting on the floor.

"Okay . . . now . . ." Young Sams was trying to think like Ballard. "We must assume that whoever is in that car is watching for you to leave. Is there a way out of here other than by the front door?"

"Well, we could go out the back way," the woman said hesitantly, "to get to the street behind us."

"Could you make your way to the second street away?"

"If we walked through a neighbor's backyard, yes."

"Then that's what I want you to do. Go to the second street and wait for me there." Charlie was speaking slowly, not wanting to be misunderstood. "I'll go out the front way and drive away. If that green Ford doesn't follow me I'll pick you up in five minutes. If I'm not there in five minutes you come back to this house and lock yourself in again."

"All right," the aunt agreed.

"You two leave right now. We have less than an hour to catch that plane to Nashville. Leave all the lights on. The TV, too. I want whoever's watching the house to think nothing has changed. Go—now!"

Trixie picked up the bag and the two women headed toward the back of the house. Sams waited until he heard a door opening and then he opened the front door. He paused to go through the charade of waving goodbye before pulling the door shut. Again he crossed the front yard slowly, getting into his car in a leisurely manner, starting the motor and making a lazy U-turn so that he would pass the green Ford again.

The man behind the wheel of the Ford turned his head toward him slightly as he went by, but Charlie still couldn't see his face. Keeping an eye on the parked car through the rearview mirror, Sams drove a block and still the car hadn't moved. Another block and even in the darkness he could see he wasn't being followed. He turned right then for two blocks and right again, moving slowly along the dimly lit street, looking for his passengers. Somewhat disconsolately, Mrs. Pitts and Trixie were standing on the curb.

"Get in—quickly," Sams said as she stopped beside them.

They obeyed and he pulled away, grinning. "I think we've done it, Mrs. Pitts," he said proudly. "Next stop for you is Nashville. You'll like my sister, Mrs. Pitts. She's a great gal."

iv   The man in the green Ford looked at his wristwatch. It was 11:30 P.M. All the lights in the Pitts house—the porch light, too—were still on. That was strange. The night before the lights had been turned off at ten, Trixie and the old lady apparently going to bed at that time. *Maybe they're watching a late show on TV.*

He waited another half hour. The lights still burned. Concerned now, he got out of the car and cautiously approached the house, going to a side window where he thought he might be able to look into the living room. He could hear the sound of the television as he got close. At the side window, he stood on his tiptoes and looked in over the sill. The TV set was indeed playing, but there was no one watching it. He edged along the side of the house to the kitchen window, peering in again. No one was there, either.

Panic seized him. He raced around to the front, clomping up on to the porch, turning the knob of the front door. It swung open. Inside, he called: "Hello—anybody here?" There was only the sound of the TV. "Mrs. Pitts!" he yelled. He got no answer.

Hurriedly, he searched the house, every room on both floors. He went into the basement, too, his stomach churning. The occupants were gone. *How long? Christ, it's been more than an hour-and-a-half!*

Returning to the living room, he dropped into the sofa, staring at the TV set, not comprehending what was being shown on the tube. On an end table next to the sofa he spotted a telephone. He picked it up, dialing the familiar number of K.C.'s Place. When someone answered, he growled: "Sheriff there? It's important."

He waited a few moments. "Yeah," a voice said.

"Terry, this here's Birch in Asheville. Trixie an' the old lady is gone."

"What do you mean they're gone?"

"Gone . . . thet's all. I'm in the house now an' they ain't here."

"You stupid bastard!" Terry railed at him.

"Hell, it ain't mah fault, Terry. A guy drove up a while back an' went in. He weren't there more'n a minute or two an' then he left agin. But they wasn't with 'im."

"What guy?"

"Ah ain't rightly sure," Birch whined. "But it mighta been thet Charlie Sams."

"Holy Christ!" the sheriff cursed. "Did it ever occur to you that they might have gone out the back way and he picked them up somewhere?"

Birch pondered that for a few seconds. "Shit! Ya think so?"

Foster groaned loudly. "Get your ass out of there before some prowl car spots you."

"Yeah—"

"And if you run into an Asheville cop, I don't know you."

"Go t' hell, Terry!" Birch angrily slammed the phone into its cradle.

The intruder's long vigil had left him hungry. He made his way to the kitchen, studying the well-stocked refrigerator. Removing the ingredients for a sandwich, he leisurely put together two large ones. The sandwiches in one hand and a quart bottle of milk in the other, he returned to the sofa in the living room, trying to pick up the story line of the black-and-white Western playing on the television set.

He ate slowly, contentedly, washing the sandwiches down as he chug-a-lugged the milk. The movie came to an end; with a shrug he got to his feet. "Oh, what the hell . . ." he said aloud.

Going to the TV set he turned it off, unhooking it from its antenna connection. Picking it up he carried it out of the Pitts home, walked the few yards to his car and placed the set in the back seat.

Birch Staley drove away from Asheville, North Carolina, with mixed emotions. Maybe he had been duped by the visitor—was it really Charlie Sams?—who had spirited away the old lady and Trixie. But it wasn't a total loss. He needed a new TV.

13

i   It was 6 A.M. when the black butler awakened Elmo Ralston, Jr., only semiapologetically because he had spent a difficult half hour with the hysterical woman who had disturbed the servant household by banging on the mansion door when there was just a hint of the new day in the eastern sky. His efforts to calm her had been in vain. Finally, he had no choice but to enter his employer's bedroom, risking the wrath of the often irascible Ralston.

"Mistah Elmo, Ah's sorry, but there's a . . . uh . . . woman downstairs what sez she gotta see ya," the butler said firmly. "Ah tried t' send her 'way, but—"

"Woman?" Ralston responded sleepily. *"What* woman?"

"Ah don't rightly know, suh, but Ah thinks she's a sportin' lady."

"Good Christ, John," Ralston snarled, "can you take care of a nigger whore?!"

"Beggin' yer pahdon, Mistah Elmo," the butler answered with some satisfaction, "but she's a white lady."

"A white woman?"

"Yassuh, she sure is."

"Well," the master of the house demanded, "who *is* she?"

"Ah ain't never seen her 'fore, but she keeps sayin' somebody's gonna kill her less'n ya talks to her, suh."

Ralston sighed deeply. "Get me a cup of coffee first, then bring her up."

The butler hurried away, holding the door open as a maid entered carrying a previously prepared coffee tray. Ralston was annoyed even more; the blacks always seemed to be one step ahead of him, anticipating what his wishes would be. Some might have thought that an advantage of having servants; he didn't. The hovering maid was dismissed with a flip of the hand. Sullenly, he poured a dollop of heavy cream into a large cup of black brew, adding a single sugar cube that he didn't stir. He sipped at the coffee, wondering why each succeeding year seemed to bring him more grief, when he really deserved some peace in his declining years.

There was a light knock on the door. "Come in!" Elmo called angrily.

A disheveled young woman entered with the butler, her dress wrinkled, her hose torn, her shoes caked with mud, her blonde hair (obviously not natural, Ralston thought) in disarray, her face dirtied by streaks of mascara, indicating she had been weeping.

She approached the bed. "Mistah Ralston, ya gotta help me. He's gonna kill me 'less ya—"

"Stop right there!" he interrupted. "First, I want to know who you are."

"Mah name's Yolanda Young an'—"

"From Mountain County?"

"Ah's from Carolina, jest a piece way over the border." This time she halted voluntarily, waiting for permission to continue.

Elmo studied her, not liking anything he saw. Or what he heard. She was a hill girl, without doubt, slovenly in her speech *(Why is it they've got to sound like niggers?)* and in her appearance.

"Now, Miss Young," he said sternly, "who wants to kill you and why?"

"Sheriff Foster," she started, " 'cause Ah knows thet he killed mah papa an' them other men . . ." She raced on, telling of her association with Terry, of the faked cockfights robbery that went awry, of the necessity Terry felt to eliminate the robbers (including her father), of the intercession the night before of Casey Ballard, of the attempt to flee K.C.'s Place with Ballard, and of Ballard's run-in with Alvin and Daniel Staley.

"An' then Ah jest beat it the hell out o' there," she concluded, " 'cause Ah knew thet if Terry found me, figurin' Ah told thet Ballard feller . . . well—" She shrugged forlornly.

"And since you ran away from K.C.'s Place," Ralston asked, "where have you been?"

"Jest walkin' an' hidin' in the woods mostly, waitin' fer mornin' so's Ah could come t' ya."

"And why have you thought it necessary to come to me?"

" 'Cause Ah know ya give Terry his orders, Mistah Ralston."

"Hmmm. I see." He paused, staring at her, feeling sorry for her now. "While you were in the woods last night, you were dressed like that?" He gestured to indicate her tattered clothing.

"Yassuh."

"You had no coat, nothing more warm?"

"No."

Ralston looked to the butler. "John, I want you to take this young lady and make sure she has a proper breakfast," he ordered. "Then have one of the girls draw a bath for her and prepare one of the guest rooms where Miss Young might rest."

The butler nodded, taking Yolanda by the elbow.

"And John, I want no servant gossip about this. No one outside this household is to know Miss Young is here. Is that clear!"

"Sure thing, Mistah Elmo."

When he was alone again, Ralston cursed lightly under his breath, contemplating the situation. He reached over to a bedside table to dial the telephone.

"Zeb," he said when someone answered, "we have a real problem. I want you to get over here as soon as possible. And bring Deputy Apple with you." He listened. "I don't want to discuss it over the phone. But, believe me, it's sufficiently important that you not delay."

ii   Casey Ballard awoke on that Thursday morning with his mind clear, determined to strip the Mountain County experience of all emotions. To be a cop again. To be rational and hard-nosed. To solve "the case" and put it behind him.

As he ate a room service breakfast at the Hillside Inn, he called the Gatlinburg Hospital to check on Rudy's condition; young Pitts was still comatose, unable to be interrogated. That, then, could be put aside for the moment. So could Trixie; she was now comparatively safe with Charlie Sams' sister in Nashville. Casey wondered about Yolanda Young but believed she was sufficiently intelligent to keep out of Sheriff Foster's clutches. Rosalie, too, could be put "on hold" for now.

What commanded his immediate attention was a package delivered early that morning by United Parcel Service. His Chicago newspaper friend had done his research well; there was a packet of photocopy papers listing ninety-seven private mental hospitals in the states surrounding Tennessee: Kentucky, Virginia, North and South Carolina, Georgia, Alabama, Mississippi, even Arkansas and Missouri.

Casey's gut instincts told him he *had* to know what had happened to Alice Ralston Alderman. He wasn't certain why that was so, but every fiber in him pointed to Alice as a key to unlocking the truth about Mountain County. No one just drops off the face of the earth, and it was rare when someone— especially a member of a prominent family—died without any notice of it at all. Thus, he had accepted the contention of cemetery superintendent Herman Armstrong that Alice was still alive. But where? He had concluded she was probably ill—perhaps senile at the age of seventy-one—and that suggested a hospital, a nursing home. Given the affluence of the Ralston family, an exclusive, private institution was likely.

He finished his breakfast as he scanned the list dispatched to him from Chicago, and then he called for another pot of coffee, making himself comfortable at the small desk in the hotel to begin his calls. Initially, he thought it best to concentrate on those hospitals within reasonably easy driving distance of Mountain County, assuming a continuing contact with her by Elmo Ralston and Zeb Alderman. Some might have thought it a boring task; Casey found it exhilarating. The hunt was like that.

One call followed another as Ballard passed himself off as a distant relative of a woman named Alice Ralston Alderman who had been named in a small will of a deceased cousin. It went much as he expected it would, with the hospital authorities being circumspect, not eager to impart information about their patients. But he was calmly persistent, even seeming to be naively ignorant of hospital procedures, and by noon he had completed a dozen calls without having found Alice. The time wasn't wasted, however; Casey used those first few calls to perfect his scenario and to adapt to the resistance of the hospital executives—they were all of a type, he found.

Just as he was thinking of breaking for lunch, newspaper editor Charlie Sams arrived at the hotel room, grinning broadly, waving a sheet of paper at the Chicagoan in a triumphant manner.

"What's the word I ought to use here," Sams chuckled, *"eureka?"*

"What'd you find?"

"You were right, Casey, it was all there in the office of the register of wills. Elmo Ralston, Sr., when he died, willed the entire Ralston Company to a single heir: his daughter, Alice!"

" 'Eureka' sounds pretty good to me," Casey laughed.

"And while Alice was to be the owner, management of the company was vested in Elmo Junior . . ." He looked down at the paper he held: ". . . 'until such time as the *issue* of Alice is deemed competent to assume management responsibilities.' "

"And if there were no children?"

"If Alice died without issue," Sams explained, "the will designates the company goes fifty-fifty to Elmo Junior and Zebulon Alderman, should Zeb remain her husband. But old Elmo was quite thorough: if Junior and Zeb predecease Alice, and there is no living issue on Alice's eventual death, then the whole damned company goes into a trust to be shared equally by all employees of the company with ten or more years of tenure."

"So a lot of people have a stake in Alice's life?"

"Uh huh. And there's one other thing," Sams went on. "Alice was specifically prohibited from disposing of the company except to what are called 'blood heirs' upon her death."

"Blood heirs? The brother, then, or any children."

"Right."

"Are there any children?" Ballard wanted to know.

"Not to my knowledge. If Alice and Zeb ever had any, I certainly haven't heard of them."

"Might she have had a child in that brief marriage to the gym teacher?"

"Again, I've never heard of anything like that."

Casey pondered for a moment. "Well, that's all very interesting, if inconclusive. What do you say we have a quick lunch? I've got to get back to the phone calls."

They left the room to go to the hotel restaurant. As they waited for the elevator, Ballard asked, "Oh, by the way, Charlie, does the will specify the issue of Alice has to be legitimate?"

The editor's eyes widened in surprise. "Nope. I guess her father could never conceive of such a thing."

"From what I've heard of Miss Alice's reputation that might be a possibility, huh?"

Sams laughed. "Ballard, you have a devious mind."

"And it gets more devious when you consider that if there were an illegitimate child the possibility exists that he, or she, might not know of the provisions of the will, provisions that would make him, or her, a millionaire today."

iii   Randy Apple had never been in the Ralston mansion before and he was awed. He hadn't known there were people in Mountain County who lived in such opulent surroundings; he took a childish delight in being served coffee by a liveried black butler (an individual unlike the niggers he knew) in a sun-filled arboretum where all manner of exotic plants and flowers were in bloom in January.

The deputy sheriff appreciated he might be on the threshold of a unique opportunity. Banker Zebulon Alderman's summons certainly was an indication of that. What it might be, though, he had no idea. He didn't care much what it might be. He was only looking for the chance to leave behind what he regarded as the stigma of being the son of a drunken sawmill laborer.

There had been a time when the handsome young man had seen a way out of his low estate, when he had been a star running back on the Mountain County High School football team and was being wooed by recruiters from the University of Tennessee and Vanderbilt and even the storied University of Alabama. But a severe knee injury in the middle of his senior year (he still wore a knee brace) had ruined all of those hopes. In a sense, Terry Foster has come to his rescue, giving him an appointment as a deputy sheriff.

At first, he had been grateful to Terry. But more and more he was nagged by the knowledge that Foster was getting rich on the largess dispensed by the likes of the late K.C. Ballard and the proprietors of the county's "two-holers" and the county's "first family." He knew, too, that only a minor percentage of that largess was filtering down to him, even though he had become the sheriff's principal muscle.

Now, gazing about the arboretum, and having seen the lavish appointments in several other rooms in the Ralston home, he was aware a door might be opening for him. He turned as he heard a slight sound, to see Elmo Ralston, Jr., being pushed in on his wheelchair by a black nursemaid, followed by the more familiar figure of Zeb Alderman.

"Well, young man," Ralston said in an outgoing manner, "I'm delighted you were able to come to visit us."

"Yes, sir." Apple stood stiffly, ill-at-ease, the coffee cup balanced in his hand.

"Now, Deputy," Elmo went on, "we want you to know— Mr. Alderman and myself—how much we appreciate the intelligent restraint you showed last night in the barroom at K.C.'s Place, in keeping the sheriff from yet another confrontation with Mr. Ballard."

"How did—?" Randy stopped quickly. It wasn't his place to speak. Not yet.

"And such . . . uh . . . talent should have its rewards." A slight nod to Alderman and the banker held out an envelope to Apple.

"Oh, that's not necessary—"

"Take it," Ralston ordered.

Randy obeyed, quickly putting the envelope into his jacket pocket, wanting to open it, but not daring to. "Thank you, sir."

Elmo sighed. "For reasons we need not detail at this time, we would not like to see a further aggravation of the situation with Mr. Ballard. Our fondest hope is that Mr. Ballard be allowed to peaceably conclude his business here in Mountain County, so that he might depart with . . . uh . . . some fond memories of our hospitality."

Alderman coughed loudly.

"Yes, well—" Ralston grinned. "Zeb is telling me, with that . . . uh . . . pregnant cough, to get to the point. And he's right. The point is, Deputy Apple, that we, as responsible leaders of this community, are distressed by what we consider to be a dangerous propensity for violence in the management of the sheriff's department."

Randy just nodded.

"While we understand a certain amount of . . . uh . . . zeal is necessary in dealing with the county's lawless elements, we believe there has been entirely too much of it, drawing unwelcome attention to Mountain County by . . . uh . . . outsiders. We have expressed those misgivings to Sheriff Foster on numerous occasions, but we seem unable to . . . uh . . . well, to get our contention across to him. Believing, as we do, in the necessity of maintaining the . . . uh . . . integrity of Mountain County, we have come to the conclusion that Terry Foster no longer represents the best interests of the county." Elmo paused momentarily. "I say that with much sadness, because I have long been an admirer of the sheriff.

"But, now we find it . . . uh . . . judicious to try to take some action to protect our county, to get away from the pattern of violence which is bringing Mountain County into disrepute." Once more Elmo grinned apologetically. "I'm afraid I'm being redundant. Am I making sense, Randy?"

"Oh, yes, sir." The verbose old man was beginning to make Deputy Apple very happy; the portal of opportunity was growing wider every moment.

"In all candor, I must tell you we need to *defuse* Terry. We need a representative within the sheriff's department who can consult with us—confidentially, of course—so that we can be aware of what Sheriff Foster is doing, so that we might step in when necessary to exert our . . . uh . . . more mature influence. We want you to be that representative."

He waited for reaction. Apple, unsure of what he should say, was silent.

"Of course, we recognize," Ralston continued, "you may have some sense of loyalty to Terry, and that's commendable. But we also recognize you may *want* to take . . . uh . . . that extra step to help Mountain County—"

"Yes, sir."

"—and to help us to protect it. Now, we can't ask you, and *won't* ask you, to contribute your . . . uh . . . skills for nothing. In that envelope in your pocket there are five hundred dollars. Each week, as we continue this project, there will be similar monies made available to cover your . . . uh . . . expenses. And down the line, when the sheriff's position comes before the electorate again, we may find it worthwhile to support a new candidate."

Deputy Apple just stared. Everything was moving so swiftly.

"Will you be able to see your way clear to help us in this matter, Randy?"

A moment of hesitation. Then: "Yes, sir, I will."

"Fine." Ralston nodded to his brother-in-law.

"Before we end this meetin'," banker Alderman drawled, "we wanna be clear on a couple of things. We wanna know jest how much protection we might have t' provide fer ya."

"Protection, sir?"

"Yeah. What was yer role in the Rudy Pitts beatin'?"

"I . . . uh . . ."

"We *must* know. There ain't gonna be no workin' t'gether without knowin'."

Apple thought of his financial windfall. "Terry ordered me to do it."

"Then ya *were* involved in the beatin'?"

"Yes. Me and Daniel Staley," Apple confessed.

"An' thet matter o' the three men in the robbery at the cockfights?"

Randy swallowed hard. "Yeah . . . that, too." It was no more than a whisper.

"Okay, we want thet in writin' 'fore the day is out," Alderman said coldly. "We'll use it t' provide ya with protection from any criminal prosecution."

The deputy's eyes opened wide. "Can you do that?"

"We can," Zeb assured him. "Providin' yer tellin' us the truth 'bout Terry orderin' it all."

"Oh, I am!"

"Good." Alderman stood and extended his hand. Apple came to his feet hurriedly, pumping the banker's hand, and turning to also shake hands with the frail man in the wheel-chair.

"Uh . . . there's one small problem," Ralston said, "which requires your immediate attention, Randy."

"Yes?"

"I was rather rudely awakened at six o'clock this morning . . ." Elmo detailed the story of Yolanda Young. "The unfortunate Miss Young is sleeping now, but when she awakens I won't be able to keep her here, of course. You'll have to take her off our hands."

"But—?"

"You're a single fellow, aren't you?"

"Yes."

"Then it should be no problem for you to . . . uh . . . take her in and keep her safe from Terry, should it?"

"No, I guess not," Apple said slowly.

"Fine. Sometime this afternoon you can . . . uh . . . take delivery, as it were." Elmo Ralston laughed.

The deputy's mind raced as he drove to the sheriff's office. *Christ, even with the problem of Yolanda, I'm still getting five hundred a week! Wonder what Terry's take was? Well, I'll find out when I'm Sheriff Apple! But I've got to play it cool.*

He was still reminding himself of that when he sauntered into the office.

"Where in the hell have you been?" Foster growled at him.

Apple grinned broadly. "Some personal time."

"Well, well," the sheriff chortled, "found yourself a new . . . uh . . . enterprise, huh?"

"Yeah, I guess you could say that."

iv   By four o'clock in the afternoon Casey Ballard had checked off the thirtieth listing on the directory of regional private mental hospitals. And that was the only progress he had made. He had not found Alice Ralston Alderman.

Weary now, and doubting his theory, he told himself he'd make four more calls and then quit for the day.

The thirty-first call would be to the Lamont Foundation Psychiatric Hospital near Rome, Georgia, less than two hundred miles from Hillside, Tennessee. He dialed the number and found himself speaking to Marybeth Lamont, who identified herself as the wife of the hospital's founder, Dr. Austin Lamont.

"My name is Casey Ballard," he said, beginning with the

only truth he was going to tell her, "and I'm calling from Austin, Texas. The purpose of this call is to inquire about one of your patients. My aunt, actually: Mrs. Alice—"

"I'm sorry, Mr. Ballard," she interrupted sternly, "but it is the policy of this hospital not to discuss our patients with anyone on the telephone."

"Oh, I can appreciate that," Casey replied in a friendly manner, "and applaud it, really. It's a very wise policy. And if you'll hear me out, Mrs. Lamont, I don't believe I'll be asking you to violate your rules."

"Yes, well . . ." She gave tacit permission for him to continue.

"You see, ma'am, I'm the executor of an estate of an uncle who has made a bequest in his will to a second cousin, one Alice Ralston. I understand her married name is Alderman. Now this is all very complicated, and I suppose I shouldn't really say Mrs. Alderman is my aunt. I'm not sure just how to describe my relationship."

"Then you're not acquainted with Mrs. Alderman?"

Casey had to fight down a gasp. For the first time he had reached someone who was not denying knowledge of Alice. *She was alive!*

"No," he answered, trying to remain calm. "This is rather embarrassing, but my knowledge of Mrs. Alderman is contained in what I've found in my uncle's papers, and I do want to conclude this matter as soon as possible. When might I come and see Mrs. Alderman?"

"This is not a public institution," Mrs. Lamont said coldly. "We don't have visiting hours, per se. I don't believe I can permit you to visit Mrs. Alderman without permission from her guardian."

"Of course, I understand. May I have the guardian's name so that I might get his permission?"

Efficiently, Mrs. Lamont gave him the name, address and telephone number of Elmo Ralston, Jr., of Hillside, Tennessee. Thanking her profusely, Casey hung up the phone.

Okay, smartass, so you've found Alice Ralston. So what?

V   Randy Apple had done what his newly found generous patrons had wanted him to do. He had returned to the Ralston mansion in late afternoon to take Yolanda Young away from there.

He was in his apartment now, sprawled in an easy chair, watching the news on a Knoxville TV station. Yolanda was huddled on a sofa opposite him, seeming not to care what was happening to her. Her eyes were closed; Randy had the impression she was somewhere far away. He wondered what she was thinking.

His own thoughts told him he had placed himself in a dangerous position with the sheriff. It was bad enough he was now the paid informant inside Terry's office, but if Foster learned he was harboring Yolanda—

She stirred as he turned off the television set when the news was concluded.

"So, you *are* here," he said, smiling at her.

"Ah were thinkin' 'bout Terry."

"What about him?"

"Did ya know he wanted me t' work fer Lulubelle?"

He knew, but he didn't want to admit it. "You mean, as a whore?"

"Yeah."

Randy shrugged. "It pays good, I guess."

"Ah ain't a whore!" she said heatedly.

"Hmmm?" The deputy studied her, thinking that maybe she was a bit too buxom for his tastes. Yet there was a rawness about her that was appealing to him. It wasn't that she was unspoiled—she had, after all, been with Terry Foster for some months—but she hadn't been used up. One thing was universally true about hill country girls: sex wasn't an embarrassment. It was natural, necessary and, with the proper partner, even enjoyable. Stored up in Yolanda's soft, pink flesh, Randy believed, was a full reservoir of passion.

"Just what are you, Yolanda?" he asked her.

"Ah'm a . . . a . . ." She couldn't find the words.

"You know, don't you, that you've been Terry's whore."

183

"No! Ah loved 'im!"

"And he loved you, I suppose."

Yolanda stared at him, without an answer.

"Maybe I just ought to open the door," Randy said, "and kick you out. Let Terry find you."

"No . . . please."

"I'm taking a hell of a chance keeping you here."

"Please . . . please . . . he'll—" She shuddered, beginning to cry.

"Of course, he doesn't have to know you're hiding here if you're . . . well, shall we say 'cooperative'?"

Yolanda glared at him. The only sound in the apartment was the ticking of a clock. Perhaps thirty seconds passed. Then, getting to her feet, she kicked off her shoes and reached back to unzip her dress, dropping it to the floor. It was a practiced move.

Deputy Apple leered at her, moving to the sofa, filling his arms with her.

"Don't feel bad, Yolanda," he said quietly. "But I would have thought you learned something from Terry."

"What's thet?"

"That everything has its price, darlin'. Everything."

14

i   Casey was a cop who assimilated facts as a food junkie soaks up calories. It was already dark on that Friday when he drove into Rome, Georgia, but he knew all about the moderate-sized city some seventy miles northwest of Atlanta. He knew the morning light would show him a picturesque community, beautifully situated on pine-clad hills overlooking the confluence of the oddly named Etowah and Oostanaula rivers, joining to form the Coosa, names stemming from the Cherokee Nation, which once inhabited that territory before the intruding white men decided it was necessary to remove the Indians forcibly to reservations to the west.

And he knew, too, something more of Rome's colorful history: of Spanish explorer Hernando DeSoto having camped on that site as far back as 1540, of the city having grown into a major Southern cotton port, of Confederate General Nathan Forrest having captured sixteen hundred Union soldiers in a battle there while commanding a Reb force of only four hundred ten, and of Union General William Sherman's army having taken Rome in Sherman's infamous, often cruel, certainly vindictive, march through Georgia.

None of that had anything to do with Ballard's visit to Rome, but he had felt a need to know it.

Of one other thing he was certain: he would be welcome in the morning at the Lamont Foundation Psychiatric Hospital. On the preceding evening, Mountain County publisher Layton Sams, glibly passing himself off as Elmo Ralston, Jr., had called Mrs. Marybeth Lamont to assure her that one Casey Ballard was a reputable gentleman from Texas who should be permitted to visit Ralston's sister, Alice.

Layton's cooperation had cost him an evening at dinner with the old man and his editor son, Charlie. But it wasn't too much of an imposition on Casey; the mealtime had been entertaining, Layton holding forth with a lengthy monologue on the first of the Mountain County sheriffs named Foster. That, too, added to Ballard's store of knowledge and he reasoned it might prove of value in the days ahead.

"Ben Foster wasn't just a sheriff, you know," the publisher had said. "I suspect he did a lot of other things more than he did sheriffing. For one thing, he did some doctoring—a lot of folks thought of him as a doctor. Today you might call him a specialist, because he was adept at performing abortions. Ben did a lot of them, for anyone who needed that service. There was a two-fold value to that: Ben got paid for it—rather well for those times—and the grateful women, who didn't need another child underfoot or another mouth to feed, were his most zealous supporters at the polls. Even in the days when women couldn't vote here, their influence was felt. There was more than one story about a hill woman withholding . . . uh . . . her favors until her spouse would guarantee a vote for Ben Foster."

Layton had grinned. "Ben always seemed to have two angles on everything. If it was one of the whores at the two-holers who became pregnant, old Ben would doctor the . . . uh . . . lady through the birth and then sell the baby, keeping the sales price for himself. There was a whole network of lawyers in Tennessee, *and* surrounding states, who dealt with Ben for babies. And with the makers of moonshine he had a similar association. If he heard of federal agents fixing to raid a still or two in the county, he'd sell that information and then also extract a share of the booze produced after that. Once he had his hooks into a bootlegger, he never let go.

"Indeed, he had a price for everything, a fee schedule, you might say. Robbery was overlooked for one price, assault for another. Those who wouldn't, or couldn't, pay the fees went to jail. I heard Ben expound one time on the pure and simple logic he employed. 'Ain't no sin, no transgression, thet ain't got its price,' he said, 'an' there ain't no escapin' it. The price is money or jail. All Ah do is give a feller his choice.' "

The old man had sobered. "Ben Foster was . . . well, adamant on the subject of what he called 'a proper shootin'.' He could never understand why one man would want to *wound* another. 'If'n ya kills a man,' he'd say, 'chances are Ah kin git ya off. But if ya jest wound a feller, yer gonna have grief from thet quarter all the rest of yer miserable life.' A lot of folks subscribed to Ben's theory on that, which accounts, I believe, for the sad statistics on murder in Mountain County.

"Now, I have to say that his son, Billy, and his grandson, Terry, followed old Ben with somewhat different styles. But a difference in styles didn't change the basic fact of life. The law was what the Fosters said it was, through thirty-two years of Ben, and nearly forty years of Billy, and now some thirteen years of Terry. It's not something of which we can be proud, Mr. Ballard, because we—the so-called *good* people of Mountain County—have allowed it to happen. We've taken some kind of . . . damn it! . . . some kind of *pleasure* in retelling these colorful stories.

"But now, Mr. Ballard, maybe you'll get us to see, clearly and honestly, the folly of our wasted years. At least, I hope so."

Casey had sighed. "I'm a long way, I'm afraid, from nailing Terry Foster."

"But you're trying," the elder Sams insisted. "And Charlie is trying. My son has made me very proud, Mr. Ballard, while at the same time making me feel very *guilty.*" He shook his head sadly. "Wasted years. Mountain County deserves something better than the Fosters, something better than the people who have allowed the Fosters to . . . uh . . . besmirch our reputations."

Casey Ballard had left the Sams home then, to lie sleeplessly in his bed at the Hillside Inn, wondering whether he could unlock enough of the secrets of Mountain County to really make a difference. At six A.M. he had been roused by a telephone call from State Police Investigator Robert Buckhorn: "Rudy Pitts has come out of the coma. He wants to talk."

An hour later Ballard was standing by a bed in the Gatlinburg Hospital, listening to Rudy slowly and painfully telling his story of the incidents in the early hours of Wednesday, January 23, 1985. Casey felt ill as the young man's weak voice detailed the beating he had received at the hands of Deputy Sheriff Randy Apple and the brutal Daniel Staley. He seemed determined to describe every blow on the state cop's tape recorder.

"Is there any doubt in your mind, Mr. Pitts," Buckhorn had asked him, "that Deputy Apple and Daniel Staley were the men who beat you?"

"No. Ah knew 'em both fer years."

"Was there anyone else there in your apartment?"

"Yeah . . . Sheriff Terry Foster."

"Did you see him?"

"Did Ah . . .? No, Ah didn't see 'im. He came in after Ah passed out." There was anger in the words.

"How did you know that, Mr. Pitts?"

" 'Cause Randy wouldn't be there without Terry. Ah know how they operate."

"But you didn't actually see Sheriff Foster?"

"No."

"Could you hear his voice, perhaps?"

"No," Rudy answered sadly.

"One more question: when Deputy Apple entered your apartment did he have a warrant of any kind?"

"No."

Buckhorn looked at Casey. "Anything else, Lieutenant?"

Ballard leaned over the bed. "Rudy, would it be too much for you to tell of the car accident on Sunday?"

"Oh, God, Casey, Ah'm hurtin' somethin' awful," he moaned.

"That's okay, Rudy. We'll pick that up later." He nodded negatively to the state trooper.

"That concludes the statement taken from Mr. Rudy Pitts on Friday, January twenty-five, 1985." Buckhorn turned off the recorder, unpinning the tiny microphone from Rudy's hospital gown.

"Get some rest," Casey said to Rudy. "I'll be back to see you soon."

Outside in the hallway, Buckhorn said to Ballard: "We have enough to get warrants for the arrest of Apple and Staley, but not a damn thing to connect Sheriff Foster to the assault on Pitts."

"Yeah . . . shit!" Casey agreed disgustedly. "Could you hold off for a while on the warrants for those two? Maybe long enough to see whether I can tie in Foster?"

Buckhorn shook his head in doubt. "Our problem is that you really don't have any jurisdiction, Lieutenant. Maybe if you were still in the Chicago force I could—"

"Just give me a few days," Casey pleaded.

"How many are a few?"

"Oh, two, . . . three."

"Well, it might take me that long to get this transcript made and the warrants drawn."

Ballard patted him on the shoulder. "Thanks, Buckhorn."

The state trooper grimaced. "Don't thank me. I'm only able to do that because my superiors don't really want to get involved in this Mountain County mess and they won't care if I'm in no hurry."

Casey had left then, heading for Rome, Georgia. It seemed off the mark, somehow; his trip to Georgia held no promise for getting at Terry Foster. But maybe Charlie Sams would uncover something worthwhile in Memphis.

In the meantime, Ballard was looking forward to the morning—and a meeting with Alice Ralston Alderman.

ii   The editor of the *Hillside Truth* had made an assumption that proved false. He had believed he would find Kathy Ringer within the complex structure of the Holiday Inn corporation in Memphis. But the Holiday Inn people had never heard of her, and he had spent the rest of Friday searching for her at individual hotels and motels in the colorful city on the Mississippi. Without success and without certain knowledge she was even in Memphis.

He stood now, on Saturday morning, in the beautifully restored lobby of the elegant Peabody Hotel, gazing at the soaring Italian Renaissance columns and the impressive fountain carved from a single block of travertine marble. He had never been in the Peabody before, although his father had often spoken of it lovingly, insisting "there are river folks who believe that when they die, heaven will be like the Peabody lobby."

In truth, he had deliberately bypassed the Peabody in his earlier search for Kathy Ringer, because he could not imagine the Mountain County girl working in such an establishment. The lobby was crowded, some folks seated at tables eating Eggs Benedict and drinking large lime-garnished Bloody Marys. But most were just standing about, seeming to be waiting for something.

Suddenly, music was heard on the public address system, a Sousa martial air, and an elevator door opened to reveal a grinning bellman herding three live ducks in front of him. To the applause of the onlookers, the ducks padded along a red carpet laid on the marble floor, looking neither right nor left, but heading unerringly to the fountain, where they flapped into the water and settled down contentedly.

"Isn't that charming?" a matron next to Charlie said.

"Uh . . . yes," he answered, trying to recall what he had heard of the famous ducks of the Peabody.

"I find it fascinating," the woman added. "I try to see some of it every time I'm downtown, either in the morning like this, or when they're returned to their rooftop pens in the afternoon."

"Hmmm."

"It's a great tradition, young man."

"Yes, I suppose so." Sams thought it a bit silly to regard three tame ducks as "tradition." The crowd was melting away as he walked to the hotel's front desk.

"May I help you, sir?" a smiling male clerk asked.

"I hope so. My name is Charles Sams and I have a cousin who may be employed here. Her name is Kathy Ringer."

"Oh, yes. Miss Ringer has just recently joined our reservations staff."

"Is she here today?"

"No, I'm sorry, she's not. But she'll be on duty again on Monday."

Charlie shook his head. "I'm only going to be in Memphis for a few hours," he lied. "I wonder whether you could give me her telephone number or her address?"

The smile disappeared from the clerk's face. "No, I'm sorry, I can't."

Sams grinned at him. "Maybe we could negotiate this?" He reached for his wallet.

"Sir—!" The young man took a half-step backwards to punctuate the offense taken. "This is the Peabody!"

The editor shrugged, turning from the desk and idly making his way to the fountain, appearing to be fascinated by the swimming ducks, but lost in thought. *Well, if I have to stay until Monday . . .* The prospect annoyed him.

He had drifted around to the other side of the fountain, screened from the front desk, when a voice behind him said: "Excuse me, sir."

Charlie turned to find a bellman there, an older man than might have been thought to hold that position, balding and slightly stooped as if the years of heavy luggage had deformed him.

"Lookin' for Kathy Ringer, are you?"

"I am."

"I know where she is." His information ended there.

Once more, Charlie reached for his wallet, this time withdrawing a five-dollar bill, extending it but keeping a tight grip on the money.

191

"She's in the hotel right now," the bellman reported, "havin' breakfast in the Dux." He nodded toward a restaurant just off the lobby.

Sams let go of the bill and the bellman took it in one expert move, seeming to just evaporate from the newspaperman's side. Hurrying to the Dux, Charlie disengaged himself from a menu-toting *maitre d'* ("I'm meeting a friend") and began to search the restaurant for Kathy. It didn't take him long to spot her, even though she had undergone a rather startling transformation since he had last seen her: she had modified the "country" beehive hairdo, had toned down her facial makeup and, in short, had become more sophisticated in appearance. She was sitting alone, apparently near the end of her breakfast. He approached her table.

"Mornin', Kathy."

Her eyes came up, a smile starting on her pretty face. "Charlie! What are you doin' in Memphis?"

"Actually, I'm here to see you."

The smile died. "Why?"

He sat down. "Because you're a key to a story I'm writing. Or I think you are. But more properly, I guess I should say it's a story I'm researching."

Kathy looked at him suspiciously. "About me?"

"Not really . . ." Sams was trying to remember all of the coaching he had received from Casey Ballard. "It's about K.C. Ballard, and you don't have to be in it if you tell me you don't want to be."

"I *don't* want to be!"

"Then you're not," Charlie assured her casually. "What I'm after is the truth about ol' K.C.'s fortune."

"What fortune is that?" The young girl was clearly ill-at-ease.

"I have it on what I believe to be good authority—only *one* authority, however, and I need some verification from another source—that K.C. was one of the richest men in Mountain County and that when he died, there remained behind a sizable amount of cash, which seems to have disappeared. There's speculation," he was repeating Casey's theory, "that *you* might have made off with it when you departed Hillside so suddenly."

Kathy's face flushed. "That, Charlie . . . is . . . a . . . goddamned . . . lie!" She said it too vehemently, too loudly, and she looked around the crowded restaurant in embarrassment as heads turned in her direction. Scrawling her name on the breakfast check, she rose quickly to rush out of the Dux, Sams in her wake.

On the sidewalk outside the Peabody Hotel, she told the black doorman: "Get me a cab, please." One was whistled up and the door was opened for her. She gestured for Charlie to get into the car and when he did, she followed him, ordering the driver: "Cooper and Central."

"I have a place here," Kathy announced unemotionally, "where we can talk."

She stared straight ahead as the cab made its way out of the midtown area of the River City, the pretty face set into a stern mask, sullenly silent.

iii   The Lamont Foundation Psychiatric Hospital looked less like an institution than anything Casey Ballard could have imagined. As he drove through the park-like surroundings of the hospital, after being checked through an ornate iron entrance gate by a coldly efficient uniformed guard, Casey thought of himself as being transported back into another era, perhaps to gentler times when the South was a more simple, ordered place. When there was a monied gentry used to wealth and position, and when slaves did all the work. It was not a mental process he could escape; everywhere on the grounds there were black men engaged in a manicuring of the place: sweeping wide brick walks, meticulously combing the vastness of a startlingly green lawn, picking up bits of debris only they could see.

He drove through a tunnel of giant oaks, their branches bare now on that January Saturday morning. And at the end of it, perfectly placed at the focal point of a broad, sweeping driveway, as if its position had been plotted out within a sixteenth of an inch, was a sprawling Georgian mansion of beautiful red brick, the center main portion of it three stories high, with tall chimneys standing at each end over a black slate roof. The exterior woodwork was painted with a gleaming white enamel, and the shutters at the windows were a perfect dark gray. Two-story wings extended out from each side, also with their dual chimneys and slate roofs.

As he stopped his car in front of the double doors of the mansion, the doors swung wide and a gray-haired black man, actually in livery, hurried out, coming to the driver's side.

"Good morning, Mr. Ballard," he said quietly, opening the car door. "Cephus will take your car."

With that, a younger black man appeared—from nowhere, Casey thought—sliding behind the wheel and driving the car away. It was almost as if the rental Ford wasn't to be permitted there in the driveway to spoil the symmetry of the scene.

Casey was gestured through the doors, which were immediately closed behind him. He found himself in a lovely entrance hall, pine-paneled and with scarlet drapery at the windows. The unusual quiet there was disturbed only by the ticking of a huge, old grandfather's clock in the corner. The butler took Casey's hat and coat and disappeared. From behind a massive, antique oak desk, a beautiful, light-skinned black girl rose and came forward, smiling.

"Good morning, Mr. Ballard," she said, the voice carefully modulated, the soft Southern accent appealing. "I'm Erlene. Mrs. Lamont will be with you presently. May I get you some coffee?"

"Uh . . . no. But thank you very much." Ballard was disquieted. It all seemed to be a stage setting. Unreal. And made no less unreal by the appearance, the entrance, of a woman coming down the wide, carpeted stairway leading into the hall. She was forty, perhaps, handsome rather than beautiful, dressed in a severe, dark gray suit that failed to hide her good figure. Her brunette hair was tastefully coiffed, her makeup was without a flaw, and when she extended her hand to him, the smell of the fragrance she used fitted her perfectly.

Everything is perfect, Casey thought. *Too damned perfect!*

"I'm Marybeth Lamont, Mr. Ballard," the woman said. "We spoke on the telephone."

"Yes."

"Did you have a pleasant trip?"

"Yes, I did. This is beautiful country. And this is a beautiful house."

"We're very proud of it, Mr. Ballard," she replied, leading him, with a gentle touch on his elbow, to a corner of the entrance hall where there were two easy chairs positioned by a low table on which had been placed a silver tray with a china pot and two delicate china cups and saucers. As they sat down, Mrs. Lamont poured coffee for them, handing him a cup. "Cream and/or sugar, Mr. Ballard?" she asked lightly.

"No, thank you." He dutifully took a sip of the coffee he didn't want.

"The main section of the house, and we're in it now," she explained, "was built before the Revolution. The wings were added in the first decade of the 1800s. But what you see now is the product of a good deal of restoration by my husband and myself."

"It must have been a lot of work."

"Oh, it was. I'm sorry Dr. Lamont couldn't be here today—he had to be in Atlanta for a psychiatric conference—because he can explain the history of the house much better than I can."

"Uh huh."

"But you didn't come here to talk of old houses, did you?"

"No, I—"

"I must confess," she hurried on, "that I'm glad you got the permission of Alice's brother to visit her. No one comes to see her. Indeed, Mr. Alderman has visited her only once. I suppose the experience was too painful for him to repeat it. And truthfully, the first time I talked to the brother was the other night when he called about you."

"Oh, really?"

"It's all very sad. But then, Alice is less and less aware of what's happening around her. She has Alzheimer's syndrome, you see. But perhaps Mr. Ralston told you that?"

"No, he didn't."

"Hmmm." Mrs. Lamont sighed. "It's dreadful what Alzheimer's does to a once-vital person."

"Yes, I imagine so," Casey replied, wondering when he was going to get to see the patient.

"Alice is your aunt, you said?"

"Well, as I told you," Ballard was repeating the story he had invented, "Mrs. Alderman was the second cousin of my late uncle. So the relationship is a bit blurred. But in light of what you've told me, Mrs. Lamont, is Mrs. Alderman competent to sign a document regarding the inheritance from my uncle?"

"I'm not sure." She made a small gesture to the black girl at the oak desk. "Mr. Colter, one of our aides, is more familiar with the day-to-day progress of Alice and I'll have him take you to her. I think you'll find him helpful."

A burly man wearing a white medical jacket entered the entrance hall and came to them. It was obvious to Casey that he had been summoned by the receptionist, Erlene.

"This is George Colter," Mrs. Lamont said, "one of the doctor's medical aides." She smiled. "One of our best people. George, this is Mr. Casey Ballard, who wishes to visit Alice."

Casey rose and shook Colter's hand, appraising him. He was one of those men whose age it was difficult to gauge. Not a young man, certainly, but the face was still youthful under a graying head of hair. Ballard put his age at about fifty, maybe a few years more.

"If you'll come with me, sir," Colter said in a formal manner. He started to lead Casey away.

"Oh, Mr. Ballard," Mrs. Lamont called to them, "have George show you the formal gardens before you leave. We have a spectacular view from there."

The medical aide led the way down a hallway leading from the entrance hall. "We'll take the elevator," he said. "Alice's suite is on the second floor."

When they were in the elevator, Colter said. "Mrs. Lamont tells me you're a nephew of Alice."

"Well, not really . . ." Once again Casey repeated his false story.

"I see. And you're from—?"

"Texas," Casey answered, perpetuating his lie.

Colter said nothing more as they exited the elevator and moved a few feet to a door. Again, there was nothing institutional about it; there was no number on the door, no nameplate to indicate who was on the other side of it. Colter knocked lightly and then turned the knob, making way for Casey to enter a large sunlit living room.

"All of our patients have suites," Colter explained. "Living room, bedroom, kitchen and dining nook, and a full bath, of course. All of Alice's meals are prepared right here by one of our cooks. We try to maintain a home-like atmosphere."

Casey nodded, thinking the Lamont operation was hardly a Medicare operation. He wondered how much Elmo Ralston, Jr. was spending to maintain his sister here. Looking across the room, he saw a figure seated on a small sofa facing the window, a wheelchair to one side of it. There seemed to be no awareness that anyone had entered the room.

They went to the sofa, Colter deliberately standing in front of the woman there, blocking her view through the window, commanding her attention.

"Alice," he said gently, "there's someone here to see you. This is Mr. Casey Ballard."

The old woman looked up, smiling. But dumbly. Not comprehending that someone had been introduced to her.

Casey was astounded by how beautiful she was, even in the throes of her Alzheimer's deterioration. He was remembering the things he had heard about her. Zeb Alderman's rather plaintive recollection: "Alice was the sweetest thing . . ." And ancient Herman Armstrong's more earthy description: "At thirteen she were a woman! Ah mean, she were the kind t' give a lot o' married men in the county wet dreams. A pluperfect beauty. Curly brown hair an' big hazel eyes—kinda innocent eyes, ya know. An' smooth skin the color o' buttermilk, an' a figure—Lord! She had a way o' walkin' that were . . . well, suh, she were appealin' an' she knew it. She had a . . . uh . . . instinct,

Ah guess ya'd say, thet gave 'er the advantage over any man what crossed 'er path."

Ballard found himself staring at her. The hair was white now and the eyes were still hazel, but rheumy. Nevertheless, Casey saw a hint of the innocence of which Armstrong spoke. And the skin was still smooth, even though she was . . . what? . . . seventy-one years old. Looking at her at that moment, at a time when she was dying most cruelly, her visitor could actually believe she might have had an instinct giving her an advantage over any man crossing her path.

"Alice," Casey heard Colter saying, "aren't you going to say hello to your guest?"

"What?" The single word was slurred, the voice weak.

"Mr. Ballard has come all the way from Texas to see you."

"Texas? I know someone from . . ." The thought left her, unfinished. She tilted her head to try to see around Colter and then she angrily waved him away from in front of her.

"She loves to just look out the window," Colter explained.

"Bunny!" Alice said testily, wiggling her fingers at him.

The medical aide smiled. " 'Bunny' is the term of endearment she uses with me when she wants something," he told Ballard. "She's allowed two cigarettes a day. It's time for the first one." He pulled a pack from his pocket, removed a cigarette, placed it between his lips and lit it. He handed it to her and she took it from him.

With her left hand, Casey noted.

"Is it all right if I just try to talk to her?" he asked Colter.

The attendant shrugged.

Casey sat down on the sofa next to her. "Mrs. Alderman," she turned her head to look at him, blowing smoke through her nostrils, a contented smile on her face, "I'm here because of the will of my uncle, John Ballard."

She shook her head negatively. At least she was still listening to him.

"John Ballard, your cousin," he went on. "Maybe you remember him *and* his brother, another cousin, King David Ballard?"

Alice just puffed on her cigarette, seemingly more concerned with it than with what Casey was saying to her.

"Uncle John was a close friend of Herschel Barnes."

Alice had already turned away from him, her attention span exhausted.

"Herschel . . . Barnes . . . ," Casey said slowly and forcefully.

She was staring out of the window.

"I think that's enough," Colter said with a strange hint of anger in his voice.

"Yes, I suppose so," Casey sighed. Getting to his feet he moved toward the door. "You stay with your patient, Mr. Colter. I'll find my way out."

"Mrs. Lamont said I was to show you the view from the formal garden."

"Oh, that's okay," the visitor replied. "It's not necessary that I see it."

"When Mrs. Lamont gives an order," the attendant insisted, "I follow it."

The mistress of the Lamont Foundation Psychiatric Hospital hadn't exaggerated the view. The grounds of the institution, Casey realized for the first time, were situated on a bluff overlooking the Oostanaula River, glittering in the morning sunlight several hundred feet below. Looking over the carefully trimmed privet hedge bordering the garden Casey could see for miles over the countryside.

"It's lovely," he commented.

"Hmmm."

"And this garden certainly is unique," Ballard added, sweeping his arm to indicate the expanse of the garden, which featured many styles of statuary and more than a dozen examples of topiary: large shrubs trimmed in the shapes of swans and crescent moons and horses, even a startlingly realistic giraffe.

"It must take a lot of work to keep those shrubs in that condition."

"It does." Colter stared at him for a moment. Then: "What's the hell's your game, Ballard?!"

"What?"

"Alice doesn't have a cousin John Ballard. Nor a cousin ... what the hell was that name? ... King David Ballard, either! I knew you were a phony the moment you mentioned Herschel Barnes."

Casey tried to put up a defense of indignation. "See here, Colter, you have no right—!"

"I have every right," Colter interrupted. "Herschel Barnes was my father ..."

Casey sucked in a deep breath.

". . . and Alice Ralston is my *mother*."

15

i   It was an old frame house with a tiny front yard, to which Kathy Ringer and newspaper editor Charlie Sams were delivered by the Memphis taxi driver. An address on Cooper Street, not too far removed from the bustling Overton Square, with its collection of colorful and unusual shops and restaurants. There was a white picket fence around the house, and while its appearance bespoke of another era of Memphis history, obviously it had been carefully restored.

"Do you rent this place?" Sams asked as they got out of the cab.

"No," the young woman replied, "I own it." She led the way to the door, unlocked it and stepped into a small foyer, followed by Sams. Every passing moment with Kathy enhanced the sense of mystery about about her; he knew the woman was Kathy Ringer of Mountain County, but the perception he had held of her was rapidly being destroyed.

"You mean you bought this place since starting to work at the Peabody?" he asked. She had been employed there for only a few days.

"No, I've had it for a nearly five years."

"But—?"

Fingers gently placed on his lips stopped his further questioning. "In a moment," she said, smiling sweetly. "Right now I'm going to brew us some fresh coffee." She nodded toward the living room. "So, you just make yourself comfortable for a few moments."

Sams shrugged off his topcoat and entered the tastefully furnished living room, surprised once more by the many prints of art masters on the walls and the well-stocked shelves of books. He could hear her in the kitchen, humming lightly, and then a door opened and closed.

Nearly ten minutes passed before she came into the living room, carrying a tray holding a ceramic coffee pot and cups and saucers. She had changed once more: her hair had been let down to her shoulders, delightfully framing her pretty face; she wore a light pink satin robe, beneath which he could see tiny, heeled slippers.

Placing the tray on a table next to Charlie's chair, she instructed, "Help yourself." And he sat down opposite him, crossing her legs, the robe falling open and revealing her fine legs.

"I've got to say, Kathy, that this is all . . ." He looked around the room. "Well, it's . . . uh . . ."

"Not bad for a hillbilly girl, huh?" she laughed.

"It's not what I would have expected."

She nodded soberly. "This is all because of K.C. and I'm not going to play games with you, Charlie. I'm going to tell you all about it. But I'm also going to tell you that I'm not going back to Mountain County again. If you learn something which has . . . a legal side, I'm not going to go back and testify in anything you may be involved in with that Casey Ballard. I've left—permanently!"

"Okay." There was nothing else for him to say at that moment.

"I know what most people think." She leaned back easily, sipping at her coffee. "They think I was screwing old K.C., that I was his mistress. But it wasn't like that at all. I called him

'Pappy,' and our relationship was more like father and daughter . . ." She smiled. "Or grandfather and granddaughter.

"You see, it started about five years ago, maybe a little longer than that, when I met K.C. in the club on the roof of the Hillside Inn. He had come in with one of his young whores and there had been some argument or something, and the girl left. K.C. sat there at the table, looking so sad, so lost, that . . . well, I went over and spoke to him. And that started it. I learned a lot about the old man that night—we went to my room in the inn and spent the night, just talking."

She noted the incredulous expression on the editor's face. "Yes, Charlie, *just talking.* He never made a move on me at all, although I expected he would. After all, he had a terrible reputation. But with me he was different . . ."

A faraway look came to Kathy's eyes, transporting her back to that evening.

ii   The old man seemed uncomfortable in the ancient black wool suit he wore.

"Do you want to take your jacket off, Mr. Ballard?" the girl asked.

"Yeah, Ah guess so." He stood, taking off the coat. Kathy hung it in the closet.

When she returned to him, she sat on the floor in front of him, unlacing his high-top shoes and slipping them off. "Is that better?" she asked.

"Yeah." He sighed. "Ya know, in all mah days—an' Ah'm nearin' ninety now—Ah ain't never had nobody do thet fer me."

"Oh, come now, Mr. Ballard," she laughed. "I've heard you've had all kinds of women and one of them must have—"

"No, ma'am," K.C. said firmly. "Mah wife, Ah suppose, woulda figgered it were improper. Why, she never undressed in front o' me with the lights on. An' when we was in bed she was . . . dutiful, an' thet's 'bout it. An' mah daughters . . . well,

203

they figgered their ol' man were jest a money machine. Ah don't recollect that either one o' 'em ever kissed their daddy."

"But the other women, Mr. Ballard?"

"Jest 'bout the same. Ya know, it ain't hard t' git women if'n ya got money. An' Ah got money. It's 'bout all Ah got, an' ev'rybody seems to hanker fer it."

"Do you see me that way, Mr. Ballard?" Kathy asked softly.

"Are ya?"

"I don't know. I know you might think that the way I just came up to you and introduced myself. But you looked . . . so alone. So in *need* of someone."

"Yeah." He sighed deeply again. "Ah ain't got a lot o' time no more, an' Ah been thinkin' lately what Ah ain't had. Ah ain't never heard a story from a book. Ah ain't never seen a proper show. Ah ain't never been no place but this damned county!" Anger had crept into his voice. "An' when Ah die, there ain't nobody what'll shed a tear."

Kathy was moved. "There's still time."

"To do what?"

"To hear a story from a book. To see a show. To have somebody really care for you."

"Ya mean you?"

"Yes, if you'll allow me."

The old man's eyes filled with tears.

iii   "And that's the way it started," Kathy Ringer was telling Charlie Sams. "I read to him that night. I didn't have any books in my room then, except for the Gideon Bible. And so we began with that, starting with Genesis. And within a week I drove him here to Memphis to see some live entertainment—a jazz concert at Blues Alley. Pappy was delighted. By the second trip to Memphis, K.C. decided we ought to have a place here—and he bought this house, in my name.

"I'll admit to you, Charlie, that I took a lot of things from him: clothes and jewelry, this house, and, eventually, the Mercedes. But never cash." She paused. "I took what I did for two reasons. One was because I wanted them and they were offered freely, lovingly. I learned early in our association that he'd be offended if I didn't accept them. But the second reason was that everyone else was trying to rob him blind. Did you know that Terry Foster demanded—and got—twenty-five percent of everything from K.C.'s Place?"

"No, I didn't."

"Well, that was the deal," Kathy insisted. "And God knows what Lulubelle and those boys of hers stole from him! If there was any cache of money, as you suggested earlier, when K.C. died, Terry had it. Or Lulubelle. But K.C., God love him, spent what he had on the two of us. We'd see every major show coming to Memphis. And I even got him to spend some money on new clothes for himself, most of which is in the closet in his bedroom over there." She pointed to a closed door.

"Then, too, he bought this library you see here. He loved books. And I read to him for many hours. I read things I probably never would have read if it hadn't been for him." She smiled. "His favorite was O. Henry. Some of the stories I must have read for him a dozen times. He wasn't stupid, you know, he was just uneducated. It's funny, but it was me—with my high school education at Mountain County High School—who taught him about the good things in the world.

"And I loved him, Charlie. As 'Pappy,' and not in any physical scene people think of when you mention love. He was a virile old man, no doubt of that, and he indulged in his sexual life right to the end. But in the last year or so, he had only one lover, Trixie. In her own way, she was as good for him as I was for him in my way. Trixie loved him, too, and got no payment for it at all." She shook her head sadly.

"We were together maybe a year when he told me he was going to change his will and leave everything to me. I didn't want it. It frightened me, honestly, because I knew there would be a terrible fight if I was his heiress. So I convinced him to leave his estate, or what would remain of it, to a blood relative, and that's how Casey Ballard came into the picture."

"What about Edgar? Wasn't he K.C.'s son?"

"That's what Lulubelle claimed, but K.C. always had doubts about it. I don't know for sure, of course."

"That's a hell of a story," Charlie commented.

"Uh huh. And it's the truth."

"But why did you leave so suddenly when Casey Ballard came on to the scene?"

"Terry," Kathy said, spitting out the word. "He came to my room at the Hillside Inn that afternoon, all agitated about Ballard's arrival, cursing about him. He told me about him being a Chicago cop and how much trouble there was going to be if Ballard stayed around. He actually wanted me to make a play for Ballard, to seduce him, so that Terry could find us together and arrest him for rape!"

"Jesus!"

"He was crazy, I tell you," she raced on, "and then he threw me down on the bed and started to tear my clothes. I screamed. Loud! And kept screaming until he left." There was a wan smile. "You know, with all the screaming I did, no one came to see what was wrong. The people at the inn knew Terry was in my room and they were scared to death of him. That's when I decided I had to leave immediately. I was going to come to Memphis anyway, eventually, but now I was really frightened. I was afraid there'd be another time with Terry, when I wouldn't be able to keep him off me. And I knew he was capable of killing me if I resisted him enough."

Her eyes were wide now in what Charlie Sams thought was real terror.

There was a long silence.

Finally, Sams asked: "If I'm out of bounds, just tell me, Kathy, but in that time with K.C. what about your own . . . well . . ."

"You mean did I have any sex life?"

"Yes," he said, embarrassed.

"Some. But here in Memphis. Never in Mountain County. And, I want to repeat this because I want you to understand it—*never* with K.C.!"

"I'm sorry, I shouldn't have asked you that."

Kathy shrugged.

"And what now for you?" he wanted to know.

"Now, I'll have my job at the Peabody, I have this home, thanks to K.C., and I'll think of him a lot, with love. And maybe someday I'll find a young man—"

"Who will be damned lucky to have you," Charlie cut in.

"You think so?"

"Uh huh."

Kathy looked at him intently. "Do you think so for yourself, Charlie?"

Even though her directness startled him for a moment, the editor answered, "I'd be a liar if I said no."

"Then don't go back right away."

Sams was tempted. His swift thoughts suggested he'd be compromising his integrity as a journalist. He recognized this as pure sophistry. Finally, he simply resolved not to give in to the temptation.

"Sorry," he said, "I have to return tonight." And he found himself wondering what Casey Ballard would think of his decision.

iv   At the same hour, Casey was involved in his own drama, one that even his fanciful scenario had not covered. He sat in a motel room in Rome, Georgia, having confessed his police background, listening to the recollections of a man who claimed to be the son of Alice Ralston and one-time gym teacher Herschel Barnes. Ballard believed what he was being told by Max Barnes, a.k.a. George Colter; it had the ring of solid truth.

"I was sixteen when my father died," Barnes had said, "and I didn't remember anything about my mother. That doesn't mean I didn't know about her; Dad talked of her often. But I had no personal recollection of her. They had broken up, you see, when I was still quite young. But I knew who she was and I had a real sense of her. Dad had pictures of her from when they were married. She was only thirteen, you know . . ."

Casey nodded.

"And she was quite beautiful. I was to learn just how beautiful she really was later. Anyway, when my father died, I was on my own and that was the first time I tried to find her. But at sixteen I wasn't wise enough to know the ways of tracking her down. And, of course, I had the daily struggle to keep myself alive. I had all kinds of jobs in Texas: cottonfield worker, with roughneck gangs in the oil fields, and in '43 I was drafted.

"When the war was over I took advantage of the GI Bill to go to the University of Texas. I had found my niche in the service—I was a medic—and I took nursing courses to become a registered male nurse. That's what I become early in '49. It was rewarding work; I enjoyed it and I was good at it. But in the back of my mind there were always nagging questions about my mother. Where was she? What was she doing? Would she want to see me? I finally went to a private detective agency to try to find her.

"As it turned out, I guess it was rather easy for them. Within a few weeks, I had a report. She had been married again, to a banker named Zebulon Alderman, and she was living in Hillside, Tennessee. They gave me her address. That was in 1958. December of '58, just before Christmas. I wrote her a letter, saying I wanted to see her. I waited for weeks for a reply which never came. I was deeply hurt and tried to tell myself I didn't care, but I did. I argued with myself for a while about whether I just ought to go to Tennessee and present myself to her. I decided against that course of action. I suppose I was frightened by the prospect of a direct rejection.

"And that's the way it stayed," he sighed, "for many years. Until July of '75, when I picked up a Dallas paper one day and saw her picture there on the society page. I knew who it was immediately; that beautiful face had been burned into my mind. She was older, of course, but the face was like the one on the pictures my father had of her as a high school girl. The caption on the picture confirmed she was Mrs. Zebulon Alderman of Tennessee and told me she was the house guest of a Dallas family named Sandorvale. I went to see her."

Max Barnes shook his head sadly. "Yes, sir, I screwed up my courage and went to see her . . ."

V   The walled estate of the Sandorvale family was intimidating, but Max drove his car through the gateway and up to the white brick mansion. When a butler answered the ringing of the door chimes, the visitor said, "I'm here to see Mrs. Alderman."

"Is she expecting you?" the butler demanded.

"No, not really. But I'd appreciate it if you'd tell her Max Barnes is here."

The servant shook his head in doubt. "Mrs. Sandorvale has guests for luncheon and—"

"Please. It's important."

"Wait here." The door was closed on Barnes, and it seemed a long time before it was opened again. "Mrs. Alderman will see you."

Max followed the butler through the big house and out onto a patio area next to a swimming pool, where several dozen people sat at tables under large, striped umbrellas, laughing and chattering. As they approached one of the tables, a woman arose, smoothing out her chiffon dress. She carried a drink in her hand as she came toward them on spiked heels, moving rather unsteadily.

The visitor froze there as she got close to him, studying his face. "Bunny?"

"I'm Max Barnes," he said, swallowing hard.

"Yes," she replied, "I think you are. You look very much like Hersch."

"Father's dead," he reported uneasily. "June seventeen, 1943."

"Is he?" There was no emotion. "That's too bad. And what do you do, Bunny?"

"I'm a male nurse at—"

"How quaint," she interrupted. "A male nurse at age—?"

"Forty-seven."

"Has it been that long?" she sighed.

"Yes."

"Hmmm. And what is it you want, Bunny?"

The question shocked him. "I . . . us . . . just wanted to meet my mother."

Alice grinned at him. "You should know that your mother is temporarily cut off from her fiscal resources, Bunny. A disagreement—of limited duration, I hope—with her husband of record. But, if you're patient, I should be able to help you out in the future."

Barnes stared at her for a moment, his face flushed. "Damn you!" he snapped.

"Now," the woman said triumphantly, laughing loudly, "that's more like Hersch. You *do* have some balls!"

She grabbed him by the arm, pulling him toward the assembled diners by the pool. "Listen everybody!" she called out. "I have an interesting revelation. This handsome gentleman, believe it or not, is my *son!* His name is Max Barnes . . . or Bunny, if you wish . . . and he's a male nurse. And I'm not going to tell you how old he is."

The others laughed and Alice guided him through a bewildering series of introductions. At the end of them she came to a swarthy man, sporting a pencil-thin mustache and a bored expression.

"And this, Bunny," she said, "is my paramour of the moment, Count Alfonso Renelli, of the Italian royal family he says. The title may be phony, but the accent is reasonably authentic."

Renelli remained seated, not offering his hand, contemplating Barnes. "Darling," he said finally, addressing Alice, "I didn't think you had the genes to produce such a pleasing specimen."

Alice giggled. "Beware of this scoundrel, Bunny. He's been known to be indiscriminate in his sexual tastes."

The others roared.

"For reasons I can't fully explain, not even to myself," Barnes was saying to Casey, "I stayed with her. There always seemed to be money coming to her from Tennessee; she never told me how much. But she was firmly committed to what has been called the 'jet set.' I suppose I saw a need to try to protect my mother. And I did, in a sense, even though the likes of Count Renelli kept popping up. I like to think I kept her from the worst of them. But she drank too much; there weren't too many sober breaths drawn in any one day.

"And there were more and more incidents of her flying into inexplicable rages. Signs of madness, really. I accepted all of it because I honestly grew to love her. There were a few quiet times, a few sober moments, when she was quite sweet and I could see why my father had loved her so much.

"Then, one day in Paris, she just disappeared. That was three years ago. It didn't take me long to learn she had boarded a plane for the States. But it did take me several months to track her down to the Lamont hospital, again with a private detective agency helping. Apparently, she had gone back to Tennessee, and her family, recognizing her needs, committed her for psychiatric care. It was then I presented myself for a job here—"

"Changing your name?"

"Yes. I was afraid if the Lamonts learned I was her son, I wouldn't be permitted to care for her, but I can as 'George Colter, Male Nurse.' I thought perhaps Dr. Lamont would have known of her earlier marriage to someone named Barnes."

"Didn't your mother ever give you away?"

"No. Her problems were compounded by the onset of Alzheimer's and her memory disappeared. Of course, she does call me 'Bunny' from time to time, but she doesn't know why. She's dying now, Mr. Ballard, and if I can bring her some small comfort in her last days I want to be here. That's why I don't want you to intrude your police investigation, whatever it may be, into the Lamont hospital."

"Hmmm. Have you ever been to Mountain County, Tennessee, Mr. Barnes?"

"No. I saw no reason to go there. Her family is looking

after her by paying the bills at the hospital and, otherwise, I don't care about them."

"Didn't your mother ever speak of them?"

"Rarely, and then only in derogatory terms."

"What do you know of the Ralston Company?"

"Only that it's the family business. Lumbering, isn't it?"

"It is. But do you know anything of its ownership?"

"No. I assume the brother, who signs the checks for the hospital bills, is the owner."

Casey hesitated. "Does your mother have a will?"

"No. The Lamonts tried to have all of her legal matters in order when she was accepted here as a patient. But she had never written a will, and by the time she got here, she wasn't competent to draw one."

"But can you prove Mrs. Alderman is your mother? I mean, do you have a legal birth certificate?"

"Yes. What are you getting at, Mr. Ballard?"

"What I'm getting at, Max," Casey said slowly, "is that your mother is the sole owner of the Ralston Company; she was willed it by her father. And the control of the company passes to her issue, according to the terms of that will."

"You mean me?"

"Exactly. You face the prospect of being a millionaire."

Max swallowed hard. "I can't comprehend anything like that."

"Well, you'd better start thinking about it. Because when your mother dies, the Ralston clan, her brother and her husband, will conspire to steal the company from you. If I were you, I'd get myself a lawyer."

The male nurse shook his head in disbelief. "Is that why you came here?"

"Quite honestly, Max, you were a total surprise to me. I didn't even know you existed."

"Then, why—?"

"There was another matter, having to do with one King David Ballard."

"Oh, yes, you mentioned that name to Mother. A relative?"

"In a sense," Casey answered. "In light of the circumstances, though, it doesn't seem to be very important anymore. Maybe it wasn't ever important."

"That's a strange thing to say."

"I suppose." Ballard paused for a moment. "I would like to ask one more question, even though I believe I already know the answer. Is your mother left-handed?"

"Yes. Definitely. Does that have anything to do with . . . uh . . . King David Ballard?"

"It might." Casey shrugged. "But it's nothing to concern yourself about, Max, nothing at all. It's just a minor bit of ancient history."

Minor? he thought. *What a lie! How many lives are bound up in the minor fact that Alice Ralston was left-handed?*

16

i   It was raining on that Sunday morning in Mountain County. A cold, hard, persistent rain dripping in sheets off the loblolly pine, soaking the decaying layer of natural debris nurturing the tiny, living elements of the forest floor. In Hillside it raced in minor flood along the few gutters of the village. And at the Hillside Inn the noisy gurgling of the water through the rain spouts awakened Casey Ballard.

He moaned, regarding the day as nothing less than perverse. It was bad enough he was still there; the rain he heard simply dampened his spirits even more. He was tired, having arrived back in Hillside from Rome Georgia, at one A.M. And he had slept poorly, vividly dreaming again of Rosalie angrily chastising him for his folly. Casey thought of calling her, but abandoned the thought quickly, not wanting to engage in another conversation in which he did all the talking and she replied in disapproving monosyllables.

Nevertheless, he knew she was right. The Mountain County adventure had gone beyond reason. He *had* to conclude it quickly, put it behind him, and pick up the pieces of his own life. The cop in Casey Ballard enabled him to rationalize his determination to leave Mountain County as soon as possible. For twenty-nine years he had fought the filth and corruption of the Chicago streets. And had he changed much? Very little, he admitted to himself as he stood in the shower. He hated cynicism, but he needed a measure of it now to enable him to do what he meant to do; what he meant to pack into the hours of this Sunday.

It was eight o'clock by the time he had dressed and he looked up a number in the small local telephone directory. It didn't surprise him the name he sought was listed in boldface type. The conversation he had was short and decisive. There was an effort to put him off. The effort failed. Somehow he believed he was being guided by Rosalie's quiet strength.

ii   Banker Zeb Alderman, his thin face set in a frown, stood on the steps of the Ralston mansion waiting for the visitor.

Casey cut off the car's motor and ran through the heavy rain to the door.

"Yer phone call, Mistah Ballard," Alderman drawled heavily (Casey hated that affectation), "has Elmo upset. Ah gotta tell ya, we don't 'preciate folks callin' with demands."

There was no apology from the Chicagoan.

"Mah brother-in-law's in frail health," the banker went on, "an' 'fore we go in Ah wanna know what the hell this is all 'bout!"

"I don't have the time to say it twice, nor the inclination to do so," Ballard said forcefully. "What I have to say is for both of you. Of course, if you don't want to hear me, I can say it just as easily to the state police or maybe to the state's attorney."

"We're men of influence, Mistah Ballard."

"And maybe you'll need it."

Angrily, Alderman led Ballard through the house and into

the arboretum, where Elmo Ralston, Jr. sat stiffly in his wheel-chair, seeming to be concentrating on the rain beating heavily against the wide windows. He recognized Casey with just a nod, although the two men had never met before, gesturing to a chair by his side. As Casey sat down the butler offered a cup of coffee, withdrawing from the room after the visitor had taken it.

"Now, are ya gonna tell us what's all this 'bout?" Alderman demanded.

Ballard drew a deep breath. "I saw Alice yesterday in Rome, Georgia."

Elmo gasped.

"And I came away from that meeting with two distinct pieces of knowledge. One is that—"

"You had no right to go there!" Ralston shouted at him.

"I had every right, because the case records of the 1933 murder of King David Ballard were altered, with your family's connivery, to point the finger of blame at my father—"

"No!"

"And to hide the fact the murder was actually committed by one Alice Ralston."

"How dare you?" Elmo raged, his face livid.

"I dare, Mr. Ralston, because it's the truth."

"Alice didn't tell you that. My God, she can't even remember her own name!"

"You're right, she didn't tell me anything. But I was able to confirm something I had only suspected. Alice is left-handed."

"Oh, good Lord—!" Alderman moaned.

Casey turned to him. "You recognize the significance of that, don't you, Zeb?"

"Yeah, Ah do," the old man replied disconsolately.

"Shut up, Zeb!" Ralston ordered.

"No, not anymore, Elmo. Ah lived with this . . . this folly for too many years . . ." The affected drawl was modified. "And, while I truly loved her, I suspect the truth ought to be told at least once." He stared for a moment at Casey. "Even now, Mr. Ballard, the truth is painful."

iii   The two young people clung together in their passion, kissing wildly. The girl's long nut-brown hair was a playground for the boy's hands as they pressed tightly against each other, seeming to be trying to meld two bodies into the space of one, defying the certain laws of physics. A hugh calloused hand roamed to a firm breast and he fondled it roughly.

With a mighty shove, Alice broke away from him, giggling drunkenly, gaily dancing circles around him, her skirt swirling high, revealing the flesh of her superb legs.

"King David! King David!" she chanted in a sing-song manner. "Do you think I'm as pretty as Bathsheba?"

The young man stood watching her, his legs spread wide, his bare feet firmly planted in the dusty pathway around the barn, his hands on his hips. He was a solidly handsome fellow, dark-haired and dark-eyed, darkly tanned. He wore only a pair of overalls, his arms and shoulders bare, revealing strong muscles, which twitched now in apparent rhythm to his deep breathing.

"Ya know what the Book sez 'bout King David?" He grinned at her. "It sez he *took* Bathsheba."

She thought that was funny, laughing loudly. "But even Bathsheba had the curse every once in a while."

"Ah don't give a damn," he said, advancing on her.

She danced away from him, still laughing, unfrightened by him. At a pile of straw next to the barn door, he lunged at her, tackling her clumsily, and both of them tumbled into the straw, resuming their giddy kissing and fondling.

At the corner of the barn, out of their sight, a huge man stood watching them, eavesdropping on their passion, repositioning himself for a better view of their frolicking when a woodpile between him and the carefree couple intruded on his line of sight.

King David ran a hand under her dress and along the inside of her leg.

"David!" she protested, "I told you I have my period."

"An' Ah told you Ah don't give a damn!"

"You're worse than an animal!"

"Mebbe King David were a animal, too," he laughed coarsely. He stood up quickly, shrugging himself out of the overalls, standing naked, his penis hard and erect.

"Oooh," she giggled teasingly, "you're mighty proud of that, aren't you?"

"An' ya know Ah got reason."

He fell on her, pinning her in the straw, reaching under the dress again, grasping her thin panties and ripping them off.

Alice's giggles died in her throat. "David, no!"

He thrust the penis between her legs, probing at her.

"David!" she shrieked. "Stop!"

He drove forward and she could feel him beginning to penetrate her. Thrashing wildly, trying to push herself backwards away from him while still on her back, she was stopped by the woodpile. Trapped now, her screams grew louder. "No! Oh, dear God, no!"

"Shut up!" he growled, balling up a fist and clubbing her on the side of the head.

"David!" Her arms flailed out in panic and her left hand touched an axe lying on the woodpile. With all of her strength she curled her fingers around the handle, swinging the heavy axe in a wide arc.

It smashed against his skull.

He fell on her heavily, holding her down. The severed temporal artery pulsated its warm blood into her face and hair, and her chilling scream was one unending, terror-stricken noise.

The portly voyeur raced from his hiding place at the corner of the barn, pulling the limp form off the girl and turning it over. He felt the wrist for life.

"My God," he breathed, "ya killed 'im!"

"Daddy!" Alice wailed hysterically. "Somebody get my Daddy!"

Her fingers remained frozen on the axe handle, the knuckles deathly white.

iv   Tears ran down Zeb Alderman's face at the recollection. "An' that's when Barney Daniels called Elmo Senior," he sighed, "An' Ah was sent out to K.C.'s Place to get Alice away from there. When I arrived, she was still there on that straw and King David's sister, Sarah, was trying to wipe the blood off of her. I tell you, it made me sick in the stomach.

"An" she still had a hold on that axe. I had to pry her fingers off. I wiped it off with an ol' rag an' threw it onto a dung pile. Then, I brought Alice back here."

"And that's when you trumped up the story against my father," Casey charged angrily.

"That was Billy Foster's doing," Elmo Junior contributed. "He thought that in the light of Abel Ballard's having just left for Chicago he could be . . . well, brought into the case without any damage to him. After all, Billy never intended to press any charges against your father, and he never told the newspaper that Abel was a suspect, or anything like that. It was all supposed to be kept hidden, as it were, in that file."

"And yet the file was used to try to blackmail me when I came to Mountain County some fifty years later!"

Ralston shrugged. "I didn't know Terry was going to do that."

Casey's anger boiled over. "Damn you, Ralston—you find it convenient to use the sheriff until something happens and then you just as conveniently attempt to disassociate yourself from what the sheriff does!"

"You must understand, Mr. Ballard, that we have no control over the sheriff."

"Bullshit! The Ralstons and the Fosters have engaged in conspiracy down through the years. And this one is a *criminal* conspiracy, attempting to hide the truth about a murder."

"A difficult point to prove in a court of law, I suspect."

"Oh, I could prove it if I needed to," Casey insisted. "But for my part, right now, I'll make a deal with you . . . and let's hope I don't live to regret it."

"What kind of deal is that, Mr. Ballard?"

"I want that phony file on the King David murder expunged from the sheriff's files . . ."

Ralston nodded agreement.

"And I want you two to stop propping up Sheriff Foster and let the legitimate law enforcement officials get at him."

"A bit more difficult, perhaps," Elmo commented coldly, "but your point is well taken."

"And I want," Casey said, slowing the words, "Alice's son to have his rightful place in the Ralston Company."

Ralston's eyes opened wide in surprise. "Alice had no children!"

"Ah, but she did—a son conceived in the marriage to Herschel Barnes. And I believe I'm not the only one of this room who knows about him."

Elmo whirled his wheelchair around to face his brother-in-law. "Zeb?!"

"It's true. There was a son named Max."

"And why wasn't I told of it?!"

"Alice asked me not to," Alderman said quietly. "Have either one of us been able to deny Alice what she really wanted?"

"Where is he now?" Zeb was asked.

"I don't know. I haven't heard of him since he was a youngster."

Casey smiled. "I think I can help you, gentlemen," he started, enjoying his role at that moment. "Max Barnes is a male nurse on the staff of the Lamont hospital in Rome, caring for his mother under the pseudonym of George Colter."

Ballard told them the entire story of Max Barnes/George Colter.

Elmo Jr. stared out of the windows at the rain for several moments. "No doubt an imposter, a charlatan, who somehow learned of Alice's . . . uh . . . holdings."

"He has a legal birth certificate," Casey reported, "carrying the signatures of both parents."

"I find that very hard to believe."

"Believe it or don't believe it, Mr. Ralston. But you're going to have to contend with him. Or . . ." Casey paused.

"Or?" Ralston demanded.

"Or you're going to have to contend with the revelation of the true story of King David's murder."

"Blackmail, Mr. Ballard?"

"You ought to know." Casey had tired of the verbal sparring. "Look—Max Barnes will be the legitimate heir of Alice Ralston Barnes Alderman when she dies. There are no doubts about that. So you'd better make up your mind to accommodate him. That's my deal. Yes or no?"

Again, Elmo seemed to be studying the rain. Finally: "Yes." The word was barely audible.

Casey turned to Alderman. "Zeb?"

"Of course."

"Okay." The visitor got to his feet. "Then my business here is concluded."

"I'll see you to your car," the banker volunteered, leaving the arboretum with Ballard.

Elmo Ralston, Jr. watched them go, setting his jaw in a determined attitude as he wheeled his chair to the desk and dialed the telephone.

V   Deputy Randy Apple groaned as he reached sleepily over the nude form of Yolanda Young to answer the ringing telephone.

"Yeah," he muttered into the mouthpiece.

"This is Ralston," the stern voice said. "I have a task for you." He took less than thirty seconds to outline it.

"Jee-sus, Mr. Ralston, that's pretty damned drastic!"

"Perhaps you'd rather go to jail for the attempted murder of Rudy Pitts," Elmo replied heatedly. "Or the *actual* murder of Willie Young and his companions."

"Yeah, I see your point. How?"

Ralston sighed. "For God sake, Deputy, can't you use your imagination?"

"Yeah . . . sure." He hung up the telephone.

"What was that?" Yolanda asked, turning over to kiss him.

"Trouble, baby, real goddamned trouble."

222

Shall we gather at the ri-ver?
The beau-ti-ful, the beau-ti-ful ri-ver . . .

The sounds were muffled somehow, the joy of the words of the old hymn suppressed by the pouring rain as Charlie Sams drove his pickup truck onto the muddied grassy area serving as a parking lot for the Holiness Church. The wheels spun in the sticky goo and Charlie, muttering an oath, turned off the motor.

"We're going to have a mess getting out of here," the editor said to Casey.

"There's one consolation," Ballard replied. "We're not going to be alone."

Gath-er with the saints at the ri-ver
That flows by the throne of God.

The church building was a simple, clapboard, rectangular affair, badly needing a new coat of paint, and with no sign of any kind to announce what it was. There were only two narrow windows on each side of it and none on either end. In the front there were four steps leading up to plain double doors. Tarpaper covered the steeply sloping roof. It was utilitarian, nothing more.

As Casey and Charlie stepped from the truck, their feet sank into several inches of mud as the rain beat down on them. Trying to run through the mud only served to splash the reddish mess on their trousers. There was a tiny roof of sorts over the doorway and they took refuge under it as they vainly tried to scrape the mud from their shoes.

Finally, frustrated, Charlie said: "Well, we can believe we won't be the only folks dragging in mud today."

He opened one side of the double doors and what had been a dampened sound only a second before now assailed them as a cacophony of an out-of-tune piano being hammered mightily, in company with a diverse group of voices, high soprano to rumbling bass, many of those also straying from the confines of the familiar tune, betrayed either by their own faulty musical ears or by the errant piano.

> *Soon we'll reach the shining ri-ver,*
> *Soon our pil-grim-age will cease . . .*

The church was crowded, every space on the unpainted wooden benches filled and the overflow of worshippers standing in the narrow aisles against each side wall. There was the unmistakable sour odor of wet woolen clothing.

> *Soon our hap-py hearts will qui-ver*
> *With the mel-o-dy of peace.*

Ballard and Sams stood ill at ease in the back of the church, just inside the doors.

> *Yes, we'll gather at the ri-ver,*
> *The beau-ti-ful, the beau-ti-ful ri-ver,*
> *Gath-er with the saints at the ri-ver*
> *That flows by the throne of God.*

The hymn ended with three crashing chords on the piano, each one of them discordant.

The Reverend Ashley Smith, his tall, emaciated frame clothed all in black, stood at the small lectern on a platform raised about two feet above the main floor. He gazed to the rear of the church to the late arrivals.

"I'm mightily pleased," he called out, "to see that Brothers Sams and Ballard have made their way through the inclement weather to be with us on this occasion. Anticipatin' they would be joining us, I've saved room for them up here in the front row." He pointed to a spot directly in front of him.

"That's not necessary, Pastor," Casey answered him. "Let someone else have those places."

"Nonsense, sir!" He smiled at them benevolently. "It's not

often we have the company of two such distinguished gentlemen. Now, while our brothers make their way forward, let us all sing the verse and chorus of hymn number three-seventy-seven." Once again the pianist assaulted the instrument, playing the introduction, as Casey and Charlie started down the center aisle.

> *When the trumpet of the Lord shall sound,*
> *And time shall be no more,*

Casey felt the eyes of the congregation on him, eyes lasering hate at him, hate of the stranger. It wasn't a new sensation for him, which was why he was so certain about it. He had felt it often in his police forays into the black ghetto of South Side Chicago, making narcotics arrests or investigating murder or tracking down lascivious pimps.

> *And the morning breaks, e-ter-nal, bright and fair;*
> *When the saved of earth shall gather o-ver on the oth-er shore,*
> *And the roll is called up yon-der, I'll be there.*

In the ghetto perhaps the differences between white cops and black miscreants were more profound, certainly more immediately evident: white and black skins. Here in the Holiness Church all were white, yet the hate was the same, born of the mistrust of the outsider. That the foundation of it was ignorance made the hate no less real.

> *When the roll—is called up yon—der,*
> *When the roll—is called up yon—der . . .*

Casey and Charlie had reached the front bench, with Reverend Smith beaming down at them. They squeezed into the two spaces left for them, Ballard sitting next to a skinny little woman who wore a ridiculously flowered hat, a spring bonnet on that cold, dank January day.

"I'm Missy Smith, the pastor's wife," the little woman whispered to him.

. . . is called up yon-der . . .

She extended her hand and Casey shook it, nodding politely to her.

When the roll is called up yon-der, I'll be there.

This time, mercifully, the pianist didn't end with a flourish. The pastor stood at gaunt attention, waiting a few seconds to allow a complete silence to fall over the congregation.

"Let us pray," he said, looking heavenward. "Oh, Lord," the voice boomed out, "look with favor on us, your children, on this mornin' when we offer praise for the bounty of your life-givin' rain. An' we plead that there not be too much rain, bringin' floods upon us. An' we ask that your presence . . . your SPIR-IT! . . . fill our hearts today as we come together to remember one of us who is by your side now, baskin' in the GLOW-RY of your sweet radiance!"

Ballard sensed it was going to be a prolonged call on God and he began to gaze about, studying the congregation. The obese Lulubelle and her sons were seated on the front bench across the center aisle from him, dressed again in their funereal clothes. Only Daniel seemed to recognize Casey's presence, glowering at him malevolently. Casey countered with a nod, shifting his attention to the members of the Hillside American Legion Post filling the three or four rows behind the Staleys, wearing their distinctive campaign caps. They were of all ages, suggesting the continuing generational persistence of war. Ballard didn't know why, but he was mildly surprised to find Sheriff Terry Foster among them.

And where was the shadow, Deputy Apple?

It was a disparate group in the simple church—and yet all of a kind: farmers, lumbermen, moonshiners (that was a supposition on Casey's part), laborers, housewives, many children, mostly sober faced in keeping with the reason for their gathering. And while there was a diversity of dress, from overalls to seldom-used "Sunday best," they were a single entity: Mountain Countians, pridefully united in their suspicion of strangers. Once more Casey felt that.

He turned his attention to the side of the church on which he sat. Next to Mrs. Smith were two children, a girl of about six, a boy of perhaps nine, skinny carbon copies of the Reverend Mr. Smith, both with their heads obediently bowed as their father continued his impassioned pleas to God and Christ.

Randy Apple sat at the far end of that row, staring straight ahead. When Casey's eyes reached him, the deputy turned his head as if the eyes had physically touched him. He smiled impudently and Ballard could only wonder what would happen to that grin when State Police Investigator Robert Buckhorn came with his arrest warrant in the matter of Rudy Pitts.

Someone tapped Casey on the shoulder. He turned around to look into the lined face of the nonagenarian cemetery superintendent, Herman Armstrong.

"The good people o' Mountain County," Herman whispered, making no effort to hide his sarcasm.

"Hmmm."

"If Ah could bottle what they think 'bout ya, Mistah Ballard, Ah could sell it for critter poisonin'."

"No doubt," Casey agreed.

Annoyed, Mrs. Smith shushed them, putting a silencing finger to her lips.

"An' so, sweet Jee-sus," the pastor was concluding, "we thank you for bein' among us here this mornin'. Amen."

"Amen, Brother!" someone shouted loudly from the rear of the church.

Reverend Smith took a deep, soulful breath. "I've given a great deal of thought about what my theme should be as we come together to memorialize the earthly life of our brother, Edgar Ballard." The voice was soft now; he looked down at the papers he had spread out on the lectern. "An' I concluded that we all ought to recognize the *redemption* we are promised in this circumstance. An' how better to begin than with the joyful words of hymn two-eighteen. All rise please as we sing." He nodded to the pianist.

> *I have a home pre-pared for me,*
> *Since I have been re-deemed . . .*

The pastor's pleasant baritone led the way.

> *Where I shall dwell e-ter-nal-ly,*
> *Since I have been re-deemed.*

"Sing it OUT, brothers an' sisters!"

> *Since I—have been re-deemed,*
> *Since I have been re-deemed,*
> *I will glo-ry in His name!*
> *Since I—have been re-deemed,*
> *I will glo-ry in my Sav-ior's name.*

"PRAISE GOD," Smith roared over the fading last chords of the piano, "THAT OUR BROTHER, EDGAR BALLARD, HAS BEEN RE-DEE-MED!"

The congregation erupted: "Praise God!" . . . "Amen!" . . . "Tell 'em, Brother!"

"AN' PRAISE SWEET JEE-SUS FOR HIS RE-DEMPTION!"

"Yea, Brother!" . . . "Praise Jee-sus!" . . . "Amen, amen!"

The minister waited for his flock to become silent, standing ramrod straight, his eyes searching their faces. When he spoke again, the words were barely whispered, forcing all to listen with complete attention.

"Now, friends, 'redemption' is not a word we use ev'ry day," he said. "An' I suspect that some may not know exactly what it means. So I went to my dictionary to learn that 're-demption' is defined as 'the act of redeemin', or the state of bein' redeemed.' " He looked up from his notes, grinning. "Now, that doesn't tell us a whole lot, does it?"

There were some chuckles in the audience and one man bellowed, "You tell us, Pastor!"

"But the dictionary writers have more to say," Smith went on. " 'Redemption' is 'repurchase, as of somethin' sold.' Or 'recovery by payment, as of somethin' pledged or mortgaged.' Or 'payin' off, as of a mortgage, bond, or note.' Or 'ransom, as of prisoners, slaves, or captured goods.' "

Reverend Smith shook his head sadly. "But only then did the dictionary writers get around to the *real* meanin' of redemption. Redemption, they wrote, is . . ." He paused as seconds ticked away. "Redemption is . . . PRAISE GOD! . . . REDEMPTION IS . . . DE-LIVERANCE . . . FROM . . . SIN . . . AN' . . . ITS . . . CONSEQUENCES . . . THROUGH . . . THE SAC-RI-FICE . . . OF . . . JEE-SUS . . . CHRIST!"

There was a loud chorus of amens.

"Redemption is . . . ATONEMENT!"

Applause started.

"Redemption is . . . SAL-VA-TION!"

The applause was sustained for perhaps thirty seconds. Casey marveled at the command the hill country preacher had over his audience.

"An' then the dictionary writers," Smith sighed, "finally get around to referring us to the well of all truth, the Holy Bible. They say we should read Hebrews in the New Testament. Now, it's really 'The Epistle to the Hebrews,' or a *letter* to the Hebrews. The Jews. But a letter from whom? We don't rightly know, except it might have been from Paul, followin', as it does, other epistles, other letters, from Paul the Apostle to the Romans, the Corinthians, the the Galatians, the Ephesians, the Philippians, the Thessalonians, to Timothy, Titus, and Philemon."

The pastor was speaking rapidly now, sure of the familiar ground. "Anyway, here we have a letter about Jee-sus to the Hebrews, an' it says that in the past God spoke to men through the prophets, but *now* speaks to us, all of us, through His son, through Jee-sus, through God's heir. An' it tells of the covenants of Jee-sus, of His bindin' contracts, of His *promises* to all of us. An' when we get to chapter nine of Hebrews, we learn that one of His covenants, His promises, was the buildin' of an earthly sanctuary for us, a tabernacle, a church. *This* church, my friends. An' we also learn there's to be a heavenly sanctuary for all of us, a home for us with God after earthly death. But how could He guarantee that to mere men, to you an' to me, to the *sinners* we certainly are?

"Well, He could because when Jee-sus was nailed to the cross at Calvary He bought REDEMPTION . . . OF . . . OUR . . . SINS! Bought an' paid for our sins like we buy an' pay for a house or a car or a refrigerator or a TV. He paid for our sins, *then* an' for the sins of all men down through the centuries, WITH . . . HIS . . . BLOOD! Not with dollars an' cents, brothers an' sisters, but WITH . . . HIS . . . BLOOD!

"Hebrews, chapter nine, verse fifteen, tells us: 'He *is* the Mediator of the new covenant, by means of death, for the *redemptions* of the transgressions . . . that those who are called may receive . . . PROMISE . . . OF . . . THE . . . E-TER-NAL . . . INHERITANCE!'

"So, when we sing the happy words of the old hymn, 'I Know That My Redeemer Lives,' we are sayin', we are . . . BE-LIEVIN'!, two things. We are sayin' we know that Jee-sus lives in the house of God, even though He died an earthly death on the cross. An' we are sayin' that, because Jee-sus lives to the end of all time, we also know there's a promise . . . NO, A GUAR-AN-TEE! . . . that WE will live, as well, in the house of God!

"An' that's why we're not sad—but JOYFUL!—today as we meet here to remember Edgar Ballard. For we know that . . . BECAUSE JEE-SUS LIVES . . . EDGAR . . . BALLARD . . . LIVES!"

Once again the emotions of the congregation spilled over, with shouts affirming the pastor's contentions. One woman, overcome with her joy, came to her feet screaming, a long, unbroken exultation that ended only when she collapsed in a convulsive heap in the center aisle. Her friends picked her up and returned her to her seat.

Reverend Smith stood waiting for the hubbub to die down, moping his sweating brow with a large, white handkerchief. Casey thought that perhaps several minutes went by before order was restored.

"My friends," the pastor said softly, leaning heavily on the lectern, as if his strength had ebbed, "we can be joyful today because Edgar Ballard lives in heaven. But we can also be sad, because we miss him here, because this gentle man was taken from us in what should have been the prime of his earthly life. There are many in this church today who are twice the age of Edgar. Some, a few, are three times his age. So we *know* Edgar has gone from us before his time. That, indeed, is reason enough for sadness.

"An' we should study that for a moment an' look for a reason for it. In the same good book that tells us of the guarantee of Edgar Ballard's eternal life we also find some words in Ephesians we might heed today." His eyes looked down at the Bible. "It says: 'See then that you walk circumspectly, not as *fools* but as *wise*, redeeming the time, because the days are evil.' "

Smith looked up again, his head turning slowly as he looked over the entire crowd. "BE-CAUSE . . . THE . . . DAYS . . . ARE . . . E-VIL! . . . BE-CAUSE . . . THE . . . DEV-IL . . . WALKS . . . AMONG . . . US!"

He laughed then. "Now, I know that some of you think the devil has horns an' a fork-ed tail an' carries a pitchfork so we all may recognize him immediately. But friends, it's not that easy to recognize the devil. He's a smart ol' fellow, wearin' many disguises. The devil is in that bottle of rotten moonshine! The devil is in the swishin' skirt of the loose woman an' in the lustin' heart of the man who covets her!"

The pastor sucked in a deep breath. "An' the devil, brothers an' sisters, can be in the guise of the stranger, of the intruder into our community! Oh, Lord . . . HOW . . . DE-VI-OUS . . . ARE . . . THE . . . WAYS . . . OF . . . THE . . . DEV-IL! Our brother Eddie gave his life in a brave act. A sacrificin', unselfish act, not recognizin', in his simple goodness, that the devil was in the . . . DIS-GUISE . . . OF . . . THE . . . STRANGER . . . IN . . . OUR . . . MIDST!"

The preacher stared intently at Casey.

"Damn!" Charlie Sams breathed.

Casey said nothing, meeting Reverend Smith's stare without a blink. But he could feel the concentrated hate in the eyes of the others burning into his neck.

"Maybe God is testin' us when he allows such intruders to walk among us." He looked away from Casey then, smiling slightly. "Yes, friends, God *is* testin' us . . . AND WE SHALL PRE-VAIL . . . THROUGH . . . OUR . . . FAITH!"

"Amen!" Mrs. Smith shrieked in Casey's ear, causing him to flinch.

"Those who attend the Holiness Church regularly," the pastor went on, "those who are the *strength* of this church, know our faith has often been tested in the past. Now we want the others here this mornin', friends *and* intruders" (he spread wide his skinny arms) "to know the *certainty* of that faith."

Smith strode to a large cardboard box placed next to the piano, opening the lid and reaching in. When he withdrew his hands he held high two large snakes, their yellowish scales marked with broad crossbands of brown and black. He had them grasped firmly just behind the heads and their bodies writhed wildly, setting off the dread buzzing sound of the rattles at the ends of their tails.

There was screams in the audience as several other members of the church rushed forward to dip into the box and come out with more snakes. One grossly fat woman, rapture reflected on her face, draped a huge serpent around her neck.

"Rattlesnakes?" Casey asked in disbelief.

"You're damned right!" editor Sams answered, coming to his feet. "And I'm getting you the hell out of here!" He grasped Casey's arm.

"Sit down," Ballard ordered, "I want to see this."

Chuckling, old Herman Armstrong leaned over to Casey. "Don't let it worry ya, Mistah Ballard, them nuts milked all the snakes 'fore they brought 'em in here. Ain't 'nuff venom in 'em to kill a mouse. It's jest a show."

The pastor's wife glared at the cemetery superintendent.

"THESE ARE VIPERS OF THE DEVIL!" the minister thundered. "DEADLY TO MEN! BUT NOT TO MEN OF FAITH IN THE LORD JEE-SUS . . . FOR . . . HE . . . IS . . . OUR . . . PROTECTOR!" He held the head of one of the snakes directly in front of his face, sticking out his tongue. The flicking forked tongue of the snake touched the pastor's.

There were more screams.

Armstrong whooped, "Ain't thet a caution, Mistah Ballard?" He clapped his hands together in delight.

"Shut up, ya ol' heathen!" Missy Smith shouted at him.

The church was a bedlam and Reverend Smith was barely heard, even though he was bellowing. "THERE ARE DOUBTERS OF THE FAITH HERE THIS MORNING! I CAN SEE THEM ALL AROUND ME!"

The cemetery superintendent jumped to his feet, waving his arms. "Ya got that right, ya shameless charlatan!"

Sweat poured down Smith's face as he whirled around with the snakes, showing them to all corners of the church. "NO HARM CAN COME TO THE FAITHFUL!" His eyes were opened wider than seemed possible, bugging out it appeared. A kind of madness had seized him.

"AN' YOU, CASEY BALLARD . . ." He strode to the edge of the platform. "ARE YOU A DOUBTER OF THE FAITH?!"

Casey, struggling to keep his composure, simply shrugged.

Without warning then, Smith hurled one of the snakes into Casey's lap. The shock of it delayed his reaction for a split second and he felt a sharp pain in his right hand. Leaping to his feet, he knocked the snake away from him.

There was a shot, exploding the rattler's head.

Ballard sank down on the bench, staring at two tiny pinholes in the back of his hand, pinholes with faint droplets of blood.

"Jesus Christ, you've been bitten!" Charlie cried.

"Yeah, I guess so." That's a brilliant answer, he thought.

Sheriff Foster, the gun he had used to kill the snake still in his hand, was shouting orders. "Everybody get back! This man's been hurt." He looked around for his deputy. "Randy! Get everybody the hell out of here!" He whirled to the people on the platform, waving the gun at them. "And you, you crazy fools, put those snakes away!"

Dr. Amos Willson, wearing his American Legion cap, pushed his way through the crowd. Seeing the wound on Casey's hand, he hurriedly undid his tie, using it to fashion a tourniquet, binding it around Ballard's forearm just below the elbow. A pocketknife was produced. "This ain't gonna be sterile, but—"

"Ah'll jest bet, Doc," Herman Armstrong said, "thet there weren't no venom in them snakes."

"Ah don't *know* thet," Willson reacted angrily, "do you?"

"Nope," the old man admitted.

Holding Casey's hand firmly in his own, the doctor expertly made short crossed cuts at the point of both punctures, sucking at them, spitting the blood (and maybe the extracted venom) on the floor. He did that several times.

Finally, he looked up to a young boy who had been watching intently. "Ya know which is mah car out there, son?"

"Yeah, Doc."

"Then go fetch mah medical bag. Black. On the front passenger's seat."

The youngster raced away.

"Got some antivenin in mah bag," Amos explained to Casey. "Ain't a doctor in these hills thet don't carry it. Use it a lot, too."

When the boy returned with the bag, Dr. Willson gave Casey a shot and put a small bandage on the hand. The tourniquet was released. "Ah want ya t' rest today, Mistah Ballard. No violent exercise. An' no whiskey, no alcoholic stimulant o' any kind. Ah think you'll be okay."

"Thanks, Doc."

"Well, this is somethin' Ah never expected to be doin' today." He looked around the nearly empty church. "Goddamned fools," he muttered.

Terry Foster, who had been absent during the treatment, came up to them now. "I finally got Smith to admit that the snakes had been milked of venom earlier this morning."

"See, Doc, what'd Ah tell ya," Armstrong said proudly.

"Yeah, Herman," Willson sighed, "ya told me."

"Do you want to file charges, Ballard?" the sheriff asked.

"Do I have to? You were an eyewitness."

"I was, yes," Foster said. "But, under the circumstances, what I saw was . . . well, maybe harassment, huh?"

"You're the lawman," Casey countered sarcastically.

The sheriff's face flushed. "Goddamnit, do you want to file charges or not?!"

"No," Ballard said slowly, "I just don't have the stomach for screwing around with the sheriff's office anymore."

Terry turned angrily and started out of the church.

Casey began to chuckle.

"What the hell's so funny?" Charlie Sams wanted to know.

"I was just remembering that when my father would take me to the Lincoln Park Zoo in Chicago I'd stay a mile away from the reptile house. I always hated snakes."

17

i   Sheriff Foster sensed a kind of madness in it all, a madness threatening to tear apart his carefully structured world.

In his verbally muscular interrogation of the Reverend Ashley Smith about the incomprehensible rattlesnake incident Terry had learned it had been done at the insistence of Deputy Randy Apple. He found it hard to believe what the pastor was telling him.

"Look," the sheriff had shouted at the gaunt man of God, "I *know* my deputy! It doesn't make sense for him to go off half-cocked on his own."

"I swear to you on the Holy Book, Randy came to me this mornin' an' strongly urged me to include the faith ceremony in the memorial services."

"Why in the hell would he do that?"

"He pointed out that this Ballard was a disruptive influence in our community," the pastor answered, "somethin' I already knew, of course, in light of poor Edgar's death."

"Randy told you to throw the snake at Ballard?"

"Yes. I assumed he meant to frighten him, to demonstrate to him that he wasn't welcome here. I could see the value of such a course, even though we barely had time to extract the venom."

"Did you tell Randy you were going to do that?"

"What?"

"Milk the snakes, for Christ sake!"

"Please, Sheriff, your language—this is a house of God."

"Don't give me that crap, Ashley," Foster railed at him. "Just answer the question: did you tell Randy you were going to milk the snakes?!"

"Uh . . . no," he replied sheepishly. "It's not something we . . . uh . . . reveal outside our own circle of faith."

"So as far as Randy was concerned, the snakes were deadly?"

Reverend Smith hesitated. "Yes, I suppose so."

"Then Randy must have believed that if the snake struck Ballard, Ballard would die!"

The minister's face flushed. "You mean he—"

"Exactly! He was asking you to *kill* Ballard for him!"

"Oh, sweet Jee-sus! That was never the intention, Sheriff, you've got to believe that!"

Foster sighed. "I do. But let me tell you this: if I ever hear again of you staging that snake thing, I'll have you all in jail."

Now, as the sheriff left the church, his mind raced through a series of disconcerting developments. *Where was Trixie? Where was Ballard hiding her? And why hasn't Yolanda surfaced? And Randy— what gave him the balls to pull such a stupid stunt?*

What he found outside the church didn't make him feel any better. The rain was still coming down—hard—and the parking lot was a quagmire, an insane circus of mired cars and trucks, with backs being strained to free them, and even the four-wheel-drive vehicles having difficulty moving.

His own squad car sat in six inches of mud.

"Hey!" he yelled, "I need some help over here!"

No one paid any attention to him.

Slogging through the goo, cursing with every difficult step, he jerked open the door of the police car, flipping the switch

238

to activate the siren. Its screaming wail turned all heads in his direction.

"Bring that jeep over here!" he commanded. "I've got an emergency!"

With the jeep, and with sufficient manpower, and with the passage of ten minutes, the squad car was finally freed, and Terry drove too fast along the macadamed country road, the mud flying off his tires slapping loudly against the underside of the fenders.

He activated the radio. "This is Terry," he barked into the microphone, "where's Randy?"

"I don't know," the dispatcher answered. "Ain't heard from 'im since he went out to the church."

"Find him. Real fast-like."

He listened as the call went out for his deputy and the two other squad cars on duty at that time reported negatively.

"He don't answer," the dispatcher reported. "Mebbe he's home. Want me to raise 'im on the phone?"

"No, no," Foster said. "I'll check that out myself."

He was frustrated, wildly angry. He turned the siren on, tromping on the accelerator, skidding into the tight turns of the narrow road. In just minutes he was coming into Hillside, where he silenced the siren and brought his speed under control. He drew several deep breaths, also trying to control the anger.

At Apple's apartment house, where Randy's car was parked by the curb, the sheriff changed his boots, tossing the mud-caked ones into the trunk.

Foster entered the building, climbing the stairs to the second floor, where he pounded on the door of 2-B.

"Yeah . . . who's there?" a voice called out.

"Terry."

"Oh . . . just a minute."

Foster could hear some scurrying about inside the apartment. *He's hiding that new broad of his.* And then the door was opened.

"Terry," Randy grinned, "that was a damned mess out there, wasn't it?"

"Hmmm." Foster looked around the tiny living room, noting the door to the bedroom was tightly closed. "Yeah," he said, dropping onto the sofa and propping his feet on the coffee table, "a damned mess. And I want to know, with no shit, what the hell prompted you to have the pastor stage that snake bit!"

"Jesus, Terry, I don't know what you're talking about."

The sheriff sighed deeply. "I don't have the patience this morning to play games with you. Smith told me what happened. And I want to know why?"

"Yeah . . . okay . . ." Deputy Apple shrugged. "I *suggested* he might want to bring out the snakes. You know, just to liven things up a bit." He laughed. "It did, didn't it?"

"It did," Foster agreed stonily. "And I suppose you just wanted to scare Ballard a bit?"

"Scare him? Yeah, something like that."

"Who put you up to it?"

"What?"

"Are you deaf?" The anger returned. "I asked, who put you up to it?!"

Randy waited a few seconds before answering. "I don't know what you're getting at, Terry. I thought you wanted Ballard out of the way."

"Out of the way? A moment ago you said it was just to scare him."

"What is this?" Apple was angry now, too. "Why are you suddenly so concerned about Ballard? He's dead! And we can get things back to normal again. Isn't that what you wanted, what you always wanted ever since that sonofabitch started poking his nose into everything?!"

"Let me understand something," the sheriff said in even tones. "Who's running this department?"

"Why . . . you are, of course."

"And did I ask you to kill Ballard?"

"Uh . . . no, but—"

"Then *who* did?!"

"I don't know what you want me to say," Randy protested. He was frightened now, the anger sublimated to fear. Something had gone wrong, but he didn't know what it was.

Foster shook his head in disgust. "I can't believe I have a deputy who's so stupid! You really thought that snake was going to kill?"

"It was a timber rattler, for Christ sake."

"And it never occurred to you that phony preacher might milk the venom before going into his act?"

Apple's mouth gaped.

"Well, that's what he did," the sheriff told him. "And if you hadn't beat it out of there so fast you'd know that Ballard *isn't* dead. At worst, he's a little uncomfortable."

The deputy stayed silent.

"So Randy, you're not only stupid, you're also a liar! Who put you up to it?! I want to know right now!"

The color went out of the subordinate's face. "Well . . . it was Ralston . . ."

Foster wasn't surprised by the admission.

"And he said he wanted Ballard out of the way. You know Ralston. He demanded it! And I thought the snake—"

"You're on his payroll?"

Randy nodded disconsolately.

"Since when?"

"Just for a couple of days. Ever since Yolanda—" He stopped abruptly.

It all came clear to Sheriff Foster in that instant. Slowly, he pulled himself to his feet, turning to stare at the closed bedroom door. "YOLANDA!" he bellowed.

The door opened and the girl stepped into the living room, quaking. She wore only a pair of scant panties and a lacy bra.

"Well, well," Terry grinned, "the two of you, huh?"

"You've got to understand the way it was, Terry," Apple said. "Yolanda showed up at old man Ralston's place, and told him all kinds of stories about you, and Ralston offered me money to take her off his hands. And I figured—why not? Hell, you were making all the bread," the words were turning defiant, "and I was doing all the muscle work. And I thought that if the state cops push too hard on that Rudy Pitts thing, I'd need some protection. You might be in the clear, but it was going to be my ass! So Ralston said he could fix it so I—"

"So you wouldn't have to take the fall," Foster finished the sentence.

"Yeah."

"You're *doubly* stupid! Elmo Ralston's not the power in this county—I am! Do you hear me? I AM!"

"Maybe you are and maybe you aren't. But I'm not going to be your patsy if the state cops come in here! What I did was under orders from you, and if I go down, so do you!"

"As simple as that, eh?"

"As simple as that!" the deputy said coldly.

Foster sighed. "Oh, my, Randy, I can't believe how stupid you are." He drew his gun.

Yolanda screamed.

But the deputy kept his composure. "You're not going to kill us, Terry. Because if you did, you'd be the prime suspect. And Ralston would make sure the authorities figured it that way."

"You know, you're right for the first time today," Foster said easily. "If you could stick around for a while there might be hope for you." He gestured with his weapon. "Into the bedroom!"

The girl began to weep.

"Move!" the sheriff ordered.

Yolanda scurried into the bedroom and Apple followed more slowly. He was prodded with Foster's gun.

"You're not going to do it, Terry."

Foster didn't answer him. In the bedroom, he took the deputy's gun from the holster lying on the dresser, and put his own away. "Undress," he said.

"Now wait a minute, Terry."

"Take your clothes off, all of them!"

Apple knew he had overplayed his hand. "Terry, for God's sake, you don't want to do this!"

"Just shut up!" He put the pistol against Randy's temple. "Do it now!"

The deputy began to unbutton his shirt.

Terry glanced at Yolanda. "You, too, baby."

Her hands were shaking so much she couldn't undo the

fastener on her bra, and Foster reached over with his free hand and ripped it off her. "Torn in a moment of passion," he said, chuckling. He watched as Yolanda stepped out of her panties, tears streaming down her pretty face. *What a waste!*

In a few moments, Apple also stood naked.

"Into the bed," he said, gesturing with the gun.

"Terry," the deputy pleaded, "don't! I promise you I won't say anything!"

"Into the bed. I want you together."

"I'll take the fall!" Randy screamed in anguish.

"You have one second to get into the bed!"

Unable to think of anything else to do, Apple got into bed with the hysterical Yolanda.

"Now, hold her."

Apple obeyed again. As the sheriff came close to them, he muttered weakly, "Sweet Jesus, Terry, don't do this."

The trigger was squeezed, the bullet ripping through Yolanda's throat diagonally, tearing away part of her jaw, the blood spattering the wallpaper.

"Lover's quarrel," Terry Foster breathed, pulling the trigger once more. A gaping hole appeared in Deputy Apple's right temple, exposing the brain.

Quickly, the sheriff wiped the gun on the sheet and holding it carefully in the corner of the sheet, pressed it into Randy's dead hand, disgusted by the rank odor of evacuated bowels. Hurriedly, the left the apartment, racing down the flight of stairs to the street. He saw no one. He drove away at moderate speed.

Two minutes later the police radio came to life: "Dispatcher to sheriff!"

"This is the sheriff," Foster answered easily.

"There's a report of gunshots at the Third Street Apartments."

"I'm way out on I-40," Terry reported. "Send someone else. No, wait . . . isn't that Randy's place?"

"Yeah."

"Give him a call. Maybe he's there. Hell . . . I'll bet he's already on it."

"Didn't you go see him, Sheriff?"

"No, Roy," the lie came easily, "I decided it wasn't really important."

"Okay, Terry."

"Keep me informed, huh?"

"Sure thing."

"And Roy—"

"Yeah?"

"I'm maybe . . . oh . . . twenty, twenty-five minutes away if you really need me."

ii   News of the deaths of Randy Apple and Yolanda Young had a vigorous birth on that early Sunday afternoon. Like the squalls of a newborn infant it commanded the attention of all who heard it. And it was relayed swiftly. The circumstances of the incident were just too compelling, too scandalous, not to be shared.

Banker Zeb Alderman heard of it in a telephone call from a gossipy woman depositor. He needed to share it, too, rushing to the Ralston mansion where he found his brother-in-law watching an Atlantic Coast Conference basketball game on television. The fortunes of North Carolina State and Virginia seemed of little consequence in the light of Zeb's news.

Elmo Ralston, Jr., moaned softly. "Oh, Christ . . . isn't it ever going to end?"

"Ah jest hope Terry doesn't find out 'bout our . . . well, our li'l deal with Apple."

The color drained from Elmo's face. "I'm afraid he has already."

"What?"

"You see, Zeb," the man in the wheelchair sighed, "I took it upon myself to instruct the deputy to . . ." He confessed to Alderman the task he had given to Randy Apple to eliminate Casey Ballard from their midst.

"Ya stupid ass!"

244

"Yes, I have been," Ralston admitted. "I suppose you heard about the debacle at the Holiness Church this morning?"

"Yeah." The banker's eyes opened wide. "Ya mean thet was Apple's doin'?!"

"Sadly, I'm sure it was."

"Jesus Christ, ev'ry kid over the age o' ten in the county knows 'bout them snakes being milked! There was no way Apple was gonna carry it off!"

"Sadly, I suppose we overestimated the intelligence of Deputy Apple."

"*You* did the overestimatin'," Zeb roared. "Ah didn't have a damned thing t' do with it!"

"No, you didn't," Ralston said quietly, "but do you think Sheriff Foster is going to be that . . . uh . . . discriminating?" We have to devise some protection before Terry figures it out."

"Damn you!"

"Now Zeb, control your emotions. We haven't played our last card." He wheeled himself to a small end-table, looked up a telephone number in an address book there, and dialed it. "I think the state police commissioner might be interested in the situation here."

Someone answered the telephone.

"Fred, Elmo Ralston here. I apologize for bothering you on a Sunday afternoon . . ." He listened. "Yes, thank you, I'm quite well. But, in a community sense, we have a rather distressing matter here. Our law enforcement setup seems to have broken down . . ." Elmo talked for several minutes.

And then he listened again.

"Well, I certainly do appreciate that, Fred. What's the name of that young man again?" He printed a name on a notepad by the phone: ROBERT BUCKHORN. "Fine. You have him contact us here and he'll have our utmost cooperation."

iii   "I can't really explain it all," State Police Investigator Buckhorn was reporting, "but there's been a complete turnaround in attitude about dealing with Mountain County." He was seated in the den of the home of publisher Layton Sams, speaking to the elder Sams, his son Charlie, and Casey Ballard. "I've been put in charge of a special detail to supersede the established law enforcement here and, in the commissioner's words, to clean up the county. Manpower is on the way from Knoxville, Nashville, and Memphis."

"That's good news," Layton said.

"And I've asked to see you gentlemen," Buckhorn went on, "because I need some quick advice. I've been instructed to contact Mr. Elmo Ralston, Jr., and Mr. Zebulon Alderman for assistance. It was those two gentlemen who prevailed on . . . uh . . . higher authority to take this action. Frankly, I'd like to know why before I see them. I thought you three could give me the background I need."

"It's simple," Layton said, "they've been substantial contributors in the right political circles for years. They *do* have influence."

"And, yet," the state police investigator said, frowning, "you, Mr. Ballard, have already given me the impression that Mr. Ralston and Mr. Alderman are somehow allied to the sheriff's office."

Casey smiled wanly. "It's a sure thing in my book, but hard, admissible-in-court evidence—?" He shrugged.

Layton interjected, "It's been going on for years, an unholy binding of the Ralstons and the Sheriffs Foster." He launched into several of his lurid stories about the Fosters and their support by the county's number-one family. When it threatened to grow into a protracted monologue, Buckhorn cut him off.

"Thank you, Mr. Sams, your point has been made." He looked at his watch. "My Knoxville troopers will be here within the half hour. I want to see Ralston and Alderman before that time." He got to his feet, looking directly at Casey. "Mr. Ballard, I have the authority to engage whoever is needed to expedite this operation. In light of your experience, I'd like to have you—"

Casey, although exhilarated by the prospect of concluding one more case, objected: "I'll give you whatever help I can in the next forty-eight hours, Buckhorn. But after that, my personal matters must take priority." He saw Rosalie's face in his mind's-eye once more.

"I accept whatever limitation you think you need to impose, but I am going to need you in the initial stages."

"Agreed," Casey said.

Robert Buckhorn left the Sams home then after directing Ballard to meet him in an hour at the Hillside Inn.

"A tough nut," Casey commented to the newspapermen when Buckhorn closed the door behind him.

"Will there be violence, Mr. Ballard?" Layton asked.

"I suspect Buckhorn will put the lid on quickly and decisively. Of course, Terry will be unpredictable." He grimaced. "If he resists, your history of Mountain County, Layton, is going to have another bloody chapter."

The telephone rang and Layton answered it. A smile came to his face. "Darling, how nice to hear from you!"

The smile quickly turned to a frown. "What?!"

He listened. "How long ago was that?"

Again, he listened. "Well, darling, don't be so upset. I'm sure she'll be found quickly. Safe and sound, I'll bet. Notify the police and we'll watch for her here."

He hung up the phone. "Trixie has run away from Nashville."

Casey groaned.

"My daughter and her husband went out to dinner, taking Mrs. Pitts with them," Layton explained. "Trixie stayed behind, telling them she wasn't feeling well. When they returned, she was gone."

"She'll come back here," Ballard insisted.

"I believe so, too," the publisher said. "But God knows what could happen to her on the way."

"She's so naive," Charlie added.

"But not stupid." Casey thought for a moment. "She's got only one place to go, Charlie. I suggest you go out to K.C.'s Place and just park yourself there. When she shows up, get her the hell out of there again."

"Yes," Layton said. "And bring the poor child here. This will be the safest place for her for the next day or two."

iv   Before the clock at the Mountain County Courthouse could chime midnight on that Sunday, State Police Investigator Robert Buckhorn's efficient paramilitary operation had seized control of the county's law enforcement apparatus.

It had gone almost too smoothly. They had marched into the sheriff's headquarters—riot guns in hand, flak jackets making their uniforms appear bulky—and had taken over. A young state's attorney with the contingent had read the court authorizations for the takeover to the dispatcher and two deputies found in the office. Three other deputies patrolling in squad cars were called in and likewise stripped of their authority. All were disarmed and detained. Two off-duty deputies were apprehended at their homes, also disarmed, and taken with the others to the Hillside Inn, where they were placed in a kind of "house arrest" in guarded hotel rooms. Buckhorn had deemed the small county lockup as being inadequate to his needs.

Casey had been impressed by Buckhorn's calm, authoritarian manner. There were three lieutenants and a captain in the special squad, all outranking Buckhorn under normal circumstances. Yet Buckhorn was clearly in charge.

By midnight then, the sheriff's radio was being operated by a state trooper. A state trooper answered the telephone at the sheriff's office. And three two-man state police cars were engaged in the normal overnight patrol of Mountain County.

There was only one problem: Sheriff Terry Foster was not among those housed at the inn. As the courthouse clock tolled the first note of midnight, Terry was at large, the subject of an all-points search.

18

i   The rain had stopped an hour before Casey Ballard awakened on Monday morning. But the day wasn't bright and clear. The sun remained hidden behind a gray-green canopy of heavy clouds. Monday could only be called somber.

As Casey showered and dressed, he felt as if he was running a marathon, approaching "the wall," when his second wind would come. He was weary, no doubt of that, but he was certain now he was approaching the finish line. Maybe even as a winner. He was on a case again and he whistled gaily as he vigorously toweled himself off.

He checked with the state policeman acting as the dispatcher at the sheriff's office: Terry Foster still hadn't been apprehended. He called Charlie Sams at K.C.'s Place to learn that Trixie hadn't showed up during the night.

"Get any sleep?" Casey asked the editor.

"Some. A catnap or two on a damned overstuffed chair. I don't think it's ever been cleaned. It smells of all kinds of odors, for Christ sake."

"Do you want me to have Buckhorn relieve you for a few hours?"

"No," Charlie said firmly, "I want to stick it out."

Ballard went to breakfast then, ravenously hungry, polishing off a large country ham breakfast, and signing a state police chit for the meal. Buckhorn had thought of everything.

And then he was on the case. Before he had gone to bed, Investigator Buckhorn had assigned him to the apparent murder-suicide of Yolanda Young and Randy Apple. It was 7:30 when Casey drove to the Third Street Apartments, cordoned off now by the state police. Casey identified himself to a state cop, who lifted the rope and allowed the Chicagoan's car to be parked near the apartment building.

He entered, to be challenged again by a state trooper in the small foyer.

"I'm to see Lieutenant Richard Stefan," Casey said.

"Upstairs. Two-B."

Stefan, when Casey found him, was in plain clothes. Younger than Casey had imagined him. Tall, slim, blond, self-assured.

"What do you have?" Casey asked after introducing himself.

"Almost nothing, sir. The gun used belonged to Deputy Apple. There's a clear set of his prints on it."

"How clear?"

"Precisely clear, you might say," Lieutenant Stefan replied.

"Hmmm. Not smudged in any way?"

"No."

"And only one set of prints?"

"Yes."

"Indicating what, to you?"

"That the gun was placed in his hand after he was shot," Stefan said matter-of-factly.

Casey nodded agreement. "Any other prints here?"

"Lots of them. All belonging to Apple or to the dead girl."

"So whoever else might have been here was careful not to leave his prints behind."

"Or *her* prints," the state cop said.

Ballard's syebrows raised. "Her? Why do you say that?"

"Only because there are two genders," Stefan answered, grinning.

"Witnesses?"

"Well, there's the old lady who lives in 2-A. She was the one who reported the gunshots."

"But she didn't see anything, I'll bet."

"Nothing. She's . . . uh . . . taciturn, to say the least."

"Maybe I ought to try her." Casey started out of the room, Stefan following. "I think it's best if I see her alone, Lieutenant. What's her name?"

"Minnie . . . Minnie Fallow."

Casey chuckled. "F-a-l-l-o-w?"

"Yes."

"Maiden lady?"

"Christ, I never thought of that," the state cop laughed.

"Well, so much for humor," Casey shrugged, making his way the few feet to the apartment at the front of the building, rapping lightly on the door.

It was opened just a crack, two eyes glaring at him suspiciously. "Yeah?"

"Miss Fallow, I'm Casey *Ballard*," he stressed the last name, "and I'm helping the state police investigate the terrible thing that happened here."

"Ah told 'em ev'rythin' Ah know."

"Yes, I'm sure you did, but may I talk to you for a minute or two?"

Reluctantly, the door was opened to him and Casey entered apartment 2-A, moving nonchalantly to the curtained window and looking down on the activity below. "You have a nice view of the street from here."

"Yeah."

"Say, Miss Fallow," he said, turning from the window, "I wonder if you knew my grandfather, K.C. Ballard?"

"Yeah."

"He was quite a fellow, wasn't he? People are always telling me that I favor him somewhat."

The elderly woman studied him. "Yeah, ya do."

"Hmmm. This thing that happened here," he jerked a thumb toward the next-door apartment, "it really isn't a very nice thing for Mountain County, is it?"

"No," she answered hesitantly, still uncertain of his motives.

"Now that I'm one of you, so to speak," Casey pressed on, "I hate to see this kind of thing . . . well, spoil Mountain County. It's such a beautiful place."

"Yeah." The muscles in her stern face relaxed.

"Now, Miss Fallow, would you mind telling me what you did after you reported the gunshots to the sheriff's office?"

"Well, Ah—" She stopped.

"Did you open the door and look out into the hall, perhaps?"

"No, Ah was too scared."

"Maybe you went over to the window and looked outside."

"Mebbe."

"Did you, Miss Fallow?" he asked, a kindly tone in his voice.

"Yeah, Ah guess Ah did."

"Uh huh. And what did you see?"

"Well . . . Ah saw Randy's car out there," the woman said slowly, "an' 'nother police car, too."

"Oh? Then did you see somebody come out of the building and drive the second police car away?"

She hesitated once more. Then: "Yeah."

"Someone you recognized, perhaps?"

"No, Ah don't think so."

"Do you know Sheriff Foster?"

"Uh . . . yeah."

"Was it Sheriff Foster you saw coming out of the building and driving that second police car away?" Casey was trying not to be too insistent.

"Ah ain't sure."

"Miss Fallow," Ballard sighed, "I know this is difficult for you, but would you mind telling me whether you're afraid of Sheriff Foster?"

She went to a chair, sinking it into it, her eyes concentrated on her hands. They were clasped together so hard the knuckles were white.

Finally, she looked up at him, her eyes on his. "Ah'm scared to death of 'im!"

"I can understand that. But, Miss Fallow, you should know that Sheriff Foster has been relieved of his duties. And so have his deputies. The state police are in charge here now and Terry Foster can't hurt anyone anymore."

He paused, waiting for his announcement to sink in.

"If it was the sheriff you saw driving that second police car away, you really ought to tell me."

The Fallow woman was silent for a long time. "Yeah," she said in a whisper, "it were Terry."

"You're certain of that?"

"It were Terry," she insisted. "Jest a li'l bit aftah Ah heard the shots. Ah 'member wonderin' what terrible thing he done."

"Thank you, Miss Fallow. Maybe later, if we need it, you'll be willing to repeat your story on a tape recorder?"

"If ya need it to git Terry," there was defiance in her voice now, "Ah'll do it."

Moments later, the police broadcast was putting out an all-points bulletin for the arrest of Terry Foster for the double murder. *The suspect must be presumed to be armed and dangerous and must be approached with extreme caution.*

ii   As the day lengthened, the hours moving it into late afternoon, Terry Foster remained at large. But the dismantling of the power of the sheriff proceeded apace. Several more state lawyers arrived in Mountain County to assist in the monumental task of poring through the sheriff's files to piece together the criminal conspiracy Foster had headed.

"I can't believe what we're finding," Robert Buckhorn was telling Casey in the Hillside Inn restaurant, where they met for the first meal since breakfast. "The arrogance of these people simply astounds me. I mean, they operated for so many years without regard for law that . . . well, they saw nothing wrong in documenting it. It's all there in the files. My God, Ballard, there are going to be hundreds of indictments—literally hundreds! Reaching far down into the community."

"Ralston and Alderman?"

"Especially those two." Buckhorn laughed. "They had the sheriff on their payroll. And do you know how they paid him? With Ralston Company checks, for God sake! And Foster actually made photocopies of the checks and kept them in his files! Can you believe that?"

"You said it right. It was arrogance." Casey took a deep breath. "Robert, you're going to find one file in there—and it's going to seem insignificant in the light of today—about the murder of one King David Ballard. The case file points the finger of guilt at a young man, a brother of King David, named Abel Ballard. He was my father."

Buckhorn stared at him in disbelief.

"It all happened in '33 and the file is a complete phony, trumped up by Sheriff Ben Foster and Elmo Ralston, Sr., the current Ralston's father. It was done to hide the fact that King David was killed by the Ralston daughter, Alice, later to become the wife of Zeb Alderman."

"This is a fantasyland," Buckhorn commented.

"Somewhat. Alice Ralston Alderman is still living, in a private mental institution in Georgia, where she's dying of Alzheimer's. For what it's worth, I can prove Alice was the murderer. So when your people get to that file—and I realize it may be weeks before they do—I want the opportunity to give you what I've got. I just want to clear my father's name."

"Sure thing, Ballard."

Casey clapped his hands together, "What's next?"

"K.C.'s Place," the state policeman announced. "It seems to be the biggest cancer in Mountain County and Daniel Staley ought to be there, right?"

"Yes."

"And we already have a warrant for his arrest in the assault of Rudy Pitts."

"Do you know I'm the owner of that place?"

"I do. You inherited it just recently, didn't you?"

"Yes." Ballard hesitated for a moment. "I've been thinking, Robert, that when we go out there I want to padlock the place. Close it down, once and for all. Clean it out, as it were. Do you have sufficient manpower to do that?"

"Certainly. Since it appears I'm going to be administering the law here for some months to come, I'd rather that it be padlocked."

"Good." Casey sighed. "And once that's done, Robert, I'm going home. Tomorrow morning, I'd hope."

iii   Terry Foster lounged insolently in Lulubelle Staley's huge contour chair, a pistol held loosely in his hand, resting on his lap. He smiled as he gazed around the garishly decorated room.

"Well, I never thought I'd spend my last hours," he said, "in this whore's nest."

"Ya crazy sonofabitch," the obese madam railed at him, "what are ya gonna do with us?"

"I'm going to use you for what might be my last bargaining chips," Foster snarled. "And you know, I think I lucked out when I decided to come here. I figured you might make a half-decent hostage, but when I found little Miss Dummy here, too . . ." He pointed the gun carelessly toward the bed, where Trixie huddled now, weeping. "Well, that was just the icing on the cake.

"I don't want you to feel badly about this, Lulu, but with just you as a hole card, I wasn't in too strong a position. I mean, I don't think any of those state cops would worry about you being killed if they decided to storm this room. But with that sweet little package here, they're going to think twice."

Terry pushed himself up from the chair, going to the bed

and staring down at Trixie. He put his face close to hers; she edged away from him in terror. "You couldn't stay away from *home*, could you, darling?"

She glared her hate at him.

"Now, if Lulubelle would just promise not to make a dash for the door, prompting me to put a bullet in her flab, I'd really like to have you entertain me for a time."

The deaf mute whore understood his intentions and she spat at him.

"Some learned gentleman once figured out that hate was akin to love, and I suspect that's true. You're a great piece of ass, Trixie, just because you hate me so much."

Lulubelle tried to distract him. "Mah boys are gonna be wonderin' where Ah am."

Foster whirled on her angrily, leveling the weapon at her, sighting over it. "And the first sonofabitch who tries to come through that door—POW!" He waved the gun at her. "Get in that chair, Lulubelle."

She obeyed, dropping her bulk heavily. The sheriff rummaged through several drawers in her dresser before finding a pair of nylon hose. With them he tied her down to the arms of the chair.

"Now, my dear," he was laughing as he turned his attention to Trixie once more, "as much as I'd like to accommodate you fully I don't think it would be wise to place myself in that . . . uh . . . compromising position."

She edged farther away from him until she was trapped with her back against the high headboard of the bed.

"Given our peculiar circumstances, then," he went on, grinning wildly, "I think I'll just have to settle for a one-way satisfaction. I apologize for that, but—" With his left hand he zipped open his fly.

Trixie was cringing, weeping profusely.

Foster placed the gun against the middle of her forehead, pressing the cold steel hard into her soft facial flesh, hurting her.

"*Now*, Miss Dummy!" He spat the words. "Right this damned minute!"

iv   Twilight was segueing into darkness as what reminded Casey of a well-rehearsed military exercise began on the graveled parking lot at the base of the knoll at K.C.'s Place. A dozen police cars pulled into the lot, followed by a bus carrying twenty other troopers. There was an equipment van, too. Quickly, the men poured out of them, going immediately to their assigned locations. Some raced up the long wooden stairway to the level of the Victorian house, surrounding it, riot guns at the ready. Technicians unloaded huge klieg lights, placing them at strategic locations; power lines were uncoiled from the lights and strung to a wheeled gasoline generator that was activated.

Casey, Buckhorn, and four fully armed troopers went up on the porch of the house, positioning themselves in front of the door. By design, four other similarly armed state policemen were ready at the rear door. Buckhorn looked at his watch, nodding in satisfaction. Only a few minutes had gone by. He stuck a steel whistle between his lips, blowing it.

Instantly, the klieg lights came on, making the exterior of the house as bright as midafternoon. Simultaneously, the troopers battered through the door, Casey and Buckhorn following them. Inside the parlor, the whores screamed.

"THIS IS THE TENNESSEE STATE POLICE," Buckhorn bellowed through a bullhorn. "Everyone in this house is temporarily under arrest! Proceed with your arms raised over your heads through the door onto the porch, where other officers will ask you to identify yourself. Anyone on the premises innocently will be immediately released. QUICKLY NOW!"

Newspaper editor Charlie Sams came up to them. "Jesus, what an operation!"

"Trixie?" Casey asked.

"I haven't seen her."

There was a new flurry of activity as the troopers who had come in through the rear door herded the patrons of the bar and the gaming rooms into the parlor, the Staley boys among them. Daniel, Birch, and Chester were cut out from the rest and handcuffed.

"Where's Alvin?" Casey asked.

They stared at him sullenly.

"And Lulubelle?"

Once again there was no answer. Buckhorn gestured and Lulubelle's sons were hustled out onto the porch.

"Any others unaccounted for?" the state police investigator wanted to know.

"Not that I'm aware of," Ballard replied.

"All right, you men," Buckhorn ordered, "search the entire house. Every room, closet, cranny. I don't want anyone left in here."

As two of the men started up the stairs, Lulubelle appeared on the second floor landing, the bulk of her partially hiding Sheriff Foster and Trixie, on whom he had a hold with his left hand. Terry waved his gun in the air.

"Okay, you sonofabitches," he shouted, "I'm coming down and out! Any funny moves and these two whores get it!"

One of the troopers halfway up the stairs took a half step forward.

Foster fired without further warning, striking the state policeman in the chest. He tumbled backwards down the steps, crashing in a heap in the parlor.

"Easy men," Buckhorn ordered quietly. To Terry: "I'm moving over to the bottom of the stairs, Foster, to check on my officer."

"You don't have to," the sheriff laughed. "I can guarantee you he's dead! Now, listen to me. I'm coming down! And I'm going out that door and down those stairs to parking lot and I'm taking a car. Anyone who makes a move toward me is dead! I don't miss! And I'll kill these women, too!"

He moved toward the top step, shoving Trixie in front of him.

"You women," Buckhorn yelled, "drop down!"

Lulubelle hurled herself to the floor with a thud. Trixie though stood there, confused, her eyes wide in fright.

"Drop down!"

It all happened at once. *"She can't hear you!"* Casey screamed. Foster fired again, striking the officer still on the stairs in the head, killing him instantly. Buckhorn's men cut loose with their automatic weapons. In a second only, or maybe two, it was over.

Sheriff Foster lay crumpled at the top of the stairs. Trixie's body slid down several steps. Casey rushed to her, cradling her in his arms, tears starting. He felt for a pulse. In vain.

Buckhorn came to him. "Oh, hell, Ballard, I'm sorry." His voice quavered. "But I couldn't sacrifice any more men. You must understand that." He was pleading.

"Yeah," Casey muttered, "I understand that." He could see his father again, bleeding on the floor of the Chicago currency exchange. And he could feel the nausea welling up in him.

"Buckhorn!" a state policeman shouted, "there's a helluva fire in the basement!"

"Is anyone down there?"

"I don't know. The whole damned basement is on fire!" With that, the first whiff of smoke appeared in the parlor.

Calmly, Robert Buckhorn directed the evacuation of the building. His men struggled to remove the bodies of their comrades and Foster and Lulubelle. Casey carried Trixie out into the glare of the klieg lights.

A state cop came up to him. "Can I help you, sir."

"No," Ballard said quietly, "I'll take care of her. She doesn't weigh much."

And he stood there, holding her body, sobbing out of control, as the state troopers tried to contain the fire with hand extinguishers from their squad cars. It was a futile effort. By the time the volunteer fire company from Hillside responded, with only the water they could carry in their pumper, the entire building was aflame.

He wondered why, but his brain recalled the words he had heard the mountain country preacher say only a day earlier:

He is the Mediator of the new covenant, by means of death, for the redemptions of the transgressions . . . that those who are called may receive promise of the eternal inheritance.

The words were so clear in his mind that Casey interpreted

them as a specific promise for the young girl he held in his arms.

"My God," he said aloud, "I don't even know your last name."

And the roof of K.C.'s Place collapsed with a roar, sending bright, burning sparks flying. New, brilliant, short-lived stars rising high into the cold night sky.

19

i   It was the next day. Two P.M. on Tuesday, January 29. Casey, wearier than any weary he had ever known before, deplaned from the Knoxville-originated flight at Chicago's O'-Hare Field.

As he came into the terminal he looked for her face. And suddenly, there it was in front of him. As beautiful as he had remembered it, her auburn hair framing it precisely, perfectly. She didn't rush into his arms as he walked up to her.

"Hiya, O'Hara," he said softly, smiling slightly.

"Hello," she replied, the face sober.

"See, I told you I'd be home tomorrow."

Rosalie made no comment.

"Have we suspended time as I asked?"

"I'm still thinking about that," Rosie said. "It's an experiment that takes a lot of thought."

They walked in silence to where she had parked their car. Rosie held up the car keys, jiggling them. "You want to drive?"

"Lord, no," he sighed. "Not unless you want us to end up against a lamppost somewhere."

They drove for several miles toward the center of Chicago without speaking. Not a word. Finally, Casey said: "I want to tell you about it, Rosie."

"All right."

"I want to tell you all of it, from start to finish. And then, I promise, Mountain County will never be mentioned again."

She nodded.

Ballard started slowly, carefully, trying to impart the detail of his odyssey. It was going to be a monologue, because it was clear Rosalie was just going to let him talk. It was three o'clock by the time they got to their apartment in Old Town, and they sat at the table in the little kitchen, where Rosie made a fresh pot of coffee. And the narration continued without interruption.

At five, he was finishing. "Before I left this morning, Buckhorn told me his arson people had determined the place had definitely been torched. By Alvin Staley, no doubt. They found the charred remains of a body in the basement, but there's no way to make a positive identification."

He reached across the table and took her hand. It was the first time they had touched since his return. "I'm sorry about the inheritance, O'Hara. There's nothing left but a burned down Victorian house and a few scraggly acres in the Tennessee hills. Not worth much anymore."

She shook her head negatively. "So?"

"If I had sold it when I had the chance we might have the beginning of a down-payment on an Arizona house."

Rosie was silent for a moment. "Did you love her, Casey."

"Who, Trixie?"

"Was there another one, for God sake?"

Casey was encouraged by that; Rosalie was beginning to banter with him again. "Love her? In a sense, I suppose I did. If anyone had really cared for her, had *really* loved her, she might have been something very special."

His wife looked into his face. Intently. "Casey?"

"What?"

"Why don't we suspend that time?"

"Sounds like a good idea."

They made love then, their passions as strong and as true as when they had first made love. And they slept. In each other's arms. It was about three A.M. when he tried to get out of bed without waking her. He failed at that.

"Where you going?" she asked sleepily.

"It's not very romantic, but I've got to pee."

She giggled.

When he returned to bed he was wide awake. Putting his hands behind his head, he stared at the ceiling. "You know, I've been thinking. I'm not an old man yet."

"I've just had a demonstration of that," she said.

"I can still do a job."

"Sure you can. And in a couple of weeks, you can start looking for one. And get out of the apartment for a few hours, so I can have my own time, like I always had."

"No, I mean as a cop . . ."

She sucked in a deep breath.

"They're going to be needing a sheriff in Mountain County and I thought—"

"Casey!"

"Just a thought, O'Hara," he chuckled. "Just an errant thought."

Here is an excerpt from
Bon Marché: From the Ashes,
the brand new novel by Chet Hagan,
available in hardcover from Tor Books.

Charles Dewey was dead.

The master of Nashville's Bon Marché stud had gone to meet his Maker and there were those among Dewey's friends who wondered how God would contend with him.

"The Lord will be glad to consign him to the Devil," one of his fellow horsemen suggested with only partial humor, "when He learns Charles intends to manage Heaven."

Dawn broke steaming hot at Chagres. It had rained during the night—in a deluge. Two had never seen such a volume of water pouring from the sky in such a short period of time. He and Weatherford had been soaked through; the natural tropical canopy under which they had tried to sleep gave them no protection at all. But there must have been some sleep because Dewey had the impression he had come awake as the hot tropical sun, burning orange, appeared suddenly in the sky.

He was miserable. There was no other word to describe his condition. He itched all over—a maddeningly persistent itch. And when he scratched through his clothing his fingers found hard swollen lumps. Quickly, he stripped off his shirt to find his torso covered with the lumps, most of them oozing secretions.

"My God, look at this!" Dewey said in alarm.

The Connecticut farmer nodded. "Chiggers," he commented flatly. He opened his own shirt to show Two similar eruptions on his flesh, some of them bloody welts from the scratching.

"What the devil are chiggers?"

"Damned if I know," Weatherford admitted, "but they're some kind of mites. Kin, I guess, to the ticks we have back home. But worse."

Two grimaced. "What can we do about them?"

"Nothing. I've been here long enough to know that. We just have to put up with them until we get the hell out of here."

Dewey groaned. Picking up his dripping blanket and his gear, he left the canopy to step out into the bright sun, spreading out his blanket and his shirt so they might dry. The sun worked no such miracle; the all-pervading humidity of the place kept them damp. Finally, Two put his shirt back on and it was immediately saturated with his sweat.

As he folded his blanket, he said, "Good Lord, there's mold growing on this!"

"Uh-huh. And it'll be on everything else in your bag, too. If you've got any metal in there, that'll have some kind of fungus on it, I'll bet."

Two was disheartened. "I don't even want to look."

Carrying their gear, they made their way to Juan Melendez's dock, to find four sullen-faced Cuña Indians, nearly naked, loading provisions into the big dugout boat.

"They don't seem to be bothered by chiggers," Dewey said quietly.

Weatherford laughed. "Maybe those critters don't like their stink."

Melendez appeared, carrying two rifles, double belts of ammunition crossed on his chest. "Good morning, señores," he called gaily.

"Are you expecting trouble?" Two asked, concerned about the weapons.

"No, no, Señor Dewey." The Spaniard grinned. "It's just that Melendez is a cautious man, especially when carrying such distinguished gentlemen as yourself. Put your bags in the cabin there"—Juan pointed aft in the boat where the canvas was stretched on the four poles—"and we'll get going just as soon as the others arrive."

"Others?"

"Sí. Six others—all seeking the *oro y plata.*" He grinned again, as if the search for gold and silver was a foolish thing. "You, Señor Dewey, do you expect to get rich in California?"

"I don't know, but I'm not after gold."

"Oh ... what then? Adventure? Or perhaps you're leaving behind a broken affair of the heart?"

Two resented the questioning and didn't answer. He went to the boat, stowing his baggage under one of the two benches on either side of the "cabin," thinking about how crowded it was going to be with eight adults in there.

At that point the others arrived and Dewey was surprised to see that one of them was a woman. Melendez made the introductions hurriedly. Four of the six were from New York City; Two didn't retain their names. The other two, husband and wife, were from Philadelphia: Mr. and Mrs. Amos Martin. The young woman's name was Julia.

"We're on our honeymoon," Martin volunteered. "And I must confess this isn't quite what we had in mind. Still—a new life awaits us."

Mrs. Martin said nothing, but Two noted that she appeared ill. Her face was flushed and her eyes were feverishly bright.

"Let's get aboard," Melendez ordered.

The passengers crowded under the canvas. Dewey and Weatherford sat on the bench opposite the newlywed couple. Next to Two was an obese gentleman (his name was Robert Mercer) who wheezed when he breathed, and who seemed to sweat even more than the others. The situation under the canvas was, in a phrase, extremely uncomfortable.

"How long to Panama City?" Two asked.

"Four . . . five days, señor."

Dewey was shocked. "But it's something less than seventy miles, isn't it?"

"*Sí.* But it's jungle, you know. And it's the distance we have to go on mules that slows it."

"Mules?"

"*Sí.* The river . . . it is not all . . . uh . . . hospitable."

The passenger from Tennessee groaned, cursing himself for not having asked those questions before. *But even if I had I'd still be going.*

The Indians poled the boat away from the dock into the swift current of the Chagres. The craft had no rudder and the poles were constantly in use.

Within minutes, it seemed, what was the civilization of the village of Chagres disappeared. The jungle closed around them, a green canopy so dense it enveloped them. No sense of direction remained; there was only the unrelieved green. Even the reference point of the sun was blotted out. It was as if they had drifted into a dream world—a nightmare world—where there was no north or south, no east or west. And, most frightening, no apparent escape.

Dewey had expected that the rain forest would be alive with sound. It wasn't. There was an eerie silence about it all; only the rush of water under the boat made a noise. And the steady buzz of the cloud of mosquitoes. But even those sounds were muffled. It got so that the occasional call of a bird—always far off—was welcome.

The silence infected the passengers; there was no conversation among the miserable, sweating travelers. They were like prisoners in an alien place. A hell, perhaps, where their accumulated past sins were being reckoned. And where the punishment for them was made more terrible because it was unknown.

272

Saturday, June 16, 1849—[Charles Dewey II wrote on the damp pages of his journal.] *We are now only a day, according to Melendez, from Panama City and the Pacific coast. All are exhausted, dirty, smelly. Several of the New Yorkers, Mr. Mercer notably, are afflicted with some sort of stomach ailment, unable to keep down any food. What remains of the provisions put aboard at Chagres is now crawling with maggots. Poor Mr. Weatherford, unable to control the scratching of his multiple insect stings, has now had many of them become infected; there are open sores on much of his body. Why the rest of us have escaped similar affliction, I do not know.*

Mrs. Martin has become desperately ill with swamp fever; I fear for her life. At Melendez's last jungle camp, he had some quinine cached and that seems to have helped her a bit. No one speaks of it in those terms, but she may not survive this terrible ordeal.

Melendez may be the most reprehensible man I have ever known. It has crossed my mind several times that he ought to be killed; God help me for such thoughts! But without the Spaniard, I know, we would never get out of this. Tomorrow morning we are to leave this final camp—in a dugout again after three days on mules—to cover the final miles to Panama City.

And then on to California, breathing the clean sea air of the Pacific!

Dewey had hoped to make a journal entry for every day of his trip, but it had not been possible. Several times he had simply fallen into an exhausted sleep before he could write. But it didn't matter; his mind would always retain the details of what he had been through.

273

He closed the journal now, but had no desire for sleep. It was only several hours till dawn and the thought that the new day would bring him to Panama City kept him awake. Blowing out the small oil lamp, he sat in the darkness of the vermin-infested shack Melendez called a camp, hearing the deep breathing of the others.

There was a slight moan, and a few whispered words of consolation, and he knew it was the Martins—those two young people trying to survive the first weeks of their marriage. He thought of Beth, and little Charles, and he wondered how he'd get them to California.

Certainly, they can't come this way!

It was late afternoon when the dugout was poled to a dock at Panama City. In the distance could be heard the booming surf of the Pacific Ocean crashing against the beaches. To Charles Dewey II it was a marvelously exhilarating sound. He stepped out of the dugout, turning to help Amos Martin lift his wife out of the boat. She was too weak to walk and they laid her gently on the dock.

"Find a carriage for this woman," Two demanded of Melendez. "She must be taken to a doctor immediately."

The Spaniard shrugged. "If there is a doctor."

"Certainly there must be a doctor in Panama City."

"Perhaps. Perhaps not. It all depends on who has left to join the gold rush since I've been here last."

"Well, do *something*, for God's sake!" Dewey shouted at him. "And do it quickly!"

"First, Señor Dewey, we have some unfinished business." He held out a hand. "The money, señor."

"No, Melendez, first the name of the boat."

"Of course." He grinned. "You will leave for California on the bark *Emily*."

"When?"

274

"As soon as she is ready. A day or two, perhaps."

"Wait, you scoundrel! I want to know for sure!"

Julia Martin, lying in the sun on the dock, moaned. Charles turned to look at her. The jaundiced face, the skin stretched like parchment over her cheekbones, frightened him. He felt guilty, too, about his haggling with Melendez while she was suffering.

"Very well, Melendez. How much?"

"As agreed, señor, eight hundred. Five hundred for the original passage, three hundred for the . . . uh . . . bonus. And if you still intend to be Señor Weatherford's patron, then three hundred more."

Reluctantly, Dewey drew his money pouch from his bag, counting the mildewed bills into the Spaniard's hand. "Now, find a doctor! Immediately!"

It took an hour before a doctor was located and before Mrs. Martin was bathed and put into a clean bed.

The doctor, an American with the ironic name of Blessing, was not optimistic. "She's very weak," he told the husband. "Very weak, indeed. And the fever has—" He stopped, the import of his words painfully clear.

It was only then that Dewey, with Weatherford, set out to investigate the ship that would take them to San Francisco. They made their way to the harbor to find the bark *Emily*.

Not a single ocean-going vessel was in the harbor. Not one!

"Jesus Christ," Weatherford cursed, "where are all the ships?"

Two grimaced. "Once more, Roger, our friend Melendez—"

Panama City, they found soon enough, was crowded with Americans like themselves, all awaiting passage to California. Hundreds of them, perhaps thousands. The main thoroughfare, Calle de la Merced, was jammed with American-owned hotels, and American-owned saloons and gambling parlors, and American-owned whorehouses—all catering to those afflicted with gold fever. Calle de la Merced was a madhouse. It was well after dark when they learned, after making numerous inquiries about Juan Melendez, that he was merely an agent for an American named Cabel Starnes, who owned one of the larger hotels, The California House.

Once more, Dewey felt the fool. He had come all this way from Nashville, and had endured the rigors of the trans-Isthmus passage, without really knowing with whom he was dealing. And it angered him again.

Starnes, when they found him in his hotel, was a portly man, dressed in the highest fashion, jeweled rings on all of his fingers, and a permanent smile fixed on his florid face. That smile annoyed Two as he told Starnes of their dealings with Melendez.

"Well, let's just see," he said agreeably. A large ledger was produced from under the counter in the lobby. "Dewey, eh?" he asked as he flipped it open.

"Yes. And Weatherford, too."

A stubby finger traced down the page and then the page was flipped. There were pages upon pages of names. Finally: "Ah, here's Mr. Weatherford. Yes, yes, all paid in full. For the bark *Emily.*"

His search continued. Two pages later he also found the name of Charles Dewey. "Yes, Mr. Dewey, all is in order."

"I thought, perhaps, Señor Melendez might not—"

Starnes laughed loudly. "He's not a man who inspires a lot of confidence, is he?"

"Hardly," Dewey answered.

"But he does his job."

"We've been to the harbor, Mr. Starnes," Two reported, "and there's no *Emily* there. No ships of any kind, for that matter."

The fat man closed the ledger. "Yes, well, that's one of the disadvantages of my service. Uh . . . not all of the vessels leaving here return, you know. Crews often jump ship when they get to San Francisco. The lure of gold is very powerful. I've been told the harbor of San Francisco is a sea of masts of abandoned ships."

Dewey frowned. "Then you don't know whether the *Emily* will return?"

"If you wish a guarantee, no. But the captain is a very strong man and he manages to keep a crew together. Of course, each trip, it seems, the bonuses paid to crews are greater and, therefore, sometimes . . . uh . . . adjustments must be made in the price of passage."

Weatherford spoke up. "Do you mean I might have to come up with *more* money?"

"That's always a possibility."

"Jesus Christ!"

"Yes, well . . ." Starnes shook his head sadly. "I'm afraid I'm portrayed as a villain in many quarters of Panama City, but I'm merely an agent for the captains. If they charge more, I charge more." For the first time the voice grew cold. "This is not a charitable enterprise."

"Can you give us a guess, Mr. Starnes, about the *Emily*?"

"Maybe tomorrow," he said easily. "Or next week. Or next month."

"And in the meantime—?" Two was disheartened.

"The services of The California House are available to you."

"For how much?"

"Ten dollars a night."

Weatherford whistled through his teeth.

"Of course, if you two are friendly enough to share a room," Starnes went on, "I could offer a special rate of fifteen for the both of you."

Dewey laughed now, seeing humor in the madness of Panama City. "Mr. Starnes, you've found your gold field right here, haven't you?"

"That's true," the man confessed. "Very true, indeed."

Two booked the room. The California House even offered the availability of a bath, for two dollars each. Dewey, as he soaked in the hot water, thought what a luxury being clean was; it was not something that had ever crossed his mind before.

The room was comfortable. As they went to bed that night, after applying a soothing lotion to their many insect wounds, Roger Weatherford expressed his gratitude for Two's friendship.

"Charles, I'm keeping a complete record of everything I owe you. You'll have every cent back. Maybe it'll take me some time, but I want you to know that I'm not one to live on charity."

"It hasn't been charity, Roger."

"I know you don't look at it that way, and I appreciate that." He paused. "I know now that a true friend is worth more than all the gold there is in the world."

BESTSELLING BOOKS FROM TOR

HISTORICAL NOVELS
OF THE AMERICAN FRONTIERS

DON WRIGHT

☐	58991-2 THE CAPTIVES	$4.50
☐	58992-0	Canada $5.50
☐	58989-0 THE WOODSMAN	$3.95
☐	58990-4	Canada $4.95

DOUGLAS C. JONES

☐	58459-7 THE BAREFOOT BRIGADE	$4.50
☐	58460-0	Canada $5.50
☐	58457-0 ELKHORN TAVERN	$4.50
☐	58458-9	Canada $5.50
☐	58453-8 GONE THE DREAMS AND DANCING	$3.95
	(Winner of the Golden Spur Award)	
☐	58454-6	Canada $4.95
☐	58450-3 SEASON OF YELLOW LEAF	$3.95
☐	58451-1	Canada $4.95

EARL MURRAY

☐	58596-8 HIGH FREEDOM	$4.95
☐	58597-6	Canada 5.95

Buy them at your local bookstore or use this handy coupon:
Clip and mail this page with your order.

Publishers Book and Audio Mailing Service
P.O. Box 120159, Staten Island, NY 10312-0004

Please send me the book(s) I have checked above. I am enclosing $_____ (please add $1.25 for the first book, and $.25 for each additional book to cover postage and handling. Send check or money order only—no CODs.)

Name _____

Address _____

City _____ State/Zip _____

Please allow six weeks for delivery. Prices subject to change without notice.